Praise for
New York Times and USA Today Bestselling Author

Diane Capri

"Full of thrills and tension, but smart and human, too."
*Lee Child, #1 New York Times Bestselling Author of Jack
Reacher Thrillers*

"[A] welcome surprise….[W]orks from the first page to
'The End'."
Larry King

"Swift pacing and ongoing suspense are always
present…[L]ikable protagonist who uses her political
connections for a good cause…Readers should eagerly anticipate
the next [book]."
Top Pick, Romantic Times

"…offers tense legal drama with courtroom overtones, twisty
plot, and loads of Florida atmosphere. Recommended."
Library Journal

"[A] fast-paced legal thriller…energetic prose…an appealing
heroine…clever and capable supporting cast…[that will] keep
readers waiting for the next [book]."
Publishers Weekly

"Expertise shines on every page."
*Margaret Maron, Edgar, Anthony, Agatha and Macavity Award
Winning MWA Past President*

FATAL ERROR

by DIANE CAPRI

ALSO BY DIANE CAPRI

The Hunt for Jack Reacher Series
(in publication order with Lee Child source books in parentheses)

Don't Know Jack (The Killing Floor)

Jack in a Box (*novella*)

Jack and Kill (*novella*)

Get Back Jack (Bad Luck & Trouble)

Jack in the Green (*novella*)

Jack and Joe (The Enemy)

Deep Cover Jack (Persuader)

Jack the Reaper (The Hard Way)

Black Jack (Running Blind/The Visitor)

Ten Two Jack (The Midnight Line)

The Jess Kimball Thrillers Series

Fatal Enemy (*novella*)

Fatal Distraction

Fatal Demand

Fatal Error

Fatal Fall

Fatal Edge

Fatal Game

Fatal Bond

Fatal Past (*novella*)

Fatal Dawn

The Hunt for Justice Series

Due Justice

Twisted Justice

Secret Justice

Wasted Justice

Raw Justice

Mistaken Justice (*novella*)

Cold Justice (*novella*)

False Justice (*novella*)

Fair Justice (*novella*)

True Justice (*novella*)

The Heir Hunter Series

Blood Trails

Trace Evidence

CAST OF PRIMARY CHARACTERS

Jess Kimball
FBI Special Agent Henry Morris
Wilson Grantly
Enzo Ficarra
Colonnello Santino Vanelli
Romeo Pausini
Luigi Ficarra (deceased)

FATAL
ERROR

"It is not enough that we do our best;
sometimes we must do what is required."

— Winston S. Churchill

CHAPTER ONE

Tuscany, Italy
May 12

A DOG BARKED, LONELY in the night. The sound rolled down the hill. Echoing over the lawn. From the house at the top, to the woods at the bottom. It was more a timorous complaint than a demand for attention. The kind of sound made by the upper half of a body. Short. Thin. High pitched. Pushed out with an expectation of kindness borne from years of loving attention. Enzo Ficarra smiled. It was not the growl of a broad rib cage and strong lungs. It was not a big dog.

The sound quelled the last of his concerns.

He had scheduled this meeting for the following day. They would not be expecting him a day early. They would not be prepared to fight.

He walked slowly up the hill. Measured steps. Neither rushing nor sauntering. The walk of a guest expecting to be welcomed. Deception and surprise were the stock of his trade, and he walked to deceive any eyes that might be upon him.

Surprise would come soon enough.

The house had square walls and round balconies. Wrought iron railings decorated the windows. Eaves hung out from the building. Arched tiles covered the roof.

It was a traditional Tuscan home. Around the house was perhaps an acre of garden. Enough to give the occupants their privacy. Enough to keep his visit private, too.

He reached the rear door into the kitchen. Deep inside the house, a television played. A mindless show host asking mindless questions of a mindless audience.

They weren't expecting him. Which was as it should have been, the night before the meeting.

All was well.

He braced a flat metal hook against the doorframe. Three occupants inside. Fifteen rounds in his Beretta. More than enough to do the job. He would act fast. Not that he was concerned they would fight back.

Which might be interesting.

Still, best avoided.

He savored the moment. Long ago, he had learned to crave adrenaline. The chemical that quavered other's voices, deepened his. What trembled other's hands and fingers, steadied his. He was never more focused than when events promised a rush.

Tonight should be such a time.

He pulled his silenced Beretta from his pocket, and took a deep breath.

He shoved his weight behind the metal hook. Its sharp edge cut into the wood. Splintered the doorframe. Opened a gap to the lock.

He felt the solid touch of metal. He wrenched the hook down. Pulling at the lock. Tearing at the screws. Wrenching them from the cracked remains of the doorframe.

He barreled forward. All his weight. Shoulder first.

Glass shattered. The lock clattered across a tiled floor.

The door flew back.

He scanned his gun across the room. Left to right. Kitchen counters. Gas stove. Refrigerator.

No one there.

He kicked the door closed.

A middle-aged woman appeared at the doorway into the living room, dressed in her nightgown.

She froze, her eyes wide, and her mouth open. Fear overwhelmed her capacity for thought.

He leveled the Beretta and fired.

The silencer muted the gun's roar. Still loud. Still forceful. Still a soundtrack to hot metal and death.

The woman tumbled back.

Enzo stepped over the body.

The living room was empty. A single shot silenced the television.

He darted through the door to the hall.

A man stood on the bottom of the stairs, a briefcase clutched to his chest. Ten years older than the woman. Unhealthy, too. Michael Taviani, Mike to his now-dead American wife, Lane. He thrust the briefcase forward. "Please. I have it!"

Enzo glanced up. The stairs were unoccupied.

Mike edged closer. The case still in front of him. Like a shield. "Please?"

Enzo gestured to the living room. Mike stepped through. He gasped at the sight of his wife, motionless on the floor.

Enzo closed the door, sealing the living room from the hallway.

Mike swallowed. His voice trembled. "You said tomorrow. The meeting—"

"I'm here now."

Mike stared at his dead wife. "But—"

"I make the rules, Taviani. You know this."

Mike's mouth opened and closed. A goldfish. Overwhelmed. Unable to comprehend where he'd gone wrong. Unable to grasp the events occurring around him.

Enzo pointed the Beretta toward a low coffee table. "Open it."

Mike placed the briefcase on the table. The latch thumped open. He lifted the lid. "A quarter million euro. Like you said."

"Show me."

The notes were wrapped in bundles. Mike lifted out a handful. Ten thousand euros. Maybe twenty.

Enzo waved a flashlight over them. A black light. Plenty of ultraviolet energy to excite photons, and reveal invisible marks. These notes kept their muted colors. The subtle blues and reds and greens that thwarted casual counterfeiters. But he wasn't worried about counterfeits. Mike wasn't quite that skilled, or clever. The black light assuaged a different concern. The notes were not marked for tracing.

Mike had followed instructions, as expected.

"Close it," Enzo said.

Mike complied. He held out the briefcase.

Glass crunched.

Enzo spun toward the noise. The wife lay dead as before.

Mike dived for Enzo. "Run!"

Enzo leapt sideways, pointing the Beretta and squeezing the trigger at the same time.

The gun seemed to boom louder than before in the silent house.

Mike twitched and jerked. His legs gave out from under him. His arms flailed.

He tumbled past Enzo. Head first onto the carpet and into his own rapidly pooling blood, which flowed steadily while his heart continued to pump.

Enzo glimpsed a thin figure in the kitchen. The daughter. A teenager. Over-indulged, to be sure. Seventeen now.

She had been the one who answered Enzo's original email containing fake pleas for help. She'd responded to the sleazy pitch asking for money to save young girls her age from human trafficking. Of course, seventeen-year-olds had no money. But through her, he'd reached her parents' bank account.

He shook his head. Parents would do almost anything for their children. Even when the children were the cause of their troubles.

Tears marked her cheeks. Her eyes wide. Standing by the rear door.

Enzo ran to the kitchen.

She backed away from the door. He leveled his gun on her. Her eyes darted to one side. Behind him. The briefest glimpse, like the recognition of movement.

He spun, training the Beretta to the living room doorway. The space was empty. Blood had also pooled around the woman. She hadn't moved. Nor would she. Her husband was not so lucky.

Mike rolled on the floor holding his stomach. Still alive. For a few moments more.

Enzo spun back to the girl but she had vanished.

He pressed his face against the kitchen window, scanning the moonlit garden.

He heard a click to his right. Another door.

He raced to twist the handle. Locked.

He leaned his shoulder into the door. It was solid.

He stepped back and fired at the lock twice. The wood splintered and danced.

He swung his boot up, kicking hard. The door snapped open, slamming back against the wall.

A laundry room. A washer and dryer along one wall. Washing powders and laundry stacked on a work surface along the other. A closed window at the far end. No girl. And no way out.

He glanced behind the door. Nothing.

He eased down, peering into the glass of the washing machine. It seemed impossible to think she could have squeezed into such a close space, but he'd seen fear motivate people to remarkable feats.

The washer was empty.

He moved into the crowded room. His back to the work surface. He passed the washer. Passed the gap between the washer and dryer.

The dryer's large door was metal. No doubt with a firm spring latch. He would have heard it open and close.

He adjusted his grip on the gun and moved past the dryer, to the space between its white metal side and the end of the room.

A narrow space. Long and thin. Like the girl.

She had contorted her body. Knees, shoulders, legs. Twisted. Cramped. Painful. Her head angled sideways. Her eyes staring. He leveled his gun on her. She had been brave and quick. With her dash to hide when she first saw him from the kitchen, she might even have had a bright future in front of her. In another world. Not the one in which she lived.

He took a deep breath. At another time, he might even feel he should recruit her. But not here. Not now. She had seen his face. She knew who he was. He lived not far from this very home.

He had no choice. He'd known that weeks ago. Her foolish parents should have known it, too.

Her breathing was ragged. Hard work for her lungs in such confines. He turned his face away, fired twice, and spared her lungs the work.

He didn't look back. He closed the laundry room door behind him. It drifted open again, the lock gone. He stepped over the woman's body, and into the living room.

Mike had dragged himself up against a chair. He struggled to dial the old-fashioned phone.

Enzo fired twice more. He placed the shots together. Quick succession. Center of Mike's forehead. His lifeless torso slumped sideways. The phone tumbled to the floor.

Enzo jerked the phone from the wall. He returned the money to the briefcase, and closed the latches.

The meeting had not gone as smoothly as he'd planned. Such conditions meant unacceptable levels of evidence.

He returned to the kitchen, placed the sugar bowl in the microwave, and set it for ten minutes. As the microwave hummed, he turned the four gas burners to full open positions. He tucked the case under his arm and left, closing the door behind him.

He returned to his spot in the trees at the bottom of the garden to wait. The minutes ticked by.

Before the microwave timer finished, the sugar caught fire. Flames escaped the microwave and the gas ignited. Not with Hollywood flamboyance, but a smooth, relentless *whoosh*. Here, in the countryside, with neighbors miles away, no one would find the fire until it had run its course.

The fuel burned easily in the oxygen-rich mixture. Fingers of fire reached through the doors and windows.

The dog he'd heard barking earlier ran from the rear door. Small legs. Leaping more than running. Wisps of smoke trailed from its fur. It ran to the woods, and rolled in the grass.

The fire grew to the second floor. First, a yellow glow in the windows then roaring flames that spilled out of window frames and lapped upward.

The dog trotted to sit beside him.

Enzo watched the fire until flames burst through the roof. The dog stared at him expectantly, and barked.

His brother, Luigi, was returning today from New York. One last ransom to collect in Rome this afternoon. One last family to terminate tonight. After that, vacation. He'd promised his wife and his children. He'd been working too much. Luigi, too.

Enzo picked up the case, and left the dog alone and lonely in the dark.

CHAPTER TWO

Tuscany, Italy
May 12

A FEW HOURS LATER, Enzo Ficarra sipped his espresso as dawn crept over the horizon behind him. A cheap cell phone lay on his patio table. The battery was fully charged, the shrill buzzer was set to its loudest volume, and the display showed five bars. But none of those things mattered. The one person who knew the number had not called. His brother, Luigi.

He stood the phone upright, and tapped his fingers on the table while the rising sun shortened long shadows. The phone kept its silence.

A gull's caw drew his attention eastwards, across the deep green lawn, down the rocks that led to the shore, and out over the sea. A trawler sailed by, heading for port in the next town, gulls diving in its wake to pick off the scraps.

He sipped his third espresso.

Scraps.

He took a deep breath.

Not for him.

He had a good business. It worked well. People were basically honest. They wanted to believe that of other people, too. It was a useful trait. Gullibility was how he manipulated them. And the older they were, the more they believed, and the easier they were to manipulate.

He finished his drink.

Like any business, contracts were contracts. Agreements had to be honored. He never failed his responsibilities, and he expected his clients to do the same. But when they did not, the rules had to be enforced.

He rolled the still warm demitasse cup between his palms, and watched the dregs of golden foam run around the bottom of the cup.

Enzo placed the white china cup securely on its saucer. The cup was a trophy of sorts, he supposed. He'd collected the set from Marek's club in Montreal, *Les Canard*. What a miserable day that had been. Wet, cold. Betrayal by an old friend, which was the worst kind. He shuddered.

Marek caused an unfortunate disruption to their profitable business. Contracts had been broken, agreements breached, a lapse in confidence. The enterprise was shut down and loose ends were wrapped up.

A petty incident that demanded the utmost care to bring about the final, successful conclusion. So his brother, Luigi, had travelled to Florida to collect the last payment, a quarter of a million dollars. The Italian economy being what it was, a quarter of a million American dollars would fatten their ailing bottom line nicely.

Luigi was fast, strong, and an excellent shot. More than once, he had worked for days on the most meager of sleep. He had escaped situations that would have overwhelmed ordinary men, and returned to tell the tale.

Forcing the old couple to bring their life savings to Rome to exchange it for their son's life should have been a simple matter for his brother.

Boarding a plane was a tedious process. Check-in lines. Security guards on minimum wages. Jet bridges with passenger lines wide and long. Sniveling children, frightened mothers, bored pilots prone to error.

He tamped down his annoyance. His brother would have been patient. He would have stood in line. He would have had his ticket ready, his passport in hand. He would have smiled at the check-in attendant, and complied with security nonsense without complaint. He would have answered questions with a smile. A model passenger. Accepting. Accommodating. Anonymous.

And before he departed for Rome, he would have called.

Enzo turned the phone over in his hands. Flight 12 had left New York hours ago. His brother was either on it, or he was not. Plain and simple. But with no phone call he assumed the worst.

He mashed the garish purple phone's off button, and pulled the battery from its compartment. He walked slowly into his villa, dropped the pieces into the waste disposal, and ran the motor until any proof they ever existed was gone.

Enzo pulled a second phone from his pocket. A different model, a different carrier, a standard black color, purchased with cash from a different corner store.

He pressed the on button, and began making the calls required by the circumstances. He would make arrangements to meet the plane, then he would handle the disappearance of his brother.

Those who had been involved in Luigi's disappearance had made an error. A fatal one.

CHAPTER THREE

Rome, Italy
May 12

JESS KIMBALL LAY ALMOST flat in her first class seat.
She'd slept more than half of her journey from New York to
Rome. Her limbs felt like lead, and her breathing was shallow.
The announcement that the plane was on final descent lifted her
back to consciousness. She pried open one eye. The video screen
installed in the seat back in front of her said "Movie Over."

She groaned and rotated her head, stretching the muscles in
her neck. The film had been intense, and her dream doubly so—
terrorists, antimatter, and six hours in a remarkably comfortable
bed had given her imagination far too much freedom. She
pushed a button, and her seat back rotated to the upright position.

A steward moved down the aisle, handing out hot towels.
She took one and pressed it to her face. The blast of lemon-
scented steam revived her senses and helped pry her eyes fully
open. And she needed her eyes wide open, and her senses
working overtime.

The events of the past few hours rushed into her mind again. She'd booked her trip on Flight 12 at the last minute. Her plan to spend a few days recharging her batteries had changed in the hours after she met Roger and Harriet Grantly. Well into their retirement, they had collected every cent of cash they owned and booked tickets on Flight 12 to Rome, intending to pay a ransom for their kidnapped son, Wilson.

She grimaced and shook her head. *Not that Wilson was particularly worth saving.*

He'd collaborated in an extortion scam run by a pair of Italians, Luigi and Enzo Ficarra. After he'd foolishly lost all of his own money, he'd duped his clients and even his elderly parents into losing theirs. The fiasco had almost killed the pair of ninety-year-olds who had done nothing but love their son too much.

The Ficarra brothers weren't finished with Wilson. Had they limited their focus to Wilson, Jess wouldn't be sitting on this plane now. She was a victims' rights advocate. But Wilson Grantly was no victim.

Not at first.

Not until the Ficarras had kidnapped him and demanded ransom from his parents. A quarter of a million dollars. Every last cent they knew the elderly couple possessed, because Wilson had told them to save his own hide.

Jess balled up the now-cold towel, and handed it to the steward. Another attendant passed close behind with hot, black coffee strong enough to hold the spoon upright. She took the cup and sipped it, hoping it would hold her up, too.

While working with the FBI, she had uncovered the link between the Ficarras and Wilson Grantly, and in the process shot Luigi. In a last desperate act, he had chewed a cyanide capsule before the FBI could interrogate him.

From then on, the FBI, and Special Agent Henry Morris, had taken charge. The might of the American law enforcement juggernaut, with its resources, multitude of agents, and very long arms, had eased the Grantlys to the sidelines.

It was a sensible move. The right thing to do. Youth, vigor, and experience trumped good intentions, no matter how personal.

But government agencies carried a reputation. Not always deserved, and not always correct, but a reputation nonetheless. Sometimes red tape, sometimes shifting priorities, sometimes it was a simple lack of staff. Whatever the reason, they were known to fail, and one of those reasons was probably why Agent Morris hadn't joined the passengers at the departure lounge in New York.

After take-off, Jess had walked the length of the aircraft looking for him, to no avail. He wasn't on the flight. He wasn't bound for Rome and the final confrontation with the kidnapper, Enzo Ficarra.

She clenched her fists. The Grantlys' planned meeting at the Rome airport was the only opportunity to link the murderous Luigi Ficarra in New York to the rest of the brothers' operation in Italy. She knew it, and Morris knew it, too.

So why wasn't he on the flight?

She bit her lip. Morris wasn't just one man. He was part of the FBI. A big machine. Layers on layers. Surveillance. Cameras. The Internet. They could be observing everything and everyone on the flight. They could be waiting in Rome.

She hoped.

She closed her eyes and lay back against the headrest. Surveillance. It was an obvious conclusion. No need for the FBI to reveal themselves, to tip their hand. No need to give anyone a sliver of a chance. She frowned. Yet, wouldn't they have put at least one agent on the plane?

She kept her eyes closed until they landed and taxied to the terminal. The jet bridge took forever to hook up, and even though she was in first class at the front of the crowd, exiting the plane was frustratingly slow.

She followed meandering passengers through long lines at immigration, inquisitive guards in customs, and finally, finally to baggage claim.

A television monitor showed the bags from her flight would be delivered at the far end of the hall. The silver conveyor was stationary when she arrived. Several people from her flight had made it there before her. They were all either too young or too old to be the kind of seasoned FBI agents Morris would have trusted on a case like this.

A buzzer sounded, and the conveyer belt started. People crowded around. She eased herself into the middle of the throng. The bags tumbled down in front of her.

She flipped over baggage tags as they glided by. Luigi had cut up the Grantlys' luggage in New York. But it made sense that Morris would have planned to get the ransom money to Rome for a handover to Luigi's brother. Jess thought the best way was to pass it off in different luggage as if it were the Grantlys'.

After several minutes of flipping tags, Jess found the Grantly name on two new looking pieces of blue hard-sided luggage.

Morris had done a good job of finding something similar to the original.

She made a show of checking several more bags before backing away from the carousel to wait.

She searched through her messenger bag, and checked her

phone while watching the blue luggage circling on the carousel.

One by one, her fellow passengers found their luggage, and headed for the exit. A few stragglers milled around, checking tags and muttering.

The Grantlys' bags continued their lonely orbit.

An airport employee took the last bags from the belt, and stacked them on a cart. The blue luggage was near the top.

A few bored looking employees and lost travelers stood in the area. A large man with a backpack stepped out for a cigarette. If Morris had someone in place to swoop in on whoever touched the luggage, they were doing a good job of hiding.

She bit her lip. Morris's men might have been given her picture. They might even have seen her in New York. He, and they, would not appreciate her being there. But Harriet and Roger deserved to get their son back, no matter what he'd done, and she'd promised Harriet. She wouldn't let the Grantlys down.

She pulled out her phone and talked into it, pacing up and down the baggage hall, faking a conversation.

The cart remained by the baggage carousel. The employee walked off and busied himself with paperwork behind the lost luggage desk. An announcement came over the speakers. Jess pushed a finger in one ear as if struggling to hear her non-existent caller.

An old couple entered the baggage hall and headed straight for the baggage cart. Had Morris found them to replace the Grantlys?

Jess let her gaze flick over them, not wanting to pause and stare. They were excited to see the pile of bags, but neither of them looked like FBI material.

Would Morris have dragged ordinary people into their

operation? They looked like a sweet old couple, enjoying retirement, not a pair of hardened operatives in the middle of freeing a hostage, and bringing down an organized crime ring.

The couple checked bag tags, tutted, and walked over to the man doing paperwork at the lost luggage desk. They struggled through a conversation with sentences from a phrase book and much finger pointing. The man pulled out a form, and began making notes.

Jess stretched out her fake phone call, standing by a giant window that looked down on an endless parking garage. Vehicles flowed in and out, their drivers taking tickets and paying tolls.

She watched the blue bags in the window's reflection.

If the couple were connected to Morris, they were doing a good job of disguising it.

The couple finished their conversation with the man at lost luggage, and walked out of the exit, arm in arm, excitement long gone.

The automatic doors hissed closed behind them. They weren't part of Morris's plan.

She surveyed the baggage hall. A few bored employees skulked around a vending machine. The heavyset man had returned from his cigarette break. He coughed and sputtered, his face a ruddy red. Hardly likely to be part of an intensive police operation.

Yet the bags had been put on the flight. Two bags, just like the Grantlys', and labeled with their name. Morris must have done it. He'd found similar luggage, dragged it around the floor to scuff up the corners, filled it with whatever he could find, and placed it on Flight 12. There was no doubt. No other reasonable explanation.

So, where was he? Why no surveillance? Why no twenty-something with a backpack? Or two businessmen, deep in conversation, dark suits covering automatic weapons until the bags were picked up? Anything that would be good enough cover to keep his agents' eyes on the bags while giving Luigi's contact enough confidence to reveal himself?

One of the airport employees looked at her too long. She turned away, and resumed her imaginary phone conversation. She'd become too conspicuous. She'd need a new plan. Soon.

The exit doors hissed open. A middle-aged man wearing sunglasses and a dark suit strolled in. He consulted a clipboard, and circled the baggage claim area. He passed the baggage cart with its blue bags.

The lost luggage clerk remained head down, engrossed in his paperwork.

Jess paced in a small circle as the man returned to the cart. He rechecked his clipboard, and turned over the tags on the Grantlys' luggage. Jess's skin prickled. He disentangled the blue bags from the others on the cart.

Jess's breathing raced. She kept up her circles, staring into the distance, watching the man in her peripheral vision as he scanned the room.

She squeezed her phone tight.

Where was Morris? Or his men?

And the Italian police? Wouldn't he have told them?

Yet, she scanned the room, there was no sign of anyone remotely likely to be law enforcement. No one.

The man pulled the blue bags from the pile of luggage.

Jess took a deep breath. She looked at her phone, and swore. She didn't even know the Italian equivalent of 911.

The man carried the bags toward the exit doors.

She looked around the baggage hall. No one moved. No one closed in. Through the glass doors, she could see no one was waiting outside.

The exit doors hissed open.

The man walked through the broad opening.

The bags were leaving. The Grantlys' life savings. Wrapped and bundled and counted. Their dreams swapped for one solitary hope. A ransom exchange. Their son's life for an uncertain future.

It was an FBI case. Better trained, better equipped, experienced. They were the people to bring about the best outcome to any hostage situation. They were the people the Grantlys had trusted, and rightly.

But the FBI wasn't there. Jess was.

Her pulse raced. If she lost sight of the bags, the money would be gone, and they'd never get Wilson Grantly back.

She stuffed her phone in her pocket, and headed after the man.

By the time she reached the automatic doors, he was at the elevator to the parking levels below. She breathed deeply, and slowed her pace. If he was as ruthless as Luigi, did she really want to be alone in the same elevator with him?

The man had short jet-black hair held in place with plenty of gel. His suit had shiny patches on the seat of his pants and elbows. He resembled Luigi Ficarra. About six-feet tall, slender, dark, Italian. The two men could have been brothers.

He stabbed at the elevator call button. Jess saw a large display count up three floors before the doors opened. He stepped inside.

Jess stopped by a staircase door and cursed herself for not

taking the man's picture. She had no gun, and no chance of calling the police in time.

She pulled her phone from her pocket, and bounded down the first flight of stairs.

The door into the parking area had a circular window. She pressed her face against the glass and strained to see into the garage. Cars filled most of the parking spots, a family was exiting a minivan with a mountain of suitcases, but there was no sign of the black-haired man.

She sprinted down the next set of stairs, hitting the door at full speed. It banged back against the wall, hinges squealing.

Cars packed the floor. A ticket inspector moved between the vehicles, checking tickets. Several men piled from a black SUV.

She moved along the rows of cars. People were parking, people were leaving, but still there was no sign of the man with the hair gel.

She turned back. The men from the SUV had split up. Two headed into the stairway. Two looked over the open edge of the parking level. One stood by the elevator. The man at the elevator pointed at her.

Her heart jumped. A flash of heat ran over her. She stood still.

None of the five carried luggage. The man closest to the elevator headed toward her. She hurried down the sloping road to the floor below.

She rubbed her damp palms down the sides of her jeans.

What if Luigi's single contact was really a team of five?

She took a breath, and glanced behind.

The elevator man followed, walking fast.

She threw her bag over her shoulder, better for running if it came to that.

The sloping roadway offered an obstructed view of the floor below. She bent over as she walked, peering through the gaps in the concrete pillars.

The main exit was a hundred feet away. Barriers rose and fell as a line of drivers inserted tickets into orange boxes. On the opposite side, she glimpsed glossy jet-back hair.

The man following her called something she didn't understand. She glanced back at him and started jogging.

The terminal building was a few hundred yards away. But she couldn't run to safety there. Not yet. She needed at least a picture of the man with black hair. He was her only potential lead to the hostage, Wilson Grantly.

Jess circled around a slow moving car, away from the terminal, chasing the jet-black hair. He fumbled keys from his pocket. He looked up, saw her, and froze.

She stopped and held up her phone.

The man swiveled his face away. He'd found his keys. He pressed the key fob and lights flashed on the old brown Lancia. He tossed the blue luggage into the rear, and jumped into the driver's seat.

She ran toward the car, her phone camera held out ready to shoot.

Footsteps pounded behind her.

The Lancia's engine roared to life. The Lancia screeched out of its parking place, and roared around the garage toward the exit.

Jess ran faster. She darted between parked cars and concrete pillars. She heard shouting behind her. Two men from the SUV were chasing her now.

She cut for the exit. A lane opened up. The Lancia line-jumped immediately behind the car at the gate to a chorus of horns.

She flipped her phone camera to video and held it as steadily as possible. The man with jet-black hair stuffed a ticket into the orange box.

She was only twenty feet from his car. The barrier rose, and he screeched away, barely glancing in her direction.

The two men shouting behind her became frantic.

She bolted through the vehicles lined up at the exit gates. The safety of the steel and glass terminal was just five lanes of crawling traffic away.

Jess plowed on, bouncing off cars with her hands. Her bag swung wildly.

She dodged the last lane, and dived for the open outer doors to the terminal, willing the inner ones to open.

But they didn't.

She hit the glass, forearms outstretched, and ricocheted off. The thick glass vibrated but didn't open.

Jess spun around, eyes wide, gripping her bag, ready to swing.

The two men blocked all daylight outside the doors. They glowered at her. One pointed a gun, and motioned her to lie on the ground.

Her heart thumped against her ribs. There was no space around the side of either man to make a run for it. No way in. No way out.

The man with the gun shook his head and ran splayed fingers through his hair. "Lie down, *Signora* Kimball."

She turned to the inner doors. From behind the glass, two uniformed police officers motioned her down.

She sank to the floor. *Dammit!*

Morris wasn't there.

But he must have organized a police operation. He could have warned her before she broke about a dozen Italian laws.

CHAPTER FOUR

JESS SAT IN A SMALL, square police interview room. Her back ached from the hours she'd spent in one of the room's two small plastic chairs. They were light, one-piece scoops that flexed as she moved. The kind of cheap seats found on patios the world over. The second white scoop was directly facing her on the other side of a heavy-duty aluminum table bolted to the floor. The table's surface had been polished to remove graffiti scratched into the metal. The result was only half successful. The words it bore were in Italian, but they were obvious enough to keep her from resting her arms on its surface.

A single overhead light cast a yellow hue on thickly painted walls. They bore more pictures than words, and the same effort had been put into removing them, with the same imperfect results. Jess suspected it was a losing battle.

She shifted her weight in the chair. It was hard, cold, and uncomfortable, much like the rest of her experience in the room.

The Italian police had taken her phone and her belongings.

They'd also taken a mug shot, her fingerprints, and a blood sample. The latter done by a nurse who communicated only in grunts and the waving of a needle.

They hustled her into the interview room, and left her for hours before a man who introduced himself as Colonnello Vanelli had questioned her. His suit flattered his tall physique, broad in the shoulders and trim at the waist.

In the moments when he wasn't glowering at her, his face was good enough for the front page of any magazine. Dark hair, gleaming white teeth, olive skin, smoldering brown eyes. In any other circumstance, she would have been okay with his undivided attention. But not in a police interview room when she'd been detained on unspecified charges in a foreign country.

She'd explained about Roger and Harriet's desperate attempt to get their son back, about Luigi and Enzo Ficarra, and the ransom. She'd told him about the planned handover at the Rome Airport when the couple landed.

Colonnello Vanelli was unimpressed. He didn't believe her claim that she had become caught up in the affair. Nor did he believe that her escapade at the airport was simply a concerned citizen acting in the public's best interest.

She had been on the verge of explaining about Morris and the FBI when Vanelli had taken a call and left the room.

That was an hour ago.

She stood up, the plastic chair scraping on the hard floor. Her stomach growled, and she wanted to do the same. What right did they have to hold her? What did they really have against her? That she'd chased a man from the airport with her camera? And why the hell weren't they more interested in Wilson and the Ficarras?

The door creaked. She jerked her head in its direction.

FBI Special Agent Henry Morris walked in, his lips a thin line across his face, and his eyebrows pushed down, almost meeting in the middle of his forehead. His breaths came in snorts through his nose. He kicked the door closed without taking his eyes from her.

She took a deep breath. "Hello, Henry."

He grunted. "Sit down."

"I just got up." She sat and he perched on the edge of the table.

He didn't smile. "What the hell are you doing here?"

"He was there. Enzo Ficarra."

"I'm interested in what you're doing here."

She leaned back in her chair. "You saw the Grantlys. Do you think I'm going to abandon them?"

"This is a law enforcement issue, not interesting fodder for your magazine."

"I—"

He held his hand up. "No. That's not a discussion point."

She shrugged.

"You're in some serious trouble here, Jess." He ran both hands over his head. "Italian laws are not as lenient as ours. You've got to know that."

She looked down. Problem was, she did know. It was easy to do something illegal here. She'd been briefed.

"The *carabinieri* want to lock you up."

"For what?"

"You gave them a laundry list to choose from."

"They can't—"

"Aiding and abetting? Here, that's two to five."

"I wasn't aiding or abetting any—"

He placed a hand on her forearm. "These people don't play

games, Jess. Carabinieri take on the mafia, terrorists, serious stuff. They're the go-to guys when the CIA wants something done over here."

"Do you think I popped out of the ether the morning I met you?" She scowled at his hand and shook it off her arm. "Carabinieri. A branch of the Italian military. Sort of a very serious and well-trained police force, but more. Red and Blue colors. Colonnello Vanelli in charge. I get it."

"You know the op you screwed up was ROS, the special ops end of the carabinieri." He cleared his throat, *"Raggruppamento Operativo Speciale."*

Her lips twitched at Morris's struggle to enunciate.

He leaned down, maybe to avoid being overheard or recorded. "It's not funny, Jess."

She shook her head. "I'm not laughing."

"You screwed up their operation." He jerked his fist, thumb out, toward his chest. *"Our* operation. One reason I was late? Twisting the arm of our liaison in Rome to get the Italians to help us."

"Why?" She frowned and her eyes narrowed. "They should want to help. This is a crime. On their soil. It's their job."

"Maybe. We think. We don't know for sure." He sighed and shook his head. "We're asking a favor here. Quite a few favors. We can't bite the hand that helps us."

"Look, we're doing them a favor, aren't we? If we find this guy, they lock him up. Italians are safer, too, right?" She shrugged. "What else can I say?"

Morris's nostrils flared. He blew a long stream of air through stiff lips. "I damn well nearly didn't get approved for this operation, Jess. The things I had to promise defy belief. So how about you don't make my job any harder than it already is? Can you do that much?"

She cocked her head and said nothing.

"Between us," he lowered his voice, "the State Department isn't thrilled about the FBI working outside the U.S. They're trying to shut us down, here and all over the world. Cut costs. Leave U.S. interests to foreign governments. Replace us with paper pushers."

"I see." She frowned. "Maybe I could highlight that problem in my story. Sometimes shining a bright light on dumb ideas gets that kind of thing abandoned before it gets started."

"Story?" His jaw clenched and his nostrils flared again. "You have no story. Nothing. Nada. You dare publish one word of—"

"Take it easy, Morris." She held up her hands, palms out. "I'm not publishing anything. Not yet, anyway. Remember me? I'm on your side."

He narrowed his eyes and gazed into hers as if he might read her mind and her heart. "Okay, Jess. Let's start over. Another reason I was late getting in here to talk to you? Keeping your name out of the papers. You were arrested today. Booked. Your involvement in this is a matter of public record now."

Her breath caught. She'd been wrapped up in getting free of Colonnello Vanelli and finding Enzo Ficarra before he killed Wilson Grantly. Publicity over her arrest hadn't been as high on her radar as it should have been.

"The Ficarras aren't the sort to forgive and forget," Morris said. "Last thing we need is for Enzo to find out you shot his brother before we have him behind bars."

"You're right. Of course. My arrest would likely be international news because of *Taboo*. Thanks." She nodded and gnawed on the inside of her lip. "The only edge we have here is the element of surprise. We need to work quickly before we lose that. I'll be more careful."

"We? What 'we'?" He shook his head. "Jess, I could leave you here. You'd have to call *Taboo* and get their lawyers to persuade the Italians to let you go. By the time that happened, we'd have completed the Ficarra operation. That's what Colonnello Vanelli wants me to do, anyway."

"You could do that." Jess narrowed her eyes and nodded. Her heart pounded wildly in her chest, but her voice was steady. "You'd both have a big black eye in the press to show for it, though. And you'd be throwing away one of your biggest assets here."

"That's what I told Vanelli. I told him you were close to the Grantlys. I told him you could act as a private citizen and do things we can't do and we can't stop you, even if we might want to. I explained that you are the one who found Luigi in New York and disabled him until we arrived." Morris stopped for a deep breath. "And so far, he's been listening to me. But he's not required to, Jess. I've only got so much persuasive power here."

"He was there. Enzo Ficarra. I saw him." She stood rigidly straight, fists clenched at her sides, chin out, and defiance bubbling in every fiber of her body.

"So, you thought you'd just run after him? Chase him off? Scare him with your overnight bag?" Morris stood, too. His voice rose to near shouting. "You think Enzo Ficarra goes anywhere without some serious firepower? Where was your backup?"

She clamped her jaw tight. Lips pressed hard together. Eyes narrowed. Heat rose into her face, but she said nothing. And she didn't look away.

"Do you think I'm so damn stupid, I couldn't organize a sting in twelve hours?" Morris's nostrils flared and his face flushed. "You think I was going to let him walk away because I couldn't find enough clean underwear to go traveling around the world?"

And there you have it. Morris was pissed because she'd underestimated him. He felt disrespected. *Well, welcome to my world.*

But putting a label on his reaction calmed her. He wasn't throwing his weight around. He was defending his turf. Which was something she understood totally.

"Okay." She relaxed her posture and her tone. "He was there. At the airport."

"And we have to assume that he saw you, as well." Morris seemed to stand down a bit, too, as if he'd lost some of his iron-fisted control and he didn't like it. "By now Enzo Ficarra knows all about us. And he'll adapt. If we're not smart about all of this, he'll kill Wilson Grantly and leave us in the dust."

"He really wants that money, though. Look at everything he's gone through to get it." Jess stood and paced the room. It felt good to stretch a bit. "He'll consider it a debt of honor to best us. To avenge his brother."

Morris finally moved to sit in the chair opposite. His shoulders sank a little more. His glower softened. He unclenched his teeth.

"You did a great job stateside. You turned up things we didn't." He nodded curtly, but his voice was calmer, all business again. "And I want to find Enzo Ficarra, and drag him back to the U.S. at least as much as you do." He leaned forward. "So, let us do our job."

She nodded. She wanted him to do his job. But she fully

intended to keep her promises to the Grantlys and to do her job, too.

"Can you use the video and the photos I shot?"

Morris shook his head. "The man you chased wasn't Enzo Ficarra."

"What do you mean? It had to be him." The air in the room grew stifling. Jess tugged on her collar. She frowned. "The bags had the Grantlys' names on them. Who else would want their luggage?"

CHAPTER FIVE

MORRIS SIGHED. "I WROTE those name tags. I even bought
the damn suitcases last night at JFK. And at airport prices."

Jess blinked. "And the money?"

"Went through diplomatic channels." He leaned forward.
"You didn't think we were going to stuff cash in a bag and send
it economy, did you?"

Her shoulders sagged.

Morris shook his head. "You chased the wrong guy, Jess.
You probably scared some tourist half out of his wits."

"He took the Grantlys' bags."

"Not the first time someone's walked off with the wrong
luggage. Won't be the last."

"But…but, didn't you have a transmitter or something? In
the cases?"

Morris scowled. "Europe. Different frequency or it got
damaged or something. It worked and then it didn't. We're
looking into it."

She narrowed her eyes. "Didn't you bring your own receiver?"

"What do you take me for?" His nostrils flared again. "I've driven half the city waving the thing out of the window, and nothing."

"And the farm? Two hours north of Rome? The phone calls. You said Wilson—"

"I know what I said, Jess. And there is a farm two hours north of here. It's on a hillside. They grow olives. An old family business that supplements its income with tours. They even have a gift shop. With a phone booth." He sagged back in his chair. His red-eye flight in coach class was beginning to get to him. "Anyone could have used it."

Jess looked down at her hands. He was glad of the quiet. He rolled his head around, stretching his neck.

"We know what will happen if the ransom isn't paid," she said.

"Certainly do."

She lifted her head. "Was Enzo at the airport?"

"Don't know. Vanelli's got a team scouring surveillance videos."

"Wilson?"

Morris shrugged. "Same thing. Vanelli's men didn't see Wilson anywhere, but until they've reviewed the videos we won't know much."

She let out a long sigh. "When can I get out of here?"

"Vanelli wants you locked up until they have a line on Enzo and Wilson."

"A line?"

Morris grimaced. "One dead, one alive sounds like his preference."

"Mine, too." She nodded. "The man I chased. He took the Grantlys' luggage."

"So I heard."

"You've seen the videos?"

He shook his head. "Vanelli had a man at the lost luggage counter."

"The slow guy?"

Morris nodded. "Guess he was just in character."

She rolled her eyes. "How could I have missed that?"

Morris grinned. "I keep asking myself the same question."

She shook her head. Slow. Her jaw locked in place.

"You okay?" he said.

She swallowed. "Wilson might be a slime ball for dragging Roger and Harriet into this, but they're his parents, and I promised them. I remember Harriet's face. Her eyes."

"We're going to get him back, Jess. We are. You can't think otherwise, or this job just becomes too much."

She rolled her shoulders and stretched tension from her neck. "What's going to happen next?"

He pushed his lips out and moved them around, thinking. "Vanelli doesn't trust you. He's suspicious by nature. All cops are. He thinks you could be working with the Ficarras. Or a rival."

She slapped her hand to her forehead. "Oh, good grief."

Morris shrugged. "I'm just telling you the facts."

"Great. Can't you use your influence? Get me released."

He laughed. "This is Italy, not Little Italy. I don't have a lot of power here."

She shrugged. "So you said."

"They're good people, Jess. They want the same things we do."

She snorted. "That's pretty hard to tell from where I'm sitting."

"Stop fighting the system, Jess." He sighed and shrugged at the same time.

She clenched her teeth.

He leaned over the table. "We can both be useful. You just have to stay out of the enforcement side of the business. Understand?"

She opened her mouth a fraction. "Meaning?"

"You keep away from Ficarra."

"No. You said, we can both be useful. I have a job to do, just like you do." She squared her shoulders. "The right kind of publicity released at the right time can only help, Morris. You know that."

Morris shook his head. "You're a civilian. It's my job to keep you away from people like the Ficarras. But I'll keep you informed," he leaned forward, "as long as you keep everything off the record until we have Ficarra and Grantly where we want them."

"So I'm part of the team?"

He paused. She'd been key to bringing down Luigi, and she could be a key part in Enzo as well. But it was a risk. A big risk. He wasn't on American soil. He didn't have any power. He was wholly dependent of the goodwill of the carabinieri. And goodwill could change in a moment.

But she didn't back down, and if it came to it, the suggestion of bad publicity for the Italian authorities might be a bargaining chip he could use.

He nodded. "Part of my team. The Italians, I can't speak for. But I'll keep you informed."

"All the time?"

He nodded.

"I can live with that." She gestured to the door. "And Vanelli?"

He levered himself out of his chair. "He's persuadable."

CHAPTER SIX

JESS STIRRED IN HER bed. The thinnest slice of light crept around the edges of the drapes. She rolled on her side, and drew the duvet tighter around her shoulders. The bed was divine.

She breathed out, relaxing her muscles, and quieting her thoughts. She breathed in, savoring the scent of the linen, only to breathe out, and do it all again. She closed her eyes.

How long had it been since she had gone to bed without setting an alarm? She couldn't remember, and lying in the arms of Morpheus's own bed, she didn't care.

The light under the drapes spread across the room, thickening and fanning out. Long shadows eased into crisp edged lines of darkness that traced their way from the legs of the furniture. She lay still, leaving the chemicals that numbed her arms and legs to work their magic, washing away the Atlantic crossing, the time changes, and the memories of the carabinieri's interview room.

This was what she needed. It was what her body and her

mind craved. A break from pressure and tension. Relief from the weight of responsibility. Peace for her conscience.

Though…

She rolled onto her back. Enzo Ficarra was still at large, and Wilson Grantly was still a hostage. She sighed, and ran a hand across the gentle form of the duvet. Wilson's fate was in the hands of the FBI and the carabinieri. Despite the events of the previous day, they were good hands. Yet Harriet's eyes were ingrained on her memory, and Jess wouldn't accept anything less than her best, fullest, most complete effort to save Wilson.

She threw off the duvet, pried herself from Morpheus's grip, and staggered into the bathroom, turning the shower to maximum. The water was hot in an instant. She stepped into the water, letting the heat erase the last vestiges of her travels.

She'd made a deal with Morris. Partial inclusion, partial exclusion. A two-way proposition. A trade of restrictions for options, and she wasn't going to waste any time. But first, she breathed in the shower's steam, she had to eat and rearrange her plans.

The thought of breakfast pushed her out of the shower, and into the few clothes she'd bought hastily at the JFK airport. A discrete sign on the dressing table advertised the menu for the hotel's terrace on the second floor. She was in the elevator in minutes.

The terrace didn't disappoint. A forty-foot expanse of rustic flagstones edged with a low stone wall and hedge. The terrace was filled with small round tables and large leather chairs. White tablecloths swayed in the breeze, pinned down by silver bowls of flowers. A handful of guests were crowded at one end of the terrace. She took a table at the opposite end.

A waiter arrived, his crystal white shirt and golden tan

straight from the cover of *GQ*. She skipped the cooked food, and ordered coffee and pastries. She grinned. Apart from anything else, a light breakfast opened up the possibility of mid-morning coffee.

She admired the view. The hotel towered above her, its ornate façade a mix of pillars, arches, and wrought-iron balconies. Old, small paned windows reflected the deep blue of the sky above.

The terrace looked out over a square below. The buildings around the edge matched her hotel for age and stone. In the middle, a fountain sprayed water in a pond. The pond formed the center of a roundabout, busy with tiny cars and mopeds that seemed to take traffic patterns as a suggestion, not a rule.

The sidewalks were filled with walkers. The variety of Italian life was staggering. The colors, the faces, the pace. Businessmen strolled casually past spiky-haired punks. Girls in high heels threaded between cars, their pace undiminished by the traffic jams that appeared and cleared as if for public entertainment. Cafés marked their territory with brightly colored awnings loosely covering tables and chairs that were strewn across the sidewalks. People converged for arm-waving conversations, and drank coffee with patterns in the froth, the tap-tap of china on china marking their progress.

Jess pressed her lips together. Progress. She needed progress, but she had practically nothing to go on. Morris had the videos from the airport. They were, by far, the best potential leads they had. If they could locate Enzo, they could trace him to his car, and from there the location of Wilson Grantly. It sounded easy, but real life was a long way from cop shows on television. She texted Morris that she would meet him at the carabinieri headquarters. A moment later, he replied with a K. Jess snorted a laugh. Not even an OK? Morris wasn't one to waste words.

Her waiter returned with her coffee and a plate with several fruit and cream-filled pastries. She took a bite of a cornetto, and licked the confection from her lips. The strawberries had been soaked in something faintly alcoholic. Flakes of crust floated down to her plate. She rotated the pastry, catching the cream that oozed out.

A chorus of car horns from the square drew her attention, but she returned to finish the crumbly sticky bliss in her hand first. She wiped her fingers on a napkin that felt softer than the bed sheets in her apartment, and leaned back. She could get used to this.

Her waiter swept by, scooping up her plate without a word. She nursed the last of her cappuccino, and snapped pictures of the square with her phone. The images from the day before appeared in the viewer. She bit her lip. She had sent them to Vanelli, but had forgotten to send them to Morris. She collected them together, and sent them off.

She flipped through a stack of brochures on a stand by her table. There was no shortage of sights that begged for attention; vineyards on heartbreakingly beautiful hillsides, farmhouses nestled in olive gardens, and buildings and ruins that stretched back beyond the Romans. She flipped over pictures of the Pantheon, the Colosseum, St. Peter's, and the Vatican. There was the Forum, the Galleria Borghese, the Capitoline, Piazza Navona, plazas, and basilicas galore.

"*Ti piace*," said a voice.

She looked up. Her waiter held out a new cappuccino, chocolate powder melting into the foam. His crisp white shirt fitted tight to his torso and his bulging biceps. He gestured to the cup. "You like?"

She took a breath. "Please." She cleared a space among the brochures.

He put down the steaming cup, and tapped a picture. "Deciding where to go?" His English was far better than her Italian.

"Just looking," she said.

"You Catholic?"

She shook her head.

"Then skip the Vatican. Do the Colosseum first."

She picked up the brochure.

"Not your thing?"

"No, no. It's good. Really. Just that I'm here on business."

He grimaced. "Sorry to hear it."

"There are worse places to have to work. The history is fascinating."

He nodded. "Well, that's pretty much all there is here." He shrugged. "You know. Old things."

She gave him a look of mock indignation.

His eyes went wide. "No, no, no. I wasn't...I didn't—"

She laughed. "I'm joking."

He let out a long sigh, and combed back his blonde curls. "Sorry. The hotel doesn't like it if we don't keep the guests happy."

She picked up her cappuccino. "Just keep the coffee coming."

"Right." He smiled.

He pointed to the Colosseum brochure. "It's not that far."

She shrugged. "I have to work."

"What do you do?"

"Er..."

He eased back a half step. "Sorry, didn't mean to be nosy."

She shrugged. "I work for a magazine."

His eyebrows inched upwards. "Which one?"

"Better if I don't say."

He frowned and shifted his weight between his feet. "American?"

"Uh-huh."

"Interesting."

She sipped her coffee. "I need a taxi."

"Where to?"

"Er…"

He shrugged. "I can order a taxi, but they have to know where you're going."

She studied his square jaw and bright blue eyes. Italian families could be large, but what were the chances he was somehow connected to the Ficarras? She was being paranoid. "The carabinieri headquarters."

His eyes widened. "Ah."

She rolled her eyes. "I work for a magazine, don't forget."

"Well…you can take a taxi. Three kilometers. Fifteen Euros."

She nodded. "Thanks."

He shifted his weight. "Or…"

She frowned. "Or what?"

He took a deep breath. "I, er…I live that way. I could…I have a bike. I could drop you off."

Jess looked him up and down. He was tall and tan. The idea of darting through the streets of Rome on a moped appealed. Doing it with a bona fide Italian doubly so.

She smiled. "If it's no trouble—"

"No trouble. I finish in thirty minutes. Meet you in the car park." He left without waiting for a reply.

Jess finished her coffee, went back to her room to collect her bag, and reached the car park five minutes early.

Calling it a car park was ambitious. A couple of cars stood in one corner, but bikes occupied the majority of the space. There were mopeds in a jarring array of colors, dirt bikes that lived up to their name, and a selection of big powerful machines. The bikes clumped together by type as if some social order was in play.

She toyed with her phone, browsing the images from the airport. Most were blurred, but a few were pin sharp. She lingered over one with the mystery man's head turned toward her. A three-quarter shot. He was behind the car's window and reflections masked one side of his face. "Who are you?" she muttered.

"Romeo Pausini," said a voice.

She spun around. Her waiter stood behind her, two full-face helmets in his hands.

She shrugged. "Sorry. Talking to myself."

He laughed and handed her a helmet.

She bit her lip. "But really? Romeo?"

He frowned. "Yes, really. Why?"

"I, um…" She glanced at his sparkling blue eyes, his broad smile, and his bulging muscles. "No reason."

"Well, one Shakespearian quote, and I'll dump you off the back of the bike." He winked, and gestured to the helmet.

She put it on, pulling the strap tight, grateful to hide her blushing face behind its Plexiglas.

He donned his helmet, and spoke. She saw his mouth moving, and heard muffled sounds. She put a cupped hand to the side of her head. He moved her hand, and pressed a button on the side of her helmet. She heard a buzzing, and a female voice said, "Connected."

Romeo's voice reverberated in her ears. "Bluetooth."

She nodded.

He shrugged. "Didn't used to wear them, but now it's law. So…"

She smiled. "Right!"

He winced, and tapped the side of his helmet.

"Microphones," he said. "You can speak normally."

"Oh. Sorry."

He pointed to a bike, one of the largest in the section biker-protocol reserved for big bikes. Her heart did a flip as her brain raced back over the idea that riding through Rome with him would be exciting. "That's yours?"

He threw his leg over the bike, and reversed it off the stand. "You don't like?"

"No, it's, um, very nice. I, er, imagined something smaller. Much smaller."

He looked at her. "A moped?"

She nodded.

He laughed. "You've got the wrong waiter for one of those."

"Right."

"So?" His voice cooed in her ears.

She took a deep breath, and slipped onto the back of the bike. There were two small handholds behind her that made her feel she was leaning back.

"You can hold on if you want," he said.

"I am."

"To me."

"Er…"

"It's expected. Normal. On a bike."

She took a deep breath, and leaned forward, easing her arms

around his chest, and intertwining her fingers. The engine barked into life. She jolted, squeezing his chest harder.

"Don't worry. I'll take it easy."

"Don't have to. Not on my part."

He eased the bike out of the tight confines of the parking area, and joined a line of slow traffic moving around the pond in the center of the square. She kept her feet on the footrests, and her arms locked around his chest. A gap opened up on their right. Romeo leaned the bike. There was a roar, and she found herself crushing his chest to hold on. She pushed herself forward, balancing her weight against the acceleration, and relaxing her vise-like grip on his ribs.

On the left, she glimpsed the dome of St. Peter's between buildings before they raced across a bridge. She checked the speedometer. She did a double take at the speedometer before she realized the indicated hundred was in kilometers per hour. She didn't know the conversion to miles per hour, but judging by the rate they were passing cars, it must have been the limit inside the city.

He slowed, and took a sharp left. She squeezed him tight as the bike leaned over. The speedo needle raced back up the dial as Romeo righted the bike.

She saw a small card taped in the middle of the handlebars. It flapped in the wind. She saw the word Foto, and a vaguely familiar emblem. She eased one hand from her grip on Romeo, and held the card still.

"*Foto Oggi*," he said.

"The magazine?"

"Yeeeah."

"What's that mean?"

"Being a waiter isn't exactly a recipe for wealth. I give them a call from time to time. If we have a big name in the hotel, you know?"

"You're a tipster?"

"Just…you know, it's not a big thing. We hardly ever have anyone important."

"Thanks."

"I meant, you know, in the papers."

"Right."

Romeo weaved left and right to pass a taxi. "You're not going to tell the hotel, are you?"

She frowned. "Fear not."

He sighed with relief. "Thanks."

"Who do you know at *Foto Oggi*?"

"My landlord. He's the cover editor. That's how I started."

Romeo took a left into a narrow street, a line of bikes down one side. He crept along until he found a gap, parked the bike on its stand, and killed the engine.

Jess recognized the building from the day before, the carabinieri headquarters. She climbed off the back of the bike. "You know him okay?"

Romeo flipped up his face visor. "My landlord? He pays me when I phone in tips."

She removed her helmet, and fluffed her hair. "You think he'd do me a favor?"

"What?"

"I need to find someone."

He frowned. "You've heard of the Internet, right?"

She brought up the picture from the car park, and held her phone out. "Him."

Romeo peered at the picture. "You…like him?"

"I just want to find him."

"You think he works at *Foto Oggi*?"

"No. I think they'll have an image recognition database of every photo they've ever taken."

"Um…"

"Trust me, they will. I work for *Taboo Magazine*. *Foto Oggi* is at the sensational end of the tabloid pool. It's their business."

Romeo frowned. "And *Taboo* doesn't have one of those?"

She shook her head. "Only for the U.S."

"Why would *Foto Oggi* have this man's picture? Is he famous?"

Jess hesitated. "I'm not sure. But he could be. He might have attended a film premiere or been in a crowd at a sports event. Lots of possibilities. I want to check."

Romeo shrugged, and pulled a phone from his pocket.

Jess put her hand on the phone. "In person?"

"Just email him the picture."

She shook her head. "Rather not."

Romeo rolled his eyes, and pushed down his visor. "Better get back on."

She leapt on the bike, rammed the helmet on her head, and tightened the chinstrap as they roared away.

CHAPTER SEVEN

ON A RICH WOOD pew with the patina of centuries, Enzo
Ficarra and his family occupied the front row of his church. His
two children sat silently on his left, and his wife, Elena, on his
right. His cousin's family stood around the font for the
christening of their baby boy.

The priest's voice reverberated from ancient stone walls.
Behind him, the morning sun illuminated stained glass windows,
throwing colorful patterns on the flagstone floor.

Enzo sat bolt upright without touching the back of the pew.
His two sons did the same. He eyed them approvingly as the
priest finished the service. They remained seated, hands at their
sides, and their eyes watching the father as he passed down the
aisle. The congregation followed, moving as one as he stepped
out of the church door.

Enzo guided his two children from the church. Elena held his
arm. They followed the crowd through the centuries-old
graveyard surrounding the building to the iron gate that led out

to the parking area. They took pictures of the baby, and exchanged handshakes and small talk with friends and family.

His grandfather admonished Enzo for Luigi's absence. Enzo made excuses. The pressure of work. Business abroad.

The old man grunted, clearly not convinced. He made a fuss of his great-grandchildren, producing two chocolate bars with a sleight of hand trick that Enzo remembered from when he was a child.

But he wasn't a child, and he had business to attend to.

The crowd thinned. The newly christened boy was strapped into a car seat, and the family drove away. Enzo ushered his own children to his BMW. Elena took the passenger seat beside him, shaking her hair out of its bun as he drove.

The roads wound by. Mostly narrow. Mostly edged by thick hedges. They climbed a few hundred feet to the broad hilltop of their villa. The electric gate opened as they approached, and the car's tires crunched on the gravel.

He parked in the garage. The kids were out and running to the house before he had turned off the engine.

He leaned over and kissed his wife on the cheek.

Elena smiled. "You seem preoccupied this morning?"

He nuzzled her neck a moment. "Business."

"Today?"

He smiled. "Sometimes business doesn't take a day off."

He unlocked the side door into their villa and the kids raced to their rooms, eager to exchange their formal wear for swim gear and an afternoon in the sun.

He followed his wife up the stairs to their suite. She slipped out of her dress and into a bikini.

He stood, admiring the view.

Elena drew a sheer wrap around her slim waist. "You would

tell me, wouldn't you?"

He frowned.

"If there's a problem."

"Business. I promise."

She squeezed his biceps. "But is there a problem?"

He wrapped his arm around her waist. "No."

She pouched her lips into a mock pout. "Anything I should worry about?"

"No."

"Be aware of?"

"Nothing." He patted her behind. "I have to go away for a few days. But then I'll be taking some time off. Be around the house more. Spend time with the kids."

Elena kissed him as if her mind was already somewhere else. "That'll be nice."

He tightened his grip on her waist, and kissed her back. "And you."

She giggled, and slipped out of his arms. "Well, I'll wait until then."

He sighed. "I have to leave this afternoon."

She looked at him. "This afternoon?"

"Business." He hung up his suit. "I'll be back soon."

Elena kissed him again, more thoroughly this time. "Be careful, okay." She squeezed his arm. "We're all looking forward to spending more time together." She left the room, chasing the kids down to the pool.

Enzo took a new shirt and pair of jeans from a plastic bag at the back of his closet, and ripped off the tags. He checked his appearance in the mirror. The shirt was light brown, the jeans an average indigo. He donned a new pair of dark brown boots from a box. Satisfied his appearance wouldn't draw any attention, he stuffed the plastic bag, the tags, and the wrapping paper into the box.

He opened a safe at the rear of his closet. Inside were guns, knives, and a few hundred rounds of ammunition. He snagged a small pill bottle. He turned it over in his hand before returning it to the safe. Cyanide was too quick for what he had in mind.

He selected a hunting knife with a serrated edge and a wicked curved end for gutting animals. From the guns, he took a mini-Uzi 9mm, checked the safety, and tucked the gun in his belt. Several rounds of ammunition, just in case he needed it. He didn't expect to.

He printed two small pictures from his computer. One of the cartridges in his printer was low, so the pictures had a yellowish tint, but they were good enough. He trimmed around the edges, removing all the white paper.

From his desk, he selected a box of thumbtacks.

He headed downstairs to the kitchen, and filled a plastic bag with the remains of a bread loaf, half a pound of cheese, and a string bag of over-ripe cherry tomatoes.

From a drawer, he selected an eight-inch chef's knife with a sheath. A German make. Sharp with a good handle.

He topped the bag with an orange, three bottles of water, and a single plastic sandwich bag, the type with a leak-proof seal.

Enzo loaded his supplies into an aging Fiat hatchback that had once been a light shade of blue. He donned aviator-style sunglasses and headed out of the villa.

Fifty minutes later, he pulled off the road at a rusting iron gate on an unmade path that led into a dense forest. The land had been purchased by his grandfather before Enzo was born. Fifty acres of rough ground, unsuitable for building.

Not that he had any intention of building on the land. Special rights for hunting had been granted in the mid-1600s by the somewhat bloodthirsty King Emmanuel II. A sign warned that the land was a private hunting ground. Enzo smiled at the thought. He had no interest in stalking his dinner, but the threat of being shot kept the merely inquisitive visitors away.

The gate creaked as he swung it open, and again as he closed it.

The Fiat bounced over ruts and potholes, and he made his way slowly along a lane deeper into the woods. Just as the tree's canopy threatened to blot out all light, he emerged into a small clearing, and parked the car.

At the center of the clearing was a cabin.

Vines and brambles had long ago climbed its wooden exterior. The windows were painted black on the inside, and the door was sealed with a combination padlock.

He spun the padlock's dial three times. Forward, backward, forward. Each time stopping at a carefully memorized prime number.

The lock sprang open.

Enzo entered the cabin and bolted the door out of habit. The bolt provided little extra security for the dilapidated structure. One good push and the entire building would fall over.

He lifted a trapdoor in the middle of the floor, switched on a light at the bottom of the shaft, and climbed down the ladder into the gloom.

The air below ground was cool and humid. The stink of ploughed earth permeated everything. He groped along the rocks until he found a light switch, and flipped it on. The bulbs cast small pools of yellow light on rough rock walls and an only-slightly-smoother floor that sloped down into the earth.

He walked along the slope to a section where the tunnel widened. A rough-hewn wooden table sat incongruously against one wall. A bundle of leather straps and a silver camping light were strewn on top. The camping light looked antique, but he flicked a switch and two banks of LEDs cast a pool of cold blue light around the table. Under the glare, he selected two leather straps, one with a metal hoop, and the other with a large buckle on the end.

Beneath the table was a stack of black plastic bags. The bags slipped from their neat stack as he turned up the corners, counting.

The industrial-sized bags were thicker and larger than household trash bags, but couldn't hold an entire human body. Not one that was intact, anyway.

He shuffled the bags back into place. There were four. He patted the pile. More than enough.

He pointed the camping light down the tunnel. He heard scratching, scraping, and movement on the ground. He flicked the light back and forth. Some of the nocturnal residents were more than substantial enough to cause bites and diseases and other problems. Best to clear them the easy way, with the light instead of the gun.

A row of thick, dark doors hung open on the right side of the tunnel. Some scraped the ground, some were long separated from their hinges, but some were intact. Thick heavy wood, iron banding, and solid hinges, but they had stood the test of time.

There were five doors, ten feet apart, each with a one-inch spy hole bored through the ancient wood. Each was sealed by a heavy wooden bar running across the door's width and resting in thick metal hooks on each side. Apart from the spy holes, which were added sometime later, the doors were as old as the tunnels.

The miners who'd once plied their trade here would have recognized them.

He walked to the last door. It was his habit. Start at the farthest end. Which made sense if they were going to be filling up the rooms. But they never had. People were usually either sensible enough not to defy them, or worthless enough to die long before they reached that point.

He checked the spy hole in the last door by holding the camping light close.

A heavyset man huddled in the corner, cuffed to one of the many rusty metal spikes in the walls and floor. His bright green polo shirt contrasted with his soiled jeans. His thin hair stuck to his head, and several days' stubble darkened his jaw. His head was angled down. He shuffled backward, pressing himself against the rock as if he believed it could swallow him whole.

Enzo pushed open the door. "Hello, Wilson."

CHAPTER EIGHT

ENZO STEPPED INTO THE room, and dropped the plastic bag on the ground. "Food."

Wilson's gaze hovered over the bag before sinking back to the ground.

"I have news."

Wilson grunted.

Enzo pinned the yellowed pictures to the back of the door. "You don't want to hear?"

Wilson breathed hard. "What?"

"Your parents' luggage made it across the Atlantic."

Wilson looked sideways at him. "Leave them alone."

"My, my. You do love them, don't you?" Enzo's sarcasm belied his smile. What a fool Grantly was. The last in a long line of fools Marek had chosen, thank god.

Wilson turned his face toward the light. "If you've hurt—"

Enzo's laugh taunted. "The luggage? No."

Wilson glowered from the tiny eyes in his doughy face.

"You mean mom and dad? Interesting you should ask." Laughter faded from Enzo's voice, replaced by annoyance and anger. "They didn't arrive, you see. Just their luggage. Two suitcases. One each. With their names on them. But no money. And no sign of mommy and daddy. No sign anywhere. Strange that. Don't you think?"

Wilson scowled even as he crabbed backward into the corner again.

"It leaves us with a situation." Enzo dropped the leather straps on the ground. The hooks and loops landed with a satisfying thunk. "A difficult situation."

Wilson stared at the straps, eyes wide. His mouth formed an "O" and his chin quivered.

"You see," Enzo took an exaggeratedly deep breath and exhaled very, very slowly, "the luggage had no money in it."

Wilson shuffled his knees up, shrinking farther into the shadows.

"Maybe they don't think so much of you?" Enzo frowned. "A lot less than you gave them credit for, anyway."

Wilson breathed in rapid, shallow gasps through clenched teeth.

"I thought they did. We talked. They seemed concerned. Cooperative, even." Enzo bent to retrieve one of the straps and formed a loop. He clicked his tongue against the roof of his mouth. "I thought they understood. No money. No Wilson. Pretty simple concept, really."

Wilson shook his head fast and whimpered as he dug his heels into the floor and pushed himself as far back as he could move before the cold earth blocked all retreat.

Before he could move again, Enzo snapped the loop tight around Wilson's free hand and wrapped the strap over a metal spike on Wilson's right side.

Wilson pulled his arm toward his chest. Enzo yanked the strap back. The spike's extra leverage wrenched Wilson's arm straight. Wilson squealed. Enzo doubled the strap's loop around the spike before cinching the end.

Wilson's eyes darted between the strap and Enzo.

"You understand that, don't you?" Enzo didn't smile. His voice was colder than Arctic air.

Wilson pulled at the strap.

"Not complicated at all." Enzo shook his head with mock sorrow. "No money. No Wilson."

Wilson kept up the tension on the strap.

"Very, very simple."

Wilson hyperventilated. Enzo narrowed his eyes and gazed into the dark corner to be sure Wilson hadn't passed out too soon.

"Simple...but they didn't pay."

Wilson's mouth hung open. He breathed rapidly through the open maw. Gulping air.

"So, now..."

Wilson's panting came faster. He opened and closed his mouth like a fish. "They have the money."

Enzo nodded sorrowfully again. "So you said."

"They do. They do." Wilson's tongue darted out to wet his lips. "I know for sure. I've seen it."

Enzo scoffed. "Perhaps they don't want to spend it on their son?"

Wilson's eyes went wide. "They will. They will. They wouldn't leave me. Really. They wouldn't. Not—"

Enzo picked up the second strap. "But they have."

Wilson swallowed. "No."

Enzo slipped one end of the strap through a metal loop.

Wilson shook his head. "No."

Enzo snapped the leather tight. "Yes." He bent and whipped the leather loop around Wilson's ankle. Wilson kicked, but the metal loop clamped down on the strap. Enzo wrapped the strap around a rung in the floor, pulling hard, stretching Wilson spread-eagle on the floor. He bucked, throwing his weight against the leather and chains. "No, no!"

Enzo slipped the free end of the strap through the loops, leaving Wilson's own efforts to pull it tight.

Wilson froze. "A mistake."

Enzo shook his head. "No mistake."

"You must have got the wrong luggage."

"It had their name on it."

"It can't—"

"I was there. Their luggage. No parents. No money."

"But—"

"Someone thinks they can mess with me."

"No, no."

"I don't like it when people think they can do that and get away with it." Enzo slid the chef's knife from his bag. "So, I wondered what to do."

Wilson's eyes stretched wider. "They have the money. They can get it."

Enzo nodded. "I'm sure they can."

"Yes, yes. They can. They can."

"All they need is the correct motivation."

"Let me talk to them. They'll get the money."

"I expect my instructions to be followed."

"I know."

"To the letter."

"I know. They have the money. I can get it."

"I told them what would happen if they did not follow instructions." Enzo knelt down, putting a boot on Wilson's hand, splaying it on the floor.

Wilson thrashed from side to side, pulling hard. "No, no. I can get it from them. They have it."

Enzo shifted more weight to his boot. "We gave them instructions."

Wilson panted. "I can get it."

"They didn't follow them."

"Let me, let me talk to them. Let me talk to them."

"So, we need to make sure they understand us."

"I can—"

Enzo pressed the knife against Wilson's knuckles. "One thumb, or two fingers?"

Wilson bucked side to side in his leather restraints. He curled his fingers a fraction. "No! No!"

Wilson's terror was more valuable to Enzo than his fingers. On the farm, severed finger injuries were common. Not lethal. He wouldn't die from severed fingers. But terror would make him and his foolish parents pay.

Enzo shifted more weight onto Wilson's hand, and pressed the knife harder into the flesh.

Wilson's fingers went white with strain. "NO, NO, NO."

"It was simple. No money. No Wilson."

Enzo cut skin.

Wilson threw his weight back and forth in the harnesses. "NO, NO. PLEASE. THEY HAVE THE MONEY. PLEASE. I BEG YOU. THEY HAVE THE MONEY. THEY HAVE IT."

Blood oozed around the blade. "I know they have it."

"IT WAS A MISTAKE. PLEASE. A MISTAKE. OLD

PEOPLE. PLEASE GOD. PLEASE!"

Enzo leaned forward. "All they need is the correct motivation." He shifted his weight to the knife. Gripping. Pushing. Sliding. There was little resistance. A softness. A hardness. A pop.

And blood.

Wilson screamed. His voice coarse and hard and spitting. The air tearing from his lungs, clawing at his throat. Anger and agony. Lots of agony. He snatched breaths, short and sharp, filling his lungs to do it again. Breath, breath, scream. Breath, breath, scream.

Blood poured. A momentary gush. Pressure being released. Wilson arched his back. His pain hauling him from the floor. His core pulling at his limbs, tearing at the straps and chains.

Enzo stepped back. The leather straps were stretched close to breaking. But Wilson broke first. He lurched. Twisting sideways. One arm flailing unnaturally. Dislocated.

Enzo plucked the severed finger from the warm liquid, and dropped it into the sandwich bag. He slid his fingers across the opening, sealing it.

He pulled on each strap in the opposite direction to Wilson's agony-fueled straining, releasing the cinches, and un-looping the ends from Wilson's limbs.

Wilson clutched at his bloodied hand with his free arm, and curled as far as the chains allowed. Fetal comfort to the shock gripping his body and soul.

Enzo closed the door and dropped the wooden bar into the iron clasps.

Wilson's voice modulated between moaning, crying, and screaming.

He was weak.

Unlike his parents. Enzo respected them a bit more. They didn't show up. They didn't send money. That took nerve. He hadn't expected the ancient couple to have more courage than their worthless son. But they did.

Enzo sighed. On the other hand, what they'd done was stupid. Testing him. Challenging him. Failing to pay the ransom was a gamble with their son's life. A braver move than most would have made.

Yet their luggage had been on the flight, and the ROS were waiting at the airport. So how brave were they? Perhaps they'd foolishly believed the police could save them.

Idiots.

He walked up the incline, and dropped the leather straps on the coffee table.

And what of the young American woman? The one with the blonde curls? What was her part in all this?

Police chased her and she ran, so she wasn't police herself.

Wilson had no sister. Perhaps a more distant family member? Would his parents have risked sending a woman?

He shook his head. Instinct told him she wasn't sent by the parents.

Perhaps she had heard about their money? That they were carrying the cash in their luggage? If she knew, perhaps she was a thief.

But then, she was chasing the luggage. So she hadn't stolen the money before the luggage was taken.

He shook his head again. It was a puzzle, to be sure.

He made his way back to the ladder and climbed up. Whatever her involvement, things were not as they seemed.

The luggage, the woman, and the ransom money were connected, to each other and to Luigi's disappearance.

But how?

There were too many oddities. He needed more information.

He lowered the cover over the shaft, and clicked the padlock into place. He didn't know how the woman was connected to the parents. Not yet. But when he did, he would have his money.

And Wilson, at least, would be dead. With a bit of luck, the woman and the parents, too.

CHAPTER NINE

JESS WALKED OUT OF the *Foto Oggi* offices with the cover editor's card in her hand. The man had been abrupt until she mentioned *Taboo Magazine*. Her worldwide publication held significant influence in certain circles, which was one of the many reasons Jess worked there.

He'd dispatched a junior staffer to run the facial recognition search on her video, attempting to match the man's face to photos in *Foto Oggi's* archives. Jess had her hopes up for a few minutes until he said it would take twenty-four hours to obtain the results. A lie. He planned to do his own research on the black-haired man and see what he could turn up.

She'd have argued, but there was little point. She could agree, and stand a chance of getting an answer, or argue and get none at all.

Romeo waited outside, guarding his bike from traffic wardens, thieves, and joy riders. "Success?"

She nodded and opened her mouth to speak, but her phone

rang. Morris's number appeared on the display. Turning her back on Romeo, she answered the call.

"You still at your hotel?" Morris said.

"I'm…out and about."

"You sent me a text. You heading over here?"

"I am. Now."

There was a long silence. "What are you doing, Jess?"

She took a deep breath. "All right. That picture kept nagging me."

"What picture?"

"The man at the airport."

"Which man? Don't tell me you're holding out on me."

"No! The pictures I gave Vanelli. The man who took the luggage."

"You're searching for him? I told you to keep out of the enforce—"

"I'm sticking to my half of the bargain. Investigative journalism. I called in at the offices of the *Foto Oggi* magazine. They're searching their image banks."

"Jess! The man in your picture might be completely innocent, and now you've just fingered him to some magazine."

"I didn't tell them why I wanted to know his identity."

"They're a tabloid magazine, and you just hung a giant question mark over his head."

"It could be important."

"Which is why the carabinieri are searching their databases, too. And they don't need the help of some trashy magazine."

Jess frowned. She certainly agreed with the trashy tag.

Morris sighed. "Jess. I didn't mean it like that. I have the greatest respect for you. You know that. But you have to be careful. Some of the worst people are involved in this."

"It was one picture. At a magazine. How's anyone going to know? The Grantlys want their son back. I promised to help, Morris."

He sighed. Twice. "Can I meet you at your hotel?"

"Why?"

"Can I meet you at the hotel?"

"Why? What can't you tell me on the phone?"

"There's something you need to see."

She looked at Romeo and the running motorbike. "All right. See you in ten minutes."

CHAPTER TEN

ROMEO PARKED THE BIKE at the rear of the hotel. Jess apologized and thanked him and rushed through the lobby to stand on the curb in front.

Morris arrived in a taxi a few minutes later. He opened the rear door. "Get in."

"Nice to see you, too." She settled next to him. "Where are we going?"

Morris grunted, and gave the driver an address.

"So, has Vanelli caught up with Ficarra? Interviewed him?" She raised her eyebrows. "Shot him, maybe?"

"Nothing like that. There's no sign of him. His wife claims he's away on business."

She snorted. "Yeah, right. What about surveillance?"

"There's a process. Vanelli's working through it. Soon."

"Can't he just put a man on his tail?"

Morris laughed. "My first suggestion, but apparently there was a big case a couple of years ago where a well-known Mafia boss sued the carabinieri because they did just that. Walked away with a good chunk of money."

"It's not right."

Morris nodded.

The car came to a halt at an intersection. People crossed the road, walking every which way around the car.

"I need to call Harriet," Jess said.

"Why?"

"They deserve to know what's going on. I promised her I'd get her son back, and—"

Morris held up his hand. "All taken care of. The local field office is going to call round every day until we have him on a plane home."

She sighed with relief. It was probably better the Grantlys got their information in person rather than over an international phone line. They were the sort of people who put stock in the personal touch.

They sat in silence as the taxi inched, raced, and honked its way through traffic, finally coming to a stop outside the 300-year-old Palazzo Margherita, a huge pink building housing the American Embassy.

Jess frowned at Morris. He ignored her, paid the driver, and got out. He walked along the front sidewalk, outside the iron fences that surrounded the grand building, and past the guarded front gate.

She raced to keep up. "You're not going to use the front door?"

He shook his head. "We're not going here."

He crossed the road, and turned into a narrow walkway between two tall buildings. They came to an intersection with a second walkway. He turned right, and right again at the next intersection.

Jess walked fast and ran faster, but she was a foot shorter
than Morris. Longer legs were an asset in any speed race. "You
just wanted to show me the mazes of Rome?"

He shook his head. "Making sure we don't have a tail."

She looked behind her. The shadow-filled alleyway became
instantly less appealing.

Morris knocked on a door. An angry buzz and the door
opened, first a fraction and then wider. He walked ahead of her
into a narrow hallway. A second closed door directly in front of
them stopped all progress. Scuff marks covered dull white walls,
and a camera was mounted in the corner of the ceiling.

Jess frowned. "What is this place?"

"Field office."

"You're kidding." She looked at the dirty walls and the
empty room. "Don't you guys have a place in the embassy?"

"A public office, yes. This is the business office."

"Business?"

"I'm sure you can guess. And I wouldn't be bringing you
here if I thought there was any other way to get through to you."
He glowered at her. "Everything here is off the record.
Permanently. Nothing you see or hear in this building goes into
your magazine. Ever. Understand?"

She blew out a long breath. "Okay."

"I mean it, Jess. You'll understand why in a minute."

She looked him in the eye, and nodded.

The second door buzzed open.

They walked into what might have been a Victorian-era
home. Thick paint covered the woodwork, and paisley wallpaper
adorned the walls. Stairs ran upwards, and several doors led off
the corridor.

A middle-aged woman poked her head out of the first

doorway. Behind her, boxes were piled on the floor. "You're late."

Morris shrugged. "We—"

"Never mind." She pointed up the stairs. "He's waiting. Second door on the left." She disappeared back into her room, closing the door behind her.

Jess followed Morris up the stairs. She tapped on the florid wallpaper. "Nice."

He stopped at the top of the steps. "This isn't a good time for jokes, Jess."

She nodded. "I hear you."

He knocked on the second door on the left, and walked in without waiting for an invitation.

The room was L-shaped, a desk at one end, a table at the other, and a narrow walkway between the two, marked by boxes of files. The wallpaper had seen better days, and the once-white paintwork was tinged an aged yellow. Heavy drapes blocked the daylight, and an underpowered bulb hanging from the middle of the ceiling strained to push back the gloom.

Behind the desk, a balding man with square shoulders was hunched over a blizzard of paper. A computer with the keyboard balanced on top of the monitor was perched on the very edge of the desk. His lamp was the brightest light in the room. He switched it off. "Please sit down."

Morris pointed Jess to a chair in front of the desk, and stood by the drapes. She sat. The man had a square jaw to go with his square shoulders. In earlier years, he'd have been handsome, now he wore the signs of a hard life. His eyeglasses looked like wayfarers, and the corner of his mouth was twisted up on one side.

"Miss Kimball…" He breathed in, long and slow.

She lost patience waiting for him to finish his sentence.
"Yes?"

He flicked a switch, and a projector illuminated the wall
behind him. He turned his back on Jess.

A grainy photograph of two people in trench coats appeared.
They were walking along the edge of a country road. The picture
had clearly been taken from a great distance.

"The Ficarras," said the man.

Jess took a deep breath. "Wait a minute. Who are you?"

The man slouched down in his chair, keeping out of the
projector's beam. "Can you see well enough?"

"Yes. But who are you?" She looked at Morris.

"Call me Ahab, if you must call me something. He, too, was
a man who chased an impossible fiend."

"Very funny." Jess glared at him. Ahab wasn't his name and
he had no good reason to lie about such an easily discovered
fact. He offered no further reply. "What is this?"

Ahab flicked on to the next slide.

The Ficarras were on the same road, approaching a car.
"Them again."

Another picture. The Ficarras getting in the car. "And
again."

The picture changed a fourth time.

Jess jolted back.

Two blank eyes from a severed head returned her gaze. A
wide slash ran across the forehead. Blood ran down the face. The
head was tilted back, the muscles holding it cut, bone and sinew
exposed, pipes and veins bare and open.

Jess squeezed her eyes shut, and looked away.

"A woman, in case you can't tell," said Ahab. "A nice
woman. Respectable. Well off. Lots of friends. We know her

name. We found her after the Ficarras drove off."

Jess glowered at the man. "You watched that happen."

"Not even close." Ahab shook his head. "Those two stopped. Walked into the trees, and half an hour later walked away. We had no idea she was there. None at all."

He looked back at the screen, and returned to the slide of two men getting into the car. "But the Ficarras knew."

She took a deep breath. "The Ficarras."

He nodded again. "We told the Italians. Anonymously, of course."

She glanced questioningly at him, partly to avoid looking at the screen.

"They don't like foreign governments conducting operations in their country. Understandable. We don't like it in the U.S. either. Touchy subject." He jerked his thumb toward Morris. "Which is why your minder informed the carabinieri of his impending arrival, instead of turning up, guns blazing." He took off his glasses. "Or swinging a handbag."

She screwed up her face. "My *minder*?" She looked at Morris.

"Someone needs to look after you, Miss Kimball," said Ahab, his back to her. "You have a disturbing tendency of breaking the rules and getting yourself into trouble, don't you?"

The screen flashed. Another body appeared, twisted and bloody. Then another. And another.

She looked sideways at the images.

"We have names for some of them," Ahab said.

She kept her gaze down, avoiding the life-size butchery on the screen. "Why are you showing me this?"

"Mainly, I want you to understand you are meddling in something dangerous. Very dangerous." He grunted and gestured to the screen. "Given the state of the bodies, it's not immediately apparent, but more than half these victims were female. The Ficarras have no compassion toward women, Miss Kimball. To say the least."

She forced herself to look at the screen. "And why are you investigating murders in Italy?"

He turned back to the screen. "The Ficarras have been traveling to the U.S., as you know."

"So, why not arrest them?"

"On what charge?"

She pointed at the screen. "That."

"We see the aftermath, but we do not have the evidence, even if we had the power."

"So get it!"

Ahab scowled. "You're forgetting Miss Kimball, the FBI does not conduct unauthorized operations outside the U.S. borders."

"But you're here."

"You could say that."

"What if I do say that? In print?"

The floorboards creaked as Morris shifted his weight.

Ahab grunted again. "Look around. If the State Department wants us to vanish, we'll be gone."

He straightened his back. "And I don't believe you will say anything." He jerked his thumb at the screen. "You helped kill one of those bastards. Luigi Ficarra. We want the other one. And we want him locked up or dead just as much as you do."

She narrowed her gaze and frowned.

He nodded. "Believe me, we're doing our damnedest. If we get so much as a hint of evidence, we will share everything we know with the carabinieri. Your success with Luigi Ficarra in

New York has opened up an opportunity for, shall we call it, greater collaboration."

She nodded.

"But there is the question about what to do with you."

She leaned forward, scowling. "*Do* with me?"

"I understand Agent Morris has come to a tacit agreement with you. About the Ficarras. And your involvement." He took a deep breath. "You've agreed to stick to investigative journalism."

"So?"

"That's a broad topic."

She didn't blink.

"Don't overstep those boundaries."

"I promised the Grantlys I'd bring their son home."

"And we will do that, Miss Kimball. We. Not you. And with luck, you'll still be alive to see it when it happens."

She took a deep breath. "So, what do you want me to do?"

"I want you to take a holiday. A vacation. Splurge a little. You're a woman in Rome. Buy dresses. See stuff that's older than dirt." He leaned toward her. "Find a swarthy Italian to keep you busy at night."

She did not reply.

"Do anything you like, Miss Kimball." He leaned back. "But go near Enzo Ficarra and you'll leave me with one more slide for my collection."

She still said nothing.

He looked directly into her eyes. "Leave enforcement to us. Do I make myself clear?"

She squeezed her lips into a thin line, and nodded.

"Good." Ahab returned to his papers.

Morris jerked his head toward the door, and walked out.

She followed him to the bottom of the stairs. "You could have just told me."

Morris looked directly into her eyes. "I did tell you, Jess. You just weren't listening."

"I did listen."

"No you didn't. You chased Luigi Ficarra into that parking garage in New York when I told you not to. I told you we were on the way. That we'd handle it. And by the skin of your teeth, you shot him before he killed you. I told you not to fly to Rome, but you did it anyway. You chased a man you thought was Enzo Ficarra all over the airport yesterday. I told you to stay out of this, that we had it covered. And today, you went to *Foto Oggi* with the guy's photo looking to identify him. And you brought the tabloids into this, Jess. Muckrakers." He raked his hands over his head. "Tell me how in God's name *all of that* is *listening* to me?"

There's a big difference between simply listening and doing what I believe is best when I'm in the middle of things and you're not there.

She gestured to the upstairs office where Ahab sat smugly flashing his slides.

"Well, you could have showed me the damn pictures!" She pressed her lips into a single hard line, and swallowed.

"You've done your part, Jess. You know that. We know that." Morris touched her arm. "I gave you my word, and I meant it. I will keep you informed as and when things happen. But you're no match for these butchers. Don't you see that?"

She looked at her feet, and nodded. She saw it. But that didn't mean she would stop.

"Come on." He kept his hand on her elbow and guided her along. "I have one more thing, then I'll buy you lunch."

She followed him deeper into the house. He took a steep staircase down into the cellar, and knocked on an old, but substantial door.

A spy hole opened.

"Morris," he said.

The hole closed, and the door opened. A short man gestured for them to enter. Behind him was a counter, and behind that was a mass of smooth black metal. Rifles, pistols, submachine guns. They lined shelves, and hung from the walls, glinting under fluorescent lighting.

"Fred, this is Jess Kimball. Jess, Fred Romano."

"Good to meet you, Jess." They shook hands.

Romano pulled a box from the shelves and dumped a gun onto the counter. "We use the PPK over here." He thumped a box of ammunition beside it. Morris pocketed them both.

"And," he placed a small black object on the counter. It looked like a cardboard cutout in the shape of a gun.

"Heizer Double Tap. For emergencies." Romano picked it up, wrapping his hands around either end. "Open like so." The tiny barrel pivoted forward. He shoved bullets in the gun's two barrels. "Nine millimeter. And..." He turned the gun over, and pulled two rounds from the bottom of the grip, "Spares."

The Heizer had two short hexagonal barrels, and the sides appeared completely flat. Jess reached for the tiny object.

Romano moved the gun out of her reach.

Morris took the Heizer. "Thanks."

"Jess, are you a trainee?"

"Civilian," Morris answered before she could say she was a reporter.

Romano scowled. "We don't allow—"

"No problem." Morris grabbed Jess's elbow. "We're leaving."

He steered her out of the room. Romano slammed the door and latched bolts in place behind them.

They left the building through the same buzzing doors, the same scuffed white hallway, and same blank staring camera.

Morris picked up the pace, going vaguely back in the direction they'd come. Again, Jess struggled to keep up.

"Listen, next time you want to go jogging, let me know and I'll wear the right shoes."

He nodded and slowed slightly. "Sorry. Force of habit."

"You've been here before?"

He shrugged.

"Right. So, how come you know this place, and those people?"

"I don't. But we connected through channels." They emerged onto a wide street. He turned left. "When we realized you were on Flight 12, we asked the carabinieri to pick you up at the airport. They got held up in traffic."

She grunted.

"Anyway. Want American?"

She frowned.

"To eat."

She nodded and they sped along at his usual pace for a couple of blocks before she said, "You know, I was pretty visible at the airport."

"You could say that."

"Maybe Enzo Ficarra knows who I am."

"Possibly. Another good reason for us to keep your name out of the papers both here and back home."

"No, I mean what if he saw me at the airport? Or his man snapped photos?"

"His man?"

"The guy who took the luggage."

Morris nodded. "We don't know who that man was. Yet."

"I need protection."

"Not if you stick to our deal. You conduct your interviews, prepare to write your story. You should be fine." He glanced both ways at an intersection and hustled her across the street. "Besides, we don't have the manpower."

"I didn't mean a bodyguard." She lowered her voice. "I need a gun."

He glanced at her and kept walking.

"You kept my Glock in New York. If you hadn't, I wouldn't need to ask."

"Your gun was involved in a shooting. I was required to take it until the shooting is cleared. I didn't arrest you, did I?" He swiped his palm over his head. "Look, this is Italy, Jess. Gun laws are not as tight as Great Britain, but they're pretty tight. You're not licensed. And we don't have time to get you licensed."

She stopped on the sidewalk.

He took a few steps before he realized she wasn't walking with him. He turned back and rolled his eyes. "Jess—"

"Don't Jess me. You have two guns, I have none. Who needs protection more? You or me?" She lowered her voice. "I'm sure I could get a gun somewhere, if you're not inclined. The illegal market shouldn't be that hard to find."

Morris joined her and stood close enough to have a quiet argument. "Get caught with an illegal gun and I don't have anywhere near enough juice to get you out of prison."

"I shot Enzo's brother. His dead brother. When he finds me, do you think he's simply going to let that go?"

Morris drew a long breath through his nose. "That's why I want you to keep a low profile."

"Really, Morris. It's only a matter of time. He'll find me. You know he will."

Morris shifted his weight from one leg to the other.

She leaned in closer. "The small one. The Heffer."

"Heizer."

"You have plenty of ammo for the Walther. You won't need a second gun."

"It's for emergencies."

"I didn't think it was for entertainment. And when Enzo finds me, and you're not there, it'll sure as hell be an emergency."

"All right, all right. Not here. Let's eat." He scowled, looked up and down the busy street. "I'm not authorized to give you a gun. You get caught with it and both our asses are on the line. So don't flash the damn thing around for anything less than the absolute mother of all emergencies."

She nodded. "Trust me, if I have to use a gun, it'll be life or death."

CHAPTER ELEVEN

MORRIS'S IDEA OF AN American lunch was the Hard Rock
Café near the American Embassy. They had token
acknowledgments to local cuisine, but he stuck with a burger.
Could be irrational, but he felt protein and carbohydrates would
fend off his jet lag.

He watched Jess read the entire menu. She lingered on the
Italian options, but when the waiter arrived, she ordered last, and
simply said "same."

The food was close enough to the last Hard Rock Café he'd
been in. He wasn't quite sure if it was Philly or Chicago. He
started to eat quickly. Jess picked at her food.

He put his knife and fork on his plate, and looked at Jess.
"The pictures?"

She frowned.

"The pictures that are ruining your appetite?"

She sighed. "Just what they represent."

"Meaning?"

She stabbed a fry with her fork. "Failure."

"Er…"

She waved the fry at him. "Let's face it. If we'd done our jobs better, those people might be alive."

"We? You mean the FBI?"

She shook her head. "I meant all of us. Me included."

"We do our best." He put down his silverware. "All of us. But there's only so much that can be done. For every case we investigate, there are ten behind it, begging for our attention."

She sighed. "I know. You said that before. The never-ending caseload."

"It's the way it is, Jess. We do the best we can. We can't do anything more."

She put the fry in her mouth, and chewed.

Morris picked up his fork. "Besides, in this case, we, is law enforcement. You're the journalist. We investigate, you report what happens. We agreed, right?"

She took another fry. "Right."

"Don't renege on our agreement. I stuck my neck out to keep you out of jail, and again not to have you shipped straight back home." He leaned forward. "You break our agreement, and you're hurting me. Directly. Understand? I've vouched for you. Don't make me sorry."

She took a deep breath, and raised her gaze to his. "I understand."

"Glad to hear it." He pointed at her plate. "You going to eat that?"

She grinned and dragged her plate closer to her. "I was raised as a member of the clean plate club. So you're out of luck."

They finished their meal. Morris slid the Heizer under a

napkin, and pushed it across the table. "For emergencies only."

"Definitely." She reached for the napkin.

Morris kept his hand on the weapon. "There're two barrels, Jess. If it comes to it, don't hesitate."

She nodded. He let go. She swept up the gun and napkin, and put it in her bag.

Morris's phone rang. He recognized the number. "Vanelli. What's up?"

"Where are you?"

"Hard Rock Café. By our embassy. I'm with Miss Kimball."

Vanelli grunted. "We have the airport tapes. They're interesting. Important, even."

"What's on them?"

"Come and see. We're in the AV room. You can't miss it. And Morris? No journalists."

Morris clenched his teeth as he finished the call.

He made his excuses with Jess. She waved a corporate credit card, and insisted on paying. It went against his principles, but she thrust it into the waiter's hand before he could protest.

He left her at the restaurant, and caught a taxi back to the carabinieri's offices, arriving twenty minutes after Vanelli had called. It took another ten minutes wandering the corridors until he found a door marked "AV." He knocked, and walked straight in.

The flickering blue haze of television monitors illuminated the room. Red and blue LEDs flashed irregularly. People were hunched over keyboards, and wires trailed everywhere.

Vanelli turned to look at him. "Back so soon?"

Morris frowned.

"You had a good lunch? With your friend."

"Miss Kimball is an American citizen."

Vanelli shrugged.

Morris straightened his spine. "That means I'm obligated to protect her."

"Then send her back."

"She's here lawfully. It's a free country."

The left side of Vanelli's mouth curled up. "But not her country."

"She has rights. Even here."

Vanelli's mouth lifted at the corner. "Then let's hope you are able to protect her when the time comes."

Morris turned to the monitors. "You said you might have found something important on the video?"

Vanelli said something in Italian to one of the technicians. A pair of monitors above him went blank.

"We have reviewed the airport video. We had to go quite a way back."

Morris frowned.

The video operator ran a segment. Morris recognized one of the roads by the airport terminal.

Vanelli tapped the screen by a string of whirling digits. "Notice the time."

A white Ford bumped over a curb, and parked in a space marked for service vehicles only.

A man got out. He wore a black jacket, dark jeans, and a gray unmarked baseball hat.

He straightened his jacket, and walked into the garage.

The surveillance cameras swapped, following him across the grass, through the parked cars, and into the elevator. The doors closed, and the playback stopped.

Morris shrugged. "Where and when did he come out?"

"Good question."

The image split into several views, showing the elevator doors on each level.

People walked in and out. In on the parking levels, and out on the airport side, or in from the airport, and out to the garage and their car.

They struggled with luggage, herded children, or strolled with tiny carry-on bags. Some looked full of energy, some looked worn down by coach class, but they all had one thing in common.

None of them wore a black jacket and gray baseball hat.

People kept walking. The elevator car traveled up and down. The doors opened and closed.

The video operator sped up the recording. Travelers scurried by.

Morris pushed his lips together. "What other floors does this elevator service?"

Vanelli shook his head. "This is all of them."

"Then—"

"Watch."

The courier carrying the Grantlys' luggage appeared. He stepped into the elevator as Jess emerged on the walkway. The elevator doors closed and Jess gave chase.

The video operator returned the segment to normal speed.

Morris looked from one elevator door to the next. Seconds ticked by. His eyes swept back and forth from one set of doors to the next. "Did you stop the video?"

Vanelli shook his head.

Almost a full minute later, the elevator doors opened on the ground level. The courier walked out.

Morris pointed at the courier. "Wait."

The image froze.

Morris peered. "There's duct tape on the luggage."

Vanelli nodded.

Morris said, "He opened them."

Vanelli nodded again. "So this man knew perfectly well what was in those suitcases he took."

The operator pressed play.

As the courier walked to his car, Morris saw a shirtsleeve dangling out of one side of the suitcase.

Jess flitted across the camera's field of view. The courier's car reversed, and charged out of the parking garage. Jess came back into the camera's field of view, running toward the terminal, three men giving chase.

The elevator continued, oblivious to the excitement on the ground floor. More people passed through its doors. Single parents, babies in strollers, college kids, elderly couples, and more went about their business.

The operator pressed fast-forward. The time code in the bottom right of the screen turned into a blur. Travelers fast marched. Children danced and ran.

After about a minute, the video slowed to normal speed.

The doors opened on the ground floor, and the man in the black jacket and gray baseball cap appeared.

"Fifteen minutes later," Vanelli said. He tapped the screen by the time code. "He spent two and a half hours in that elevator."

The man walked steadily out of range. The picture snapped to a second camera, a wide-angle view across a swath of cars. The man walked out of the car park. The camera changed again, following the man along the side of the parking garage, and changed one last time to show him jumping into the small white Ford, and driving off.

"Notice anything?" Vanelli asked, without looking away from the monitors.

Morris shrugged. "Can't see his face."

Vanelli smiled. "He knew what he was doing."

The operator reversed the tape to show the figure walking across the grass to the Ford.

"Camera in the elevator?" Morris said.

"It wasn't working."

"Seems unlikely."

"It was more than that." Vanelli pointed to the man on the screen. "He came by the day before to disable it."

"Let me guess, he didn't smile into the lens as he was doing it?"

Vanelli shook his head. "Same routine. Same car. Same parking space. Only he was in and out in mere minutes."

"Fingerprints?"

"The elevator carries hundreds of people a day."

"Did he touch anything else?"

Vanelli shook his head again.

"He spent two and a half hours in an elevator. He must have left some trace."

"We've been over it. He took out a ceiling tile. Hid in the roof."

Morris watched the monitor.

The video played on. The man got into the Ford and drove off. The operator paused the video with the service vehicle parking space, and the disappearing Ford on the screen.

"License plates?" said Morris.

"Stolen."

"But you could see the face of the courier."

Vanelli shrugged. "We're checking. Nothing yet."

"His car?"

"Haven't found it. His plates were stolen as well."

"So, they're not stupid, and one of them must have been Ficarra."

"The courier wasn't."

"Which leaves baseball-cap man."

Vanelli chewed his lower lip. "Could be."

"He was there, waiting for the Grantlys' luggage."

"Even if we had pictures, it's only suspicious behavior. Not something we could use to get a warrant."

The picture glowed on the screen. Two and a half hours in an elevator, and he didn't leave any evidence? Hard to believe. The carabinieri had moved too slowly to go after the courier, even if they didn't know about the second man at the time. He cocked his head. Were they really trying to solve this case?

Morris leaned forward, and brushed a piece of fuzz from the screen. It didn't move. He swished his hand again. The fuzz wasn't on the screen, it was part of the image. He leaned in close. "Reverse the video."

The operator pressed several buttons, and the video played backwards. The man reversed into the elevator.

"Faster," Morris said.

The images grew more frantic. People passed the cameras in a blur. Baseball-cap man appeared. He raced backwards to his car.

"Slow."

The video operator pressed a button. The man resumed a normal walking speed, but he continued backwards into his car, and reversed out the way he had come, bumping over the curb.

The fuzz had disappeared from the screen. The small blurred patch on the grass wasn't there. "Forward," he said.

The video played in the normal direction. The Ford reappeared, bumping its way into the parking space. Morris leaned back and smiled.

"What?" said Vanelli.

"He left us a gift."

Vanelli raised his eyebrows.

Morris pointed to the grass beside the car. The fuzz had reappeared. "He lost a hubcap. Soil analysis might tell us something."

Vanelli nodded. "The car was stolen."

"He must have parked it somewhere." Morris smiled again. "He used the same car the day before."

CHAPTER TWELVE

AFTER MORRIS LEFT, JESS strolled away from the Hard Rock Café. The sun was strong, and she welcomed the shade of the trees along the edge of the sidewalk. The area was a mix of business and residential properties with the occasional high-end shop and café squeezed in between.

She checked the time on her phone. Her publisher would be at work. The *Taboo* offices were in Denver, and the time difference meant it was early, but Carter Pierce would be at his desk. He always claimed he wanted to avoid the rush hour traffic, but in reality, he was addicted to the publication business, and kept the hours required by such an addiction.

She dialed his number and waited as the call clicked through. His secretary answered and put her through.

Jess pictured him picking up the phone with one hand and his Mont Blanc with the other. The man was a certified genius. He could listen with one ear, distill the salient facts, and write publication-ready copy all at the same time. Discussions with him were always a game, a sport, a form of competition where he would deduce everything from nothing, even uncovering connections she herself hadn't seen. His voice came on the line.

"Jess, how you doing. Finally decided to talk to us, have you?"

"Yeah, yeah. You know what I'm doing, and you know why I can't tell you what I'm doing."

"Doesn't stop me from hoping."

"I'll be able to tell you soon."

"So, how is Rome? And don't play dumb with me, I saw your corporate card bill. First class tickets always get my attention."

"You can afford it, and you know it'll be worth every penny."

"It's Rome, isn't it?"

"Uh-huh."

"So, do I need to be preparing an edition with an Italian flair?"

"Sorry Carter. I'm serious about this one. No clues, no hints. You will have plenty of time to put an issue together when I'm ready."

Carter sniffed. "So why the call? More first class tickets?"

"Do we have an office around Rome?"

Carter groaned. "I wish. Been in the cards for a couple of years, but navigating licenses, tax issues, foreign ownership laws. Be another couple of years yet before we are anywhere near having a functioning office. Getting the approvals is a career of its own."

"Anyone in Europe?"

"We hire it all in. Freelancers. I can find someone if you want. No rubbish. Dobson from London, or Charbonneau from Paris. He's fluent in Italian."

"No. It's okay. Some local knowledge would have been good, but I'll manage."

"Really, I can find someone, whatever you want, just tell me."

She shook her head. "I'll be okay."

"Okay? You're ringing warning bells, Jess. If it is anything to do with your safety, don't be shy. I want to know."

She laughed. "Everyone is so concerned with my safety."

"Everyone? Like who? Now you're really getting me worried."

"I'm fine really. Another few days here, and I'm done. But it'll probably be a while before I can release the story."

"And what do I publish in the meantime?"

"Don't give me that, Carter. You've got a dozen of my articles in hand."

"I always want the latest thing, you know that."

Jess grunted. She heard a slap. The sound of a heavy pen thumping on a thick pad. Carter was done writing. "So what have you got?"

He laughed. "On my pad? One word. And it's nothing about what you're doing, whatever it is." He cleared his throat. "The word is danger."

She laughed. "You worry too much."

"When it comes to my top reporters, no amount of worrying is too much. Any hint of danger and you get in touch. I'll do whatever it takes. Understand?"

Her phone bleeped. She looked at the display. "Hey, I've got another call. Talk to you later."

Carter said goodbye as she swapped calls. "Morris?"

"Where are you?"

"Near where we had lunch."

"Be standing outside the embassy in five minutes. I'll swing by and pick you up. The tracker on the suitcases just triggered. No clue why it triggered now and not before. But the good news is we have a location."

Jess started jogging. "I'm on my way."

CHAPTER THIRTEEN

JESS STOOD BY THE iron fence in front of the American Embassy. A dark blue Alfa Romeo with "Carabinieri" painted on the sides in huge red letters rounded the corner, lights flashing and tires squealing. For some unknown reason, Jess had heard Italians call these carabinieri cars "Gazzella." The car looked nothing like a gazelle to her.

Two unmarked white Subaru sedans followed close behind the *gazzella*. The three screeched to a halt in front of the embassy, drawing the attention of the marine guards at the main gate.

The rear door opened in the middle Subaru, and Jess dived inside. The cars accelerated away hard, momentum slamming the sedan's door behind her.

Morris was already seated opposite her in the rear seat. She struggled to secure her seatbelt as the sedan fishtailed around a corner.

"What do you know?" she said.

"The tracker only worked for a moment, but we got a fix. It's like someone got inquisitive, and activated it. Briefly."

"You think it's real? It could be Enzo Ficarra?"

"Hard to say. It's an encrypted signal. Very difficult to fake."

"But what if it's a decoy?"

Morris shrugged. "Nothing much we can do about that until we check it out."

The man in the front passenger seat turned around. It was Vanelli. His jaw was hard set and his lips pressed into a thin line. "And when agent Morris says until we check it out, he means until the law enforcement agencies check it out. There will be plenty of time for reporting afterwards. Is that clear?"

Jess took a deep breath. Too many people were telling her what to do. Having included her in this thing, they needed to stop worrying about her welfare, and get on with their jobs.

People saw her as petite, and she was, but her height didn't make her helpless. Her skill set was formidable. Experience proved her best response was to let the comments slide and simply show her capabilities when the time came.

She smiled, and nodded toward Vanelli. "You'll barely even know I'm here."

She turned back to Morris.

"Where is the luggage located?"

"We don't necessarily know it's the location of the luggage. Someone may have taken the tracker out. But as far as we can tell, it's in an industrial unit north of the city."

"A run down area." Vanelli shrugged. "Old buildings. Mostly abandoned. It's not likely Enzo Ficarra would be there."

The uniformed carabiniere driver turned off the flashing lights, and slowed to the pace of the everyday traffic. "Two miles," he said.

"We'll set up observation first. See what happens. Who's there? How many?" Vanelli said. "Once we know the answers then we will know how to proceed."

The blue carabinieri *gazzella* ahead pulled over, and joined a line of Polizia police cars. Jess felt a familiar mix of excited fear course through her. The FBI and two Italian agencies working together could mean that Enzo Ficarra was close. The Grantly case could be closed today.

"My men will secure the area. A broad perimeter." Vanelli pointed to the carabinieri vehicles. "We will be going closer for observation."

The road looped around a series of dilapidated signs advertising auto repair shops and vinyl window manufacturers. Behind the signs were tired looking buildings. Overflowing dumpsters set at odd angles. Only the occasional window was illuminated. Roll-up doors were closed. Layers of grime indicated it'd been a long time since business boomed in the area.

They turned into a parking lot, their driver dodging debris on the tarmac. Vanelli pointed to a doorway and the carabiniere parked beside it.

Jess looked out of the window at the sorry building. "The tracker was here?"

Morris clicked open his door. "This is the observation point."

Jess, Morris, Vanelli, and their driver piled out to join the others. Now that she had a chance to look at him, the driver seemed younger than she'd expected. His name badge identified him as "Nicci." The name meant "victory." She certainly hoped so.

Vanelli's carabiniere made short work of the padlock on the

building's door. The interior was long, wide, and high, a cavernous empty space.

There was no electric light inside, only the daylight coming through the windows. The air was hot and stale. It smelled of oil and something rotten. Every sound they made echoed off the corrugated iron walls.

Two carabinieri strained to lift the roll-up door. The white Subarus were moved inside, and the door closed.

Jess took pictures with her phone as Vanelli and Morris found a way up onto a gantry that ran along the uppermost windows.

Vanelli's men lifted camera gear and long-range lenses from the trunks. Jess followed them up to the gantry.

In less than a minute, they had the camera set up on a tripod and a laptop showing the feed from its powerful lens.

The view looked across an empty parking lot, and over a road to a building that looked much as the one they had entered. The walls were a faded tan. Windows circled the upper part of the corrugated iron walls.

There were two loading docks with doors secured by thick iron bars. On the left, the entrance was covered in graffiti. Jess guessed the building had windows, but the paint was so thick it was hard to be sure.

Morris adjusted the camera, tracking it from window to window. Stopping at each.

Jess leaned down to study the picture on the laptop screen. "Looks empty."

"More than that, the windows haven't been used in a long time. See how they're all closed? It's hot, and these places don't have air conditioning. If you were inside over there for long, you'd at least open a window."

She nodded. Morris continued to track from window to window.

Vanelli's men set up a second machine on a tripod. It looked like a very sleek camera but there was no lens, only two small, silvered mirrors. Vanelli donned a headset, and plugged it into the back of the machine.

"Laser microphone," Morris said.

Her eyes searched out of the window. "Where's the beam?"

"Infrared. Not visible."

Jess nodded, and watched as Vanelli moved the microphone from window to window, just as Morris had done with the camera.

Vanelli worked back along the windows, and shook his head. "I hear noise, but…"

He handed the headset to Morris.

Morris scanned the microphone across the windows. "I hear noise at every window."

"Exactly." Vanelli explained for Jess's benefit. "If someone is talking in the building, noises would be louder by the window closest to the conversation."

"Maybe they're standing in the middle of the building?"

Vanelli shook his head. "It would still sound louder in the middle of the building."

"What's that noise?" Jess asked.

"Voices. Very muffled."

Vanelli's men carried folding chairs up to the gantry. The group sat down.

Jess felt faintly ridiculous, sitting on a lawn chair, thirty feet in the air, staring out of a grimy window in an abandoned factory.

Morris unplugged the headphones. One of Vanelli's

carabinieri plugged in a speaker, and turned up the volume. They listened to a mumbling voice booming around the empty warehouse across the parking lot.

Jess's Italian wasn't good enough to keep track of the conversation. She leaned back in her chair.

The mumbling voice stopped. There was a moment of silence.

They looked at each other, questioningly. Music blared out from the speaker. A rapid fire jingle, with a voice talking over the top. Vanelli shook his head. Morris rolled his eyes.

Jess laughed. "The local radio station?"

Nicci, Vanelli's young carabiniere driver, ran down the gantry and began searching stations on the car's radio. He found a match and turned off the radio. "*The Rome Word*," he called.

Vanelli nodded. "Local talk show."

Jess gazed out of the grimy window. "Does that explain why you hear it from all windows equally?"

Morris shook his head. "Even a radio has a point source." He paused in thought, then groaned. "The sound isn't in the building."

He knelt by the microphone, and scanned it around the surrounding buildings. The radio station suddenly jumped louder from the speaker. "The car shop on the right has the radio on. The sound is reflecting off the building."

"So, there's no sound inside that building we're interested in at all?" Jess said.

Morris shrugged. "Can't tell with so much ambient noise being reflected."

Vanelli zoomed the camera out until it framed the whole building. "We need to be patient."

Patience. Not something Jess was comfortable with or good

at, but she seemed to be the only impatient one here.

Jess watched shadows cast by the sunlight as they tracked their way across the floor and up the wall as the afternoon wore endlessly on.

Morris chewed gum.

Vanelli received sporadic calls from the Polizia stationed on the perimeter of the area, but nothing that moved him to action.

After a while, Vanelli pulled out his phone and opened an app Jess recognized. *Warped Words*. She played it often herself. She wouldn't have guessed Vanelli was a wordplay genius.

But she watched him play the anagram game expertly, moving up to higher and higher levels in record time with very few mistakes. If she challenged him to a contest, he might actually win. *Ouch*. She winced.

He must have felt her watching because he glanced her way.

"I love that game." She flashed a sheepish smile.

He shrugged. "Passes the time on stakeouts. This is the English version. Helps me to practice my language skills." He narrowed his gaze. "You might want to try the Italian language version."

Double ouch. She nodded. "Right."

He turned his attention back to *Warped Words*.

Okay, so the guy wasn't her biggest fan. She didn't feel a lot of warm fuzzies for him, either.

Jess stood, walked the length of the gantry, and sat down again so many times she'd lost count. Stakeouts were incredibly boring. This one was no more interesting than the others she'd experienced. She'd taken dozens of pictures on her phone. For something to occupy her time, she thumbed through them.

She noticed two bright dots on the images of the windows

under surveillance. She flipped to another picture. Same again. The laser. Had to be.

"Take a look at these." She handed the phone to Morris.

"Some cameras can see into the infrared." He shrugged. "Some can't."

"But if I can see the lasers, so can they."

He smiled. "If they're looking."

She took several more pictures, making sure to emphasize the laser. With no cameraman, she'd be forced to use her own images in her article. She had the time to get the best shots possible under these conditions. Cameras that recorded invisible infrared were the kind of detail her readers would appreciate.

As the light through the dirty windows turned golden, Vanelli put away his phone. He scanned the microphone from window to window again. The same muffled talk show emanated from the speaker.

He grunted. "We've waited long enough. If there is anyone in there, they'll be getting tired. The end of their day."

"Tired time is the best time," Morris said.

Vanelli made a call, then led the way down the stairs and back to the *gazzellas*. His carabinieri pulled guns and bulletproof vests from the trunks.

Jess stood to one side as they checked weapons and secured vests for the best coverage and freedom of movement. With the bulky vest on, Morris looked even larger than normal.

The carabinieri lifted the roll-up door and drove the cars out. Two more *gazzellas* were waiting outside, more carabinieri inside them. But the cars were dwarfed by the vehicle beside them, a dark blue monster of flat panels and angled metalwork painted with the same huge red "Carabinieri" on both sides.

"MRAP," Morris said. "Mine resistant ambush protected

vehicle. Specifically designed to withstand improvised explosive device attacks and ambushes. Virtually indestructible. Their military has probably been shedding them same as ours. U.S. police can pick them up for a fraction of what they originally cost Uncle Sam."

The intimidating look of the MRAP was enhanced by a battering ram across the front. The man inside the vehicle gave Vanelli a thumbs up. Vanelli talked to the men in each car before coming back to Morris and Jess.

Vanelli gestured to the MRAP. "We'll go in through the roll-up door. If there is room, the MRAP will continue into the building, if not he'll reverse out. Don't be deceived, it's quick for its size. My men go in next." He pointed to Jess. "You don't go in until I call the all clear. There will be firepower and nervous people in there. I don't want any accidents."

Jess looked at the MRAP. "What about that?"

Vanelli barely glanced at the towering vehicle. The driver sat about nine feet off the ground. "Nothing's going to damage that."

"Exactly. So why don't I go in there?"

He scowled at her.

She raised her eyebrows. "Nothing's going to damage that, you just—"

He spun on his heels, waving to the man in the MRAP's cab. She hurried after him.

The door to the MRAP popped open, an electric motor driving it outward. Vanelli shouted something to the driver, and walked off.

Jess hauled herself up a series of flat metal steps using a handrail. Despite the vehicle's size, she ducked her head as she stepped through the doorway, and sat in the passenger seat.

Her arm naturally fell on a square box snugged between her and the driver. "I'm Jess Kimball," she said.

"Angelo Graza," he said and pointed to a four-point harness. She buckled herself in, tightening the straps to their end stops.

Light green painted metal was everywhere. The dashboard was covered with lights and gauges. The switches were huge. Several had red covers that prevented accidental operation.

Graza flipped up one of the red covers, and pushed the switch underneath. Jess's door whirred closed, latching with a heavy thump and the ratcheting of metal.

The rear of the vehicle had two empty rows of seats. She and Graza were the lone occupants.

CHAPTER FOURTEEN

GRAZA TALKED INTO A headset, and nodded. He gunned the engine. The noise was loud, but not as bad as Jess expected.

The view from the flat windscreen was so far from the ground the motion of the vehicle disoriented her. The carabinieri's *gazzellas* were lost behind the square metal of the engine compartment.

Graza twisted the steering wheel with confidence. The MRAP skirted around where she imagined the cars were parked, and headed down the length of the parking lot.

The scale of the vehicle dwarfed her senses. It took her several seconds to realize they were traveling fast.

She twisted around. There was no window in the back. Graza tapped a screen, and flipped a switch. A rear-view camera activated. The white sedans were close behind the MRAP.

The end of the building loomed ahead. They slowed. But not much.

The vehicle shook as Graza spun the wheel. Her senses

swam as they turned. From the MRAP's height, the distance between the buildings didn't seem like much, but she wasn't concerned. She had the feeling knocking down a wall would be simple for the metal monster.

They emerged from the buildings, the corners whipping by so quickly she realized just how fast they were going. They covered the parking lot in seconds.

Graza veered a little left to race through the inbound lane, eschewing the out lane for speed. She fired off a couple of shots from her camera. They crossed the road and the second building's parking area in moments.

Graza switched on a bank of headlights. The loading dock loomed ahead. She glanced at the rear-view camera.

The carabinieri vehicles had split either side of the MRAP. Obviously keeping well clear in case Graza changed direction. She doubted they would feel anything as insubstantial as a *gazzella* inside the vehicle if the MRAP reversed over it.

She gripped her seat. The roll-up door on the loading dock ahead had an awning. She instinctively ducked her head. Despite the MRAPs height, it passed underneath.

Graza braked and the MRAP slowed to a few miles per hour.

She glanced at Graza. He was intently peering between the windshield and a monitor that showed views of either side of the vehicle.

The nose of the MRAP hit the door. It strained and buckled and bent. The vehicle continued its slow, relentless progress.

The door snapped from its mounting points, dropping onto the hood.

She saw the whole event without feeling a thing inside the MRAP. Metal struck metal, but there had been no noise, no jarring crash, and no rocking motion. It was as if she had watched on television. The detachment was surreal.

The door tumbled to one side. She saw it flip over. Silently. Or at least, the clamor was lost below the engine noise and the insulating layers of steel.

The MRAP's headlights revealed a massive dark space, in size, much like the building they had used for observation, but filled with heavy machines and cars in various states of disrepair.

Graza's head whipped back and forth, peering from the vertical side windows and checking the monitors. Jess fired off a burst of shots with her phone as they drove into the loading area, pushing a line of cabinets out of the way.

She strained to look into the far end of the warehouse. She saw no movement, but there was no electricity and no light. A lot could be hidden in the darkness.

Graza spoke excitedly into his microphone, encouraging the team to enter the building.

She looked at the rear-view camera, like watching a movie with the sound muted. The white sedans raced around the rear of the MRAP, hurtling through the gap between the doors and the rear of the vehicle.

The unmarked sedans lurched to a stop at her side. The ROS teams sprung from them. She saw Nicci among them, behaving as expertly as the rest. Separating. Diving for cover. Guns first. Arms waving instructions and acknowledgments.

She recognized Morris with one of the teams, working his way along a wall, heading to the far side of the building.

Jess pressed her phone against the MRAP's flat glass to take pictures.

Graza watched over everything in view, and shouted occasional instructions into his headset.

She sensed the MRAPs headlights illuminated less than a

quarter of the warehouse. From her elevated position, she saw drilling machines as large as a room. They had enormous levers and handles that protruded.

What looked like a lathe stood at the edge of the headlights' range, a kitchen table lying sideways across its mechanism. The machines were separated by wide pathways that must have once been used to move whatever heavy engineering took place in the building.

Toward the middle of the building were two dark cubes. In the gloom she couldn't tell if they were windowless storage rooms or, perhaps offices for the one-time management. Trash covered the floor. Papers, boxes, broken furniture. A large teddy bear holding a wrench had been tied to a pillar.

She saw no sign of movement. From the moment the MRAP had burst into the building through the arrival of the heavily armed carabinieri, Jess's privileged view revealed nothing but an abandoned factory. Nothing at all.

The ROS were beyond the range of the MRAP headlights now, working through the paths between the heavy duty equipment. She'd lost Morris.

Jess tapped Graza on the arm, and motioned to open the door. He shook his head. She pointed to herself, and gestured out of the window. He shook his head. She raised her hands questioningly. He shook his head again.

She looked over the bank of switches in the middle of the vehicle. The markings were Italian. Graza had pressed one to open the door, but the words she could read didn't identify the right switch.

She glanced through the windshield.

A few seconds later, Morris returned, walking straight toward the MRAP. Jess tapped the driver with her fist, and pointed to Morris. Morris waved his arm.

Graza reached for a switch, flipped up the red cover, and pressed it without looking. Jess's door buzzed open.

She thumped the release button in the center of her four-point harness, and climbed down the steps to the ground. As she stepped away, the door closed, sealing the driver in his protective cocoon.

"Nothing," Morris said.

"But the blue luggage is here, right?"

"Dunno." He gestured around the building. "Somewhere. Maybe. Vanelli ordered some lights rigged up for a thorough search."

She walked to one of the big machines. The ground was slick, a mixture of oil and dust. The machine was the same. She wiped a finger over the surface of a handle. The dust was thick.

"Been like this for years," Morris said. "They probably just brought the suitcases here to open them, and moved on."

She nodded. "Not exactly the sort of place you want to kick off your shoes and stay awhile."

His smile was flat. A radio hanging on his bulletproof vest chirped. Vanelli's voice rasped out. Jess only caught a few words, but heard Vanelli call off the search until the lights were arranged.

The MRAP's deafening engine stopped. Jess felt her muscles relax, and she wondered how people worked around such noise all the time. She craved silence. The vehicle's lights dimmed a fraction.

She turned on the flashlight on her phone. The beam illuminated her feet. She waved it around the machines. The range was pitiful, but it would stop her from tripping over obstacles in the dark.

She walked along one of the pathways through the old machinery, stepping over the debris. She studied a notice board. The most recent date she found on the papers was ten years ago. Whatever had happened to this place, it seemed a shame it had been reduced to a derelict wreck.

Light flashed over the top of the odd office cubes alone in the middle of the factory. She saw the outlines of a roof atop the cubes, wires snaking upward. She headed in that direction.

A man shouted from the far end of the building. His voice echoed. She picked up her pace. Beyond the office cubes flashlight beams flickered and danced, sweeping over walls, searching the pathways. She glimpsed a lone silver car caught in flashlight beams.

More shouting. Evening light spilled into the building near the car from one of the grimy windows.

She spun around. A car might mean someone was inside the building. The carabinieri's shouts stopped. The same thought must have occurred to them.

She turned off her phone's light, moved close to one of the drilling machines, and listened.

The building creaked. A breeze groaned over the metal roof high overhead. Something hummed and buzzed. Footsteps sounded all around her.

She looked over the top of the drilling machine. Light flickered behind the office cubes. She waited a moment. The light flickered again. Brief. Exciting her retinas, and leaving them struggling for night vision.

Then, no flicker.

A flashlight, maybe? She blinked to adjust her eyes to the near darkness.

The wires trailing up from the office cubes to the ceiling

rocked gently. A breeze from the doors the carabinieri had opened, perhaps?

She watched the wires moving, and held her hand up. No breeze. She licked her fingers and held them up. Nothing. Was there a breeze higher in the building?

She walked around the drilling machine, and onto a pathway that led to the office cubes. Morris stepped out from between two machines and walked beside her.

"Did you see it?" she said.

He frowned. "What?"

"The light. Just flickered." She pointed above the cubes. "And those wires are moving."

Morris watched then held his radio close to his mouth. He whispered, "Vanelli. The wires above the offices in the center are moving."

"On our way," Vanelli said, his voice distorted through the radio's tinny speaker.

Jess walked around one of the cubes. There were two doors, on opposite sides. The walls were smooth sheetrock. There were no windows.

She put her ear to the door nearest Morris, and lurched away. Morris cocked his head.

She gestured for him to stand still, and placed her ear back against the door. She heard crashing, crunching noises. Like heavy boots on a gravel driveway, but erratic, ill-timed paces. She waved him forward.

Morris placed his ear to the door.

The crashing continued.

He placed a finger across his lips, and walked away behind a machine, raising his radio close to his mouth. Whatever he said to Vanelli, Jess was unable to hear.

One last crunch reverberated against the door. There were other noises. Popping and ringing, and something like a freeway in the distance.

Morris reappeared, and put his finger across his lips again. He gestured for her to step away. She backed up to where he stood, ten feet from the door.

Vanelli jogged down the pathway, several carabinieri behind him. Two of them held a large metal frame that looked like a bar stool with a thick seat, a battering ram. From the way they moved, it was heavy.

Vanelli waved his men to take positions on either side of the door. They readied guns, and nodded.

The men with the battering ram lined up in a straight path to the door.

Vanelli pointed a finger.

Two carabinieri ran forward, swinging the broad end of the battering ram against the door. The wood splintered. The door shook, but held.

They jogged back, and ran again, swinging for the other side of the door. Another crash. More wood splintered off.

The door lurched sideways. Chunks of wood spun away.

One of the hinges tumbled to the floor.

The carabinieri with the ram stepped aside.

The carabinieri on each side charged forward. One man hefted a giant boot, kicking hard in the center of the door with all his weight behind the move.

The door pitched into the cube and light burst out.

Jess squinted and raised her hand in front of her eyes to block the assault on her retinas.

The carabinieri disappeared into the blinding light.

Morris followed Vanelli into the office.

CHAPTER FIFTEEN

JESS WAITED A MOMENT. Her nostrils twitched. The air smelled of noxious smoke. As her eyes adjusted, she could see wisps trailing around the doorframe.

Shouts from inside the cube.

Jess moved closer to the door, holding her phone out and taking pictures.

Inside the walls, the cube looked like a busy modern office. Computer monitors on six desks laid in a row. Fluorescent lights ran in lines across the ceiling. The floor was covered with dirty carpet squares. Wheeled office chairs were strewn around the room.

At the rear of the room was another door. Smoke poured around its edges. It took her a moment to realize this was an interior door. It couldn't be the one she had seen when she walked around the exterior of the cube.

This office they stood in was only half the total size of the cube.

The office was crowded now. Chaos reigned for a moment. When a bit of space cleared, she stepped inside with the others.

Half of Vanelli's men must have moved into the second room, to tackle whatever was burning.

Morris pulled desk drawers straight out, piling them up on top of the desks. "Empty. Everything's empty."

Jess walked around one of the desks. The computer monitor cables dangled lifelessly. She picked up the plug, and frowned.

Morris gestured to the smoky opening. "They were burning the contents of these drawers in there."

Jess peered into the second room. The fires hadn't been burning very long. Vanelli's men had already extinguished the flames.

Carabinieri were carefully lifting and separating charred and melted gray plastic boxes with computer brand names stamped on them.

"They were in here the whole time," Jess said.

Vanelli glanced at her. "Yes."

"I heard noise. Movement."

"When?"

"When Morris called you the first time."

Vanelli nodded. "Nice work."

Jess turned back to study the first office. The crunching noises she'd heard had probably been the computers being piled up and set on fire.

Which meant someone had been standing right there. Moments before Vanelli's men broke down the door.

Where were they now?

She scanned the bare, modern desks. Flat panels and steel legs. She saw nowhere even one person could possibly be hiding.

She walked around the edge of the room, rapping her knuckles on the sheetrock. It sounded as solid as sheetrock ever did. Certainly nothing out of the ordinary, like a place to hide behind the walls.

The sound of wood splintering came from the second room. Vanelli's men were breaking through the far door on the opposite side of the cube. Had Ficarra escaped through that door? Possible. But it didn't feel like the right answer.

She looked back at the desks again. Six desks. Exactly the same. Nothing charming or unusual about them. They could have been purchased from a discount furniture catalogue.

Four of the desks boasted a computer monitor. Two monitors rested atop desk number five. The surface of the last desk, number six, was bare of all computer equipment.

Jess inspected desk six. A cable dangled down its back. She poked at the wire. It swung back and forth, hitting the metal panel on the rear of the desk with a resounding chime.

She swung the cable again and the chiming noise repeated, every time.

She had heard the sound when she was waiting for Vanelli outside the closed door.

She looked around the room. Someone had definitely been here a few minutes ago. No question.

She looked back at the empty desktop again. Number six. She knelt down to inspect the floor. "Morris!"

"Yeah?" He popped his head through the doorway from the second office.

She pointed to the floor under desk number six. A square section of carpet tiles protruded a fraction above the others surrounding it. She pressed on one of the protruding tiles. The section moved as one. "Trapdoor."

Morris reached her position in three steps. He ripped the desk aside. "Vanelli!"

Jess lifted the steel loop and jerked it up. The edge of the heavy trapdoor separated briefly from the floor.

Morris helped her lift the door up and away.

They flipped it over, exposing a three-foot wide square shaft under the floor.

Jess braced her feet and bent to look into the shaft. A ladder attached to the side ran straight down into the gloom.

A sharp boom rang out, reverberating up the shaft. Jess felt the air move around her.

She lurched back reflexively

Chunks of the ceiling immediately above where her head had been rained down.

Gunfire. Shot upward, from near the bottom of the ladder. Someone was down there. Someone who intended to escape.

A second boom rang out. The second bullet dislodged more of the ceiling not two feet beyond her head

Morris pulled her away from the shaft and the line of fire.

"A man," she said, pointing toward the ladder.

Vanelli peered over the edge of the shaft. He drew his gun and shouted.

Another shot came up from below.

Vanelli returned fire.

One of his carabinieri officers produced a small green grenade. Vanelli nodded.

Morris pulled Jess farther away from the shaft's opening. He turned toward the wall, ducked and covered his head with his forearms. She did the same.

Vanelli's officer withdrew a pin, and dropped the grenade.

A long, breath-stopping moment later, a flash of light

preceded a body-shaking explosion.

Jess felt the percussive wave smack into her across the distance. Her ears rang. She stepped back. The shaft had focused the explosive energy. Expelling it out of the shaft.

The man on the ladder must have been injured or killed. Was it Enzo Ficarra?

Vanelli's man looked over the edge of the shaft. They spoke in rapid Italian. Vanelli slung the strap of his gun over his shoulder. Secure but available for action.

He flipped on a flashlight, and dropped into the shaft. Six of his men followed in rapid succession.

"Wait here," Morris said to Jess.

"Fat chance. If that's Enzo Ficarra down there, I'm going to be with you when you catch him. Or kill him. I really don't care which at this point." She gestured to the opening and grinned. "You first. If I fall, you can catch me."

Morris scowled, and set off down the ladder.

Jess followed.

Morris was quick but Vanelli's men had been even quicker. She glimpsed the last of them disappear out of the bottom of the tube.

Twenty-feet down the shaft the stun grenade had left charred marks on the walls.

Morris stopped at the bottom, standing on a platform of some type. She heard rapidly exchanged Italian. Morris replied, "*Sì*."

When she caught up with him, he waved a rope. "Long drop from here. The others climbed down this rope. Can you do that?"

"Yeah. Is he down there?"

Morris nodded. "Must have continued on after the flashbang."

"Tough guy." She heard the admiring tone in her own still-ringing ears.

"Or he wasn't in the shaft when the grenade went off. He could have been farther along already." Morris lowered himself and worked his way down the rope ahead of Jess.

She climbed down as quickly as she could. She looked over her shoulder, but Morris and the others had disappeared into the blackness.

She turned on the light on her phone, and wedged it in her belt. The rope was rough and frayed. Not nylon, a natural material.

"Come straight down." Below her, another flashlight clicked on. Morris called up to her. "It's an underground train line. Don't touch the rails. They're probably hot. You'll get electrocuted."

"Electricity kills." She grunted. "Vital safety tip."

She worked her way down the rope, gripping tightly with her hands and her knees. Shifting her weight. Before she reached the bottom of the rope, she'd exited the shaft.

The noises changed here. The close, intimate sounds of the confined space inside the shaft became deep, echoing reverberation. Morris held the rope to stop it swinging, but he couldn't stop it rotating.

She saw bouncing lights heading away in both directions. Vanelli's men were covering both options. Which meant they hadn't seen the shooter and didn't know where he'd gone.

Their flashlights glinted off the bright steel of the rails. The walls were a dirty gray with a texture like the ceilings in her apartment, rough to the touch.

She finally reached Morris and he helped her down the last few feet. To Jess's surprise, the tunnel floor was smooth.

He pointed his flashlight at the gleaming rails.

She nodded. "Got it."

The tunnel seemed a bit brighter off to her left. "A train station?"

"Yeah."

"There're a few of these alcoves along the length of the tunnel." Morris pointed his flashlight at a small open space tucked into the wall. "Find one and hop in there if a train comes, okay?"

She nodded again. "Got it."

Morris jogged toward the light ahead. Jess followed. They caught up with a group of Vanelli's officers, who were silently moving from one defensive position to the next.

Jess stayed behind Morris, who remained twenty feet back from the ROS as they cleared each alcove and hiding place. They found no one.

She passed a metal door. She rapped on it. The sound rang out, echoing louder than she'd expected. Morris grabbed her hand, and placed a finger across his mouth. She nodded and mouthed "Sorry."

She gripped the door handle, and twisted. It didn't move.

Morris pointed to a box on the ceiling. "Signal lights," he whispered. "Probably an electrical—"

Behind Morris, flashes leapt into life. Gunfire rang out. Two shots. Booming and echoing in the enclosed space.

Jess ducked onto her haunches, and pressed her head down between hunched shoulders. Morris did the same, though he pointed his gun in the direction of the noise.

Vanelli's men shouted in Italian and doused their lights.

In the near total darkness, Jess could discern movement, but not much.

More gunfire flashes erupted. Short controlled bursts,

irregularly spaced. More Italian shouting from Vanelli's team that Jess couldn't translate.

The slight movement she'd noticed in the distance became a rushing hoard. The ROS piled past her, carrying a wounded carabiniere.

She recognized him. Vanelli's young Subaru driver, Nicci. His right shoulder was pumping blood around the hand he pressed tightly against the wound. They disappeared into an alcove, and a flashlight went on.

Vanelli arrived, and sent an officer up the rope to the surface.

He knelt beside Morris. "One of my men was hit."

Morris pointed to the rope and the shaft. "Headed to find a medic?"

"And Polizia. Reinforcements." He gestured forward. "If Ficarra reaches the station before us, he'll disappear into the crowds, and we'll never find him."

"If it's Ficarra."

Vanelli shrugged. "He shot my man. It doesn't matter who he is now. He will not escape."

Morris nodded and pointed to his radio. "Does it work?"

"Maybe." Vanelli shook his head. "Too far underground."

Morris jerked his thumb in the direction of the firefight ahead. "How many are shooting back at your men?"

"One. Could be two. Probably not more." Vanelli's eyes narrowed. "Too dark to be sure."

"What's stopping Ficarra from running?"

"I have two men keeping him pinned down, but it's dark."

"You think he'll risk moving on to the station and out of the tunnel?"

Vanelli exhaled. "He had this escape route planned. He saw

us long before we saw him. Probably using night vision. He can see better than us, so he can do more than we can."

The carabinieri regrouped around Vanelli. Jess shuffled back to let them get close. She heard hushed orders. Her ears hadn't returned to normal since the first gunshots from the shaft, but she didn't understand most of the Italian that she could actually hear, anyway. She caught metallic clicks. Guns, safeties, and new magazines.

She turned around to peer into the darkness. She felt a breeze. Wind blowing down the tunnel. Her skin tingled. She shook Morris's arm. "Train."

CHAPTER SIXTEEN

THE BREEZE PICKED UP. The wind blew into her face. She heard the rustle of debris blown around on the ground.

Vanelli's men split into two groups, racing for the alcoves, gear rattling as they moved.

Jess scrambled into the closest alcove. Morris and Vanelli squeezed in beside her.

A single point of light appeared in the distance. The train's headlight.

The ground trembled and the wind intensified. The train's roar grew louder until the sound seemed to ring down the rails.

The train's light illuminated the tunnel's textured surface. The outline of the train became clear. Its single headlight was set high above two arched windows. She squinted against the glare to make out the driver. Unlike every subway she had ridden, the train wasn't speeding past, but seemed to crawl, its wheels scraping and squealing on the rails.

Vanelli put his head out of the alcove. He shrank back, and

activated his radio to talk to his men. "The train is slowing for the station. Ride it past the target."

Seconds crept by. The roar grew louder. The air blowing down the tunnel became a gale, shoved aside by tons of metal. The ground shook.

The train reached the alcove. One moment it wasn't there, the next it was thundering by, shaking the ground, swirling trash, spilling light on the trio pressed into the alcove.

The first carriage replaced the train's engine in Jess's narrow view. Vanelli slung his gun over his shoulder, and stepped out into the small space between the textured wall and the hurtling metal.

The gap between the carriages flashed by, too fast to distinguish its features. Jess twisted her head, looking for handholds on the ends of the carriages. The gap disappeared before she identified any of the carriage parts.

The train's brakes squealed. The next carriage passed. And another.

She blinked. Now she saw a step and a handrail. One at the end of each carriage. Her vision hadn't improved. The train must have slowed.

Vanelli had seen, too. He ran out of her field of view.

She leaned forward.

Vanelli grabbed a handrail and pulled himself up onto the step. By the light of the passing carriages, she saw three more of Vanelli's men jump onto the train.

The brakes squealed. The train was definitely slowing.

Now Jess could see the windows and the graffiti rolling by. She could make out people standing inside the carriages. The pressure of moving air had dropped.

The train was slowing for the station.

Morris tapped her arm. "Stay or go?"

She looked at the train moving not much more than a fast walking pace now. She could do this. "Go."

They stepped out and jumped for the train. Morris caught the end of one carriage, and Jess grabbed the front of the next.

She squeezed down, and peered through the gap between the carriages. The light from the train illuminated a clear view into the alcoves as they passed. She braced herself to pull back if she saw Enzo Ficarra or whomever they were chasing.

But she saw no one.

The train rolled on, and she saw it turn through a sharp bend and out into a station.

She pointed forward. "He must have made it to the station," she shouted.

Morris nodded.

The train emerged into the blinding white light of the underground station. Jess had to squint.

The crowds backed away from the platform's edge. Vanelli jumped off the train, waving his arms and shouting orders. The crowd drifted toward the other end of the station, shying away from the men in combat gear and guns.

Jess jumped onto the platform. Morris followed. He ran back the way they had come, his gun ready.

The tail end of the train entered the station. Passengers were lining up at the doors. Some were pointing at Morris and the ROS, the uniforms and guns clearly grabbing their attention.

The train didn't stop. It kept rolling. Not fast. Not accelerating. Just enough to stop passengers from opening a door and exiting the carriages.

Vanelli ran past her, calling to Morris. "Keep back. I've got a man on the way to the surveillance room."

Morris took up a position at the end of the platform, to one side, with the wall as protection. Vanelli waved the carabinieri into similar positions on the platforms on either side of the station.

Jess crouched beside Morris. With the train gone, the tunnel had returned to pitch dark. "No one saw him?"

"Seems not."

"Could he have ridden the train? Like we did?"

Morris shook his head. "Vanelli's men had it covered."

Jess looked into the tunnel's blackness. "There was that door."

"There were several doors."

Jess exhaled, her breath hissing between her teeth. "He probably took one of those exits while the doors were lit by the train."

"I doubt it." Morris shook his head. "He has night vision gear. Amplifies the light for him but not for us. He'd want to exit when we couldn't see him."

Jess peered into the pitch-black tunnel. "What light?"

"Right." Morris shifted his weight. "He's probably got an IR illuminator."

"Which is?"

"A light, only infrared, not visible light. Hunters use them."

"Infrared?" Jess peered into the darkness. "Same as the lasers?"

"You won't see it." He nodded. "We didn't bring—"

Jess leapt up, pulled her phone from her pocket, and activated the camera. Morris grinned. "Good thinking."

She pointed the camera down the tunnel and turned the exposure to max. In the distance, a faint glow bobbed up and down.

Morris grabbed the phone, angling it left and right, destroying the image. She eased it from his grasp and held it steady. "He's running."

Vanelli had returned. He pushed close, staring at the screen and talking into a radio.

The glow moved left, jerking up and down twice. "He's crossed the tracks."

Vanelli waved to his men. They started down the tracks in the gunman's direction.

The glow dimmed.

"He's entered an alcove on the left," Jess said.

The darkness swallowed Vanelli as he ran toward the alcove.

Morris lowered himself from the platform onto the tracks.

Jess moved the phone for a better view, but the dim glow had disappeared. "He's gone." She looked at Morris. "He's found an exit door."

Morris shouted to Vanelli, and in a moment, bouncing flashlights lit the tunnel. Vanelli's men were running, full tilt.

Jess jumped down to the tracks and followed Morris, keeping close enough to benefit from his flashlight. They ran hard, chasing Vanelli's men.

The flashlights ahead disappeared.

"They've taken the door," Morris said.

Less than a minute later, Jess and Morris reached the same door. Morris pressed his ear against the smooth surface before whipping it open.

Inside were racks of equipment, lined up in rows. Wires dangled everywhere. Some on bound bundles, some single strands that trailed to the ceiling or above their heads, or from row to row.

She heard Vanelli, somewhere ahead, ordering the station closed, and the doors to be sealed.

Morris shoved her behind him as he walked down a row of equipment.

She patted the Heizer in her pocket, to be sure she hadn't dropped it. Vanelli wouldn't take well to her being armed, and he'd produce a lot of fallout for Morris. She compromised. She kept close to Morris. And kept her hand on the gun.

They passed several doors before reaching the far side of the room. Someone shouted, and Vanelli's men ran to the right. She followed Morris.

Vanelli stood by a door, listening to his radio. A garbled voice came from the radio, and he charged through the door. The carabinieri followed. So did Morris.

Jess ran behind Morris into a stairwell. Spiral steps encircled an open central square. Jess looked up but she couldn't make out the top of the stairs. Shouts echoed. There was a brief exchange of fire. Jess flattened herself against the rear wall, away from the open space.

The gunfire stopped. Morris sprinted up the stairs. Jess followed.

Above them, were more shouts, and door slamming.

Jess kept close to the wall. After five flights, her legs began to burn. She breathed steadily through her half-open mouth and held her head up, looking up the stairs, to give her lungs room to work.

Morris slowed. Three flights later, they reached the top of the stairwell. There was only one door. Morris pushed Jess behind the door as he opened it.

He nodded. "Good to go."

They emerged into a large receiving bay. Fluorescent lights

hung from the ceiling. Half the space was filled with haphazardly stacked boxes. An eighteen-wheeler was backed up to a raised loading dock.

Beyond the truck, Jess could see the blue and black uniforms worn by Vanelli's team.

Morris ran along the side of the truck. Several dark blue carabinieri vehicles were screeching to a halt. Carabinieri piled into the vehicles and Morris dived for one of the rear seats.

Jess reached the *gazzellas* as they tore off. She waved her arms. Morris's face flashed by, looking sheepish. "Sorry" he mouthed.

She fumed. How the hell could they leave her? She was the one who found the guy in the office cube. She was the one who found him in the tunnel. If not for her they'd be back in the industrial junk yard, listening to talk radio.

She looked left. A tall chain-link fence separated her from the building they had stormed minutes earlier.

She looked back at the loading dock, an entrance for the supplies needed to run the station. She clenched her fist. She was at a train station.

Damn, she wasn't thinking straight.

She raced around the building to the station entrance and a line of taxis. She jumped in the passenger seat of the first one she reached.

The driver frowned at her. He opened his mouth to speak, but she waved her hands. "Carabinieri." She pointed in the direction the blue *gazzellas* had departed. "*Avanti, avanti!*"

The driver hesitated a moment before putting his car in gear.

"Now!"

"You American." He stared into her face. "Not carabinieri."

Jess exhaled, and pointed to herself with her thumb. "FBI. Now move."

His eyes widened, and he floored the accelerator. The car lurched away from the curb, rotating a full hundred and eighty degrees before fishtailing into a straight line, following the carabinieri.

Jess struggled to buckle her seatbelt as the driver negotiated the surface streets. They hurtled along an access road and joined the freeway with the speedo needle climbing past 150 kilometers an hour.

"Where?" he said.

Jess strained for a glimpse of the dark blue *gazzellas*. Nothing. She dialed Morris. He answered on the fourth ring.

"Sorry, Jess." She heard the weariness in his voice. "They are hot to capture Nicci's shooter. He's at the hospital. He's lost a lot of blood."

"We're all on the same page there." She pushed thoughts of Nicci aside, for now. "Where are you?"

"Some ring road."

"I'm on the same."

Silence.

"I got a taxi."

"Hang on." She heard him cover the mouthpiece and some muffled discussion in the background. He came back on. "We're turning off the ring road for the SS4. Going north. Vanelli has a helo inbound."

She turned to her driver. "SS4. Northbound."

The driver nodded, and pressed harder on the accelerator. "Chase criminals?"

"Kind of."

"We're exiting for some train yard," Morris said.

"Train yard?"

"Big shunting area, and—" Morris swore. She heard a squeal of tires and shouting. Morris grunted. "We're at a crossing. He crossed. He's on the other side of a train. We're stuck waiting. I have to go."

"Keep me updated," she said, but Morris had already hung up.

The taxi driver hunched forward, his chin only inches from the steering wheel. His eyes met hers in the rearview mirror.

"Chase criminals? *Pella, Esercito Italiano*, er, Italian Army, before." He pointed at his chest with his thumb and leaned forward as if the taxi could travel faster with a bit of encouragement. "*In treno…*" He made a back and forth motion with his hand. "Train?"

"A train yard, yes."

Pella grunted, and slowed.

"Don't slow down."

Pella shook his head. "SS4, to the train yards…" He yanked on the wheel. Jess was thrown sideways. The tires squealed and the car lurched across the lanes, crossing a white-hatched area and exiting the freeway.

She strained to see the signs but they went by too fast. "Where are you going?"

He weaved around traffic that was slowing for a traffic light, and floored the accelerator as they passed through on the last vestiges of amber. "We go the other side. Faster. Catch criminal." He waved his hand in the air. "I know the way."

She dialed Morris.

He answered the first time. "We're still waiting for the train to clear. Chopper is still five miles away."

"Well, apparently my taxi driver knows best and we're heading to the other side of the yard."

"But…"

"We turned off before the SS4. We're on surface streets. He knows a short cut to the train yard, I think."

"Jess. Don't go into the train yard." He lowered his voice slightly. "Vanelli's men are armed to the teeth and pumped. This guy shot one of theirs. They're not giving up until they get him and they don't care if he's still breathing when they're done."

Jess braced herself as Pella slung the taxi around a ninety-degree corner. Train tracks stretched to her left as far as she could see. Trains were moving. A delicate ballet of precise timing that allowed heavy goods to be routed to their proper destination.

"We're there." She sighed. "Big place."

Morris grunted. "No kidding. If you get inside, get up as high as you can. See if they have a control tower or something."

"No problem." She hung up.

Pella raced along the street. An almost endless expanse of iron railings surrounded the train yard. She saw large square notices in Italian that she guessed were the equivalent of "keep out."

The taxi slowed. Ahead was an entrance. Two lanes in, two out, separated with orange cones. Red and white striped barriers blocking the entrance lanes. A large brick built guard shack sat in the middle of the in and out lanes. The windows were slivered, and the roof bristled with cameras.

CHAPTER SEVENTEEN

PELLA SLOWED THE TAXI to a walking pace, and turned into the entrance. Two guards walked out of the building and took up positions in front of the barrier. They wore uniforms, and around their waists she could clearly see holsters.

Her "no problem," boast to Morris that she'd easily get into the train yard began to look optimistic.

As Pella stopped the taxi in front of the guards Jess saw through the doorway into the guard shack. A large red light flashed. There were several guards inside, all of them on the phone. Television screens revealed images of the shunting area fed from cameras roaming back and forth across the miles of track.

Pella rolled down his window. The guard approached. They exchanged rapid fire Italian, as the guard gesticulated toward Jess. They stopped talking. Jess pointed into the guard shack. "Carabinieri. ROS." She pointed to herself with her thumb, "FBI."

The guard looked her up and down.

"*Sì.*" Pella jerked his thumb toward her. "FBI."

The guard scowled. He snapped his fingers and said something she didn't understand.

She pointed at the train yard. "*Rapido, rapido.*"

The guard shook his head and held out his hand.

Since the guard didn't speak English, she hoped he didn't read English either. She dived into her bag, and pulled out her Colorado driving license. "FBI. *Rapido!*"

The guard reached for her license but before she handed it over, another guard stuck his head out of the shack, phone in hand.

"FBI." He gestured to his phone. "FBI."

Jess said, "Yes."

He waved his hand at the barrier. "*Avanti, avanti.*"

The guard withdrew his arm from the car. Jess nudged Pella. "Ask him for directions to the control tower."

Pella frowned.

"Control room?" Jess said.

He nodded, and exchanged more rapid Italian with the guard at the barrier across the entrance. The guard pointed to the right, and Pella launched the taxi into the train yard with a squeal of tires. He made a couple of turns, and the control tower appeared straight ahead.

It was a cylindrical building several stories high with a dome at the top, much like a water tower. Mirrored windows ringed the dome, and antennas covered the roof.

Pella raced through the parking lot, around the base of the tower, and stopped at the only entrance.

Jess handed Pella a bundle of euros. She pointed to the ground. "Wait here, okay?"

He nodded.

She jumped out. Sirens sounded in the distance. A swipe key box was next to the entrance, and the door was locked. She surveyed the empty parking lot, and hammered on the door with her fist. The sound echoed, but no one opened the door.

She walked around the base of the tower. There were no signs, no markings, no phone numbers.

The distant sirens grew closer. Pella stepped half out of the car, staring toward the noise. He looked at Jess and back at the approaching police vehicles. His brow furrowed.

"It's okay," she said. "They'll help."

The man slid back into his seat, leaving his door open, and looked at Jess.

A line of police cars poured into the parking lot, screeching to a stop and surrounding the tower. Polizia jumped out. One officer shouted instructions, sent most of the police for the rail tracks, and directed the others to the control tower.

The Polizia gathered by the tower's entrance. It sprang open, and a woman held the door open while they raced inside.

Jess made to follow, but the woman held up her hand.

Jess moved closer to the door. "I'm working with the FBI."

"Then you're in the wrong country." Her English was perfect.

Shouts came from inside the control tower.

"I have to go." She slammed the door.

Jess tried the handle, but the door had already locked.

Behind her, an engine revved. Her taxi was moving.

She ran toward the car, shaking her hands in front of her. "No, no. Pella, don't—"

Too late. Pella must have taken his cue from the woman's refusal to admit Jess with the Polizia. He reversed out of the parking lot, J-turned in the road, and sped toward the exit.

Dammit! No control tower and now no transportation.

She ran her hands through her hair and sucked in great gulps of air.

A helicopter thundered overhead, swiveling in the air. Carabinieri hung out of the doors on either side, scanning the ground below.

Jess looked around, but she was not elevated enough to see much. Low buildings and warehouses stretched along the road. Countless train tracks lined up in the other direction, endless strings of containers shunting back and forth.

In the distance was a bridge. Signs and lights hung from its girders. It spanned the tracks into the distance. Apart from the control tower, it was the only elevated structure in the area.

Two Polizia had remained with their patrol cars. She dismissed the idea of asking them for a ride to the bridge.

She stretched her calves, and rotated her waist to stretch, as she always did before running. She took a deep breath and set off. A steady jog. Her usual speed. She had run faster in college, but that was when she'd practiced every day. And when she'd worn the right shoes.

Never again had her schedule allowed the luxury of daily running, but fitness was essential to her life. She could do this.

It was hard to judge distance with the open spaces and large warehouses. In a straight line, the bridge was perhaps a mile. She soon realized that she wasn't going to run in a straight line. Various buildings had six-foot chain link fences. She turned left at the first one, thinking she could skirt around the rear parking lot, only to find the fence linked to a neighbor's, forming a dead end. She jogged back, and took the road. The tarmac was easier, smooth underfoot, but it angled away from her destination.

She picked up her pace. She looked for an entrance in the fences to cut through. She breathed hard. Keeping her oxygen up. She focused to avoid the hypnotic spell of her rhythm. Her bag bounced under her arm. She wedged it closer to her body.

She took the shortest route across a roundabout. The driver of a bright red Alfa swerved around her, waving his fist out of the window. She briefly considered begging a ride, but he was already gone.

The road arced around. Here, the buildings were smaller, closer together. Older. Not like ancient Roman ruins. More like run down sections of Detroit. She'd been mugged there once in just such a place.

She shivered and shoved the memory to the back of her mind. She patted her pocket. The Heizer was still there.

A few yards farther and she was able to glimpse the bridge between two buildings. She lurched to a stop.

The buildings were close together. The gap between them a trash-filled alleyway. But there was a path.

She checked her watch. Where was Morris, anyway? Shouldn't he be here by now?

She walked into the dim alleyway, flanked on both sides by corrugated iron walls, dark and rusty, that seemed to suck up all remaining daylight. She wrinkled her nose. Piles of cardboard boxes had decayed into formless lumps. Unidentifiable contents oozed out across the alley.

She walked carefully around the obstacles.

An open black square, a full story high, interrupted the mottled wall on the right. She inched closer. The blackness seemed total. As if no light dared enter, and none was released. Whatever it had been at one time, now it was a perfect hiding place. Their fugitive could be waiting there. She'd tell Vanelli when she caught up to him.

She took a deep breath.

She put her hand in her pocket, wrapping her fingers around the Heizer, and inched closer.

The blackness inside the square was total. No glints of light, no mottled forms. She strained to hear the slightest movement, but heard nothing.

She turned to face the blackness, back-pedaling, still gripping the Heizer.

She sighed. She made it past. She shook off her misgivings. She was being ridiculous. Her memories of Detroit were messing with her. She was wasting time.

She turned to run again.

Her heart thumped.

She emerged from the alley with a shiver. She jogged around the potholes in the old road that led to the bridge.

Up close, the structure wasn't the sort of bridge it had seemed from afar. An aluminum ladder led up to an overhead section. The overhead section was a flat walkway with railings on either side.

By the ladder were large signs with graphics warning of danger and electrocution. The warnings were pictures she could easily decipher.

She climbed the ladder carefully until she reached the walkway, and then increased her speed. The bridge ran at right angles to the lines of track, which gave her an excellent view between the carriages and trains, as Morris had expected. But the sheer number of tracks was daunting.

Her phone rang. She controlled her panting long enough to say, "Morris."

"You okay?"

"I'm fine. Couldn't get access to the control tower." The helicopter appeared overhead. She pressed a finger into her ear to mute the noise. She shouted, "I'm on the bridge over the tracks. At the north end of the yard."

"Don't run. The ROS are likely to take shots at anything moving quickly."

"Now you tell me. I just ran about two miles to get here. But I can see between the parked trains."

"Anything?"

"A lot of police."

"We're searching down here. Let me know if you see anything." He hung up.

Jess walked on. She saw Vanelli, and later Morris. She walked to the far end of the bridge. She turned and dialed Morris as she walked back.

"No sign of anyone that might be Ficarra that I can see from up here."

"Us neither. We've met up with the Polizia."

"He has to be here."

"There's been a bunch of trains in and out of the yard. He could have hitched a ride on any one of them." Morris paused. "And the shooter might not have been Ficarra at all."

"True. Whoever he was, he had a head start. And he knew where he was going."

"Best guess is that he's in the wind already and we're wasting time here," Morris said. She heard the frustration and exasperation in his voice. "Lots of Polizia on scene. Vanelli's decided to let them finish the search. His men have taken everything from the office cubes back to headquarters for analysis. Vanelli thinks the carabinieri can do more to find Ficarra from there now."

She sighed again, which might have been an effort to draw breath. "We were so close. We could have got him."

"We'll get Ficarra, Jess. This guy might not have been him, anyway. We never found the tracker, don't forget." Morris covered his phone to talk briefly with someone else while Jess made her way back to the ladder at the end of the bridge. "Do you need a ride back to your hotel?"

CHAPTER EIGHTEEN

ENZO FICARRA RESPONDED INSTANTLY when he received the message from Bruno. It was a simple message with no hint of drama. *Are you watching the game tonight?*

He had planned this, and several other meaningless phrases to pass emergency information. None of the phrases conveyed good news. This was one of the worst.

It meant the secret office north of Rome from which he ran his illegal businesses had been raided.

Enzo had weighed his options. He needed to know everything Bruno knew. But if Bruno had been caught in the raid, the message could be luring him into a trap. Enzo could be captured in the close confines of Bruno's apartment or on the streets outside.

But if he did not meet with Bruno, the police would know more than Enzo did. His only option, far from ideal, was a personal meeting with Bruno. As soon as possible.

Enzo replied to the message as planned. *Maybe we could*

watch at your house? Which told Bruno to wait at his apartment. Bruno knew Enzo would arrive in due time.

Police resources were always stretched thin. They couldn't afford to waste resources waiting to spring a trap.

Time was on his side. Patience was required. He waited until the following day to make contact.

He took a taxi to avoid the subway cameras. He surveyed the streets around Bruno's apartment block, front and rear. He sat in a coffee shop, reading a newspaper for two hours, his body charged for action.

Only when he was satisfied no one was watching the apartment building, did he venture near.

The building had a dirty yellow door and filthy windows. Like Bruno, the building had seen better times. Once Bruno's family had owned a prosperous winery. He'd been famous in Tuscany. And then he'd lost everything. Enzo shook his head. Fortunately, no one cared about Bruno anymore.

Enzo waited until another tenant approached and opened the door. Enzo followed behind before the door could latch closed.

He took the narrow steps up two flights to Bruno's apartment. The door was ajar, as he suspected. He pushed it open with the tip of his boot.

He'd been here before. The apartment was small. A bedroom, living room, and kitchen combined. The only separate room was the bathroom.

Bruno sat on the bed, waiting. "We're safe."

Enzo placed a finger over his lips. He nudged open the bathroom door, sweeping his gun across the small space. He pushed the shower curtain back, and whipped open the closet door. Only then, satisfied there was no trap, did he lock the front door.

He sat on a kitchen chair, and listened to Bruno's story.

CHAPTER NINETEEN

JESS WOKE EARLY. BREAKFAST on the terrace was as beautiful as the first day, but it didn't move her this morning. Her mind was elsewhere, racing through what she knew, what she didn't know, and how to bridge the gap.

They'd received no further demands for ransom from Enzo Ficarra. Wilson Grantly might already be dead. She shivered. Harriet and Roger Grantly wouldn't accept that for an answer, so Jess wouldn't accept it, either.

So she backed up and reviewed what she knew.

The man she'd chased at the airport was a courier for Enzo Ficarra. He'd taken the suitcases into the remote area of the warehouses where the tracking signal inside had been on the ragged edge of its maximum range. Whatever had allowed Morris's detector to locate the signal had been nothing more than a lucky fluke.

Morris had confirmed the man at the airport wasn't Enzo, although they hadn't managed to identify the courier yet. Which meant Enzo had at least one accomplice here, in addition to his brother, Luigi, now dead.

The rooms they had found inside the office cube yesterday were a professional set up, right down to the escape route. Enzo ran his extortion ring from there. Which didn't surprise her, for Enzo Ficarra did nothing on a whim. That much they'd known almost from the outset.

Vanelli's carabinieri were busy collecting evidence at the warehouse. The burnt computers were being analyzed. The hard disks had been recovered in various stages of decomposition. It wouldn't be a quick process, but they would extract all data from the delicate electronics. Eventually.

Young Nicci, wounded in yesterday's gun battle, had survived surgery, although his prognosis was guarded.

She checked her phone for messages from Morris. Nothing.

Yesterday, she'd left the train yard despondent and spent a sleepless night. After two full days in Rome, they'd failed to find Enzo. Failed to find Wilson Grantly. Failed to find the courier or the luggage. Failed to find any useful leads at all. She couldn't stay here much longer.

She needed to return to Denver. She'd spent too long away from her main job, which was first, last, and always, finding her son, Peter.

Morris, on the other hand, had been uncharacteristically confident yesterday. "We've made progress, Jess. The wheels of law enforcement grind slowly. We aren't giving up yet."

But she couldn't shake the frustration. They'd chased their fugitive to the train yard, and it should have been a simple matter of the weight of law enforcement numbers to flush him out. And there had certainly been numbers. The helicopter, and the mass of Polizia plus carabinieri, and technology en masse.

Yet they had failed.

The train yard had cameras, but they were aimed high, to focus on arriving trains, not people on the ground. Despite their efforts, train traffic in and out of the yard hadn't halted. Hundreds of tons of moving metal didn't simply come to a stop while police searched for a shooter. He must have caught a train headed away from here.

Jess clenched her teeth. She should have run harder. She could have made it to the bridge quicker. Seconds could have made all the difference.

She exhaled slowly. She, Morris, and the carabinieri had uncovered plenty of evidence already. While she sat here eating breakfast, they worked to uncover more. But where were the results?

She shoved her chair back. She'd had enough of waiting, she had to do something to flush Enzo Ficarra out of hiding. But what? She twirled, and made for the doors from the terrace into the hotel.

Her waiter, Romeo, stepped back from the entrance to let her pass. He opened his mouth to speak, closing it as she strode away.

She took the steps down to the foyer. A blonde-haired tour guide stood in the middle of a mass of people, shouting instructions in German. His party jostled for position, shoving overstuffed bags along in a winding line that finished at the check-in desk. Two harassed staff checked passports against their check-in list, and handed back keys. They parroted the same directions to each guest. When one guest moved off, dragging their belongings, another stepped forward for the same routine.

She threaded her way through the mêlée, and out onto the

hotel steps. Early morning traffic jammed the square, honking and inching their way around the fountain. The question was, what could she do now?

This was always the point in any investigation when she would suit up and run for miles. Run until she pushed every confounding thought from her mind and allowed a solution to rise up from her subconscious. But running along Rome's congested streets was impossible.

She joined the major flow of pedestrians, pushed along with the crowd. Veering around street sellers, stopping at crossings. Stretching for amber lights before they turned red. She passed shops, and offices, and cafés, and no clear plan emerged.

The air and the exercise cleared her mind enough to think.

That Enzo had an accomplice was no surprise. Likewise, that he was prepared to destroy the evidence of their operation, and had an escape route prepared.

Vanelli's ridiculous MRAP had been the wrong thinking. He and his men had been armed to the teeth for a major battle. But they should have been prepared for Enzo Ficarra, a cunning, squirming, greasy weasel.

She crossed a road, pushed by the throng of pedestrians surrounding her.

Yesterday morning, it would have been far-fetched to suggest the police block off the train lines before raiding an old warehouse where a luggage thief might or might not have ditched two suitcases. Today, the plan seemed perfectly plausible.

She blew out a long breath. First rule of Enzo Ficarra? He was not predictable. He was not governed by normal morality. He was depraved and fearless.

He needed to learn that Jess Kimball wasn't predictable, either.

She put her hand in her pocket. The immaculately machined finish of the Heizer felt comforting. Only two shots. At barely four inches long, those two shots would be fired at an uncomfortably close range. Close enough to look him straight in the eyes. She shuddered.

The gun was for emergencies. Surely, all of the law enforcement on this case could deal with Enzo Ficarra and she wouldn't be forced to do so.

The crowds changed from office workers to casually dressed, camera-toting tourists. She followed a group down a narrow cobblestone street. Waiters patrolled outdoor cafés, waving at her to join them as if she were a long lost friend. She smiled, and walked on.

She rounded a corner and followed a sign to the Piazza di Trevi. Crowds of tourists ringed a broad semicircular pool. The pool fronted a curved three-story façade. At the base of the façade, rivulets of water ran down, over, and between, all manner of mythical beasts. Behind them, three niches held gods, with yet more water tumbling over them.

She crossed the square, holding her phone high, snapping pictures above the heads of the assembled crowd. At the fountain's edge, tourists turned their backs on the pool, and threw money over their shoulders.

She slipped the phone into her pocket and climbed a fire escape on the opposite side of the square to get above the crowds for a better shot of the fountain. As she pulled out her phone, it rang. The number was local. She didn't recognize it. "Hello?"

"Miss Kimball, it's Romeo."

She took a deep breath. "I, er…"

"I hope I didn't offend you this morning?"

"No, no. I was just thinking." She ran her hand through her

hair and squeezed her eyes shut behind the sunglasses, and prayed he wasn't thinking of asking her on a date. "Sorry. I have a lot going on."

Romeo cleared his throat. "*Foto Oggi* called. They've found your man."

Jess's eyes snapped open. "They have?"

"Apparently."

"And?"

"And what?"

"Who is he?"

"They're not telling."

Jess sighed. "Let me guess…"

"They want to accompany you when—"

"They want in on the story."

Romeo made a kind of strangled groan. "You could say that."

"Did they say that?"

He made the strangled noise again. "Yes."

She held her breath. "What did you tell them?"

"Nothing! I took you there, introduced you to my landlord, and that was it. Haven't seen or spoken to him any more until just a few moments ago."

"I see."

"Anyway," he said. "What's so special about this person?"

"I can't say." She chewed the inside of her lower lip.

Romeo laughed. "So he's an ex-lover or he owes you money?"

"Closer with the second guess. And it might not be safe, so I'll go alone."

He grunted. "If it's not safe, you're not going on your own."

Jess took a deep breath. "I'll be taking the police."

"Polizia?"

"Exactly. Now what's the address?"

"Where are you?"

"What difference does that make?"

"I'll take you."

"I told you—"

"Yeah, yeah, yeah. The hotel won't like it if I get the customers into danger."

"The hotel?"

"All right. I won't like it if you get into danger. You're...you're...you know. You're nice." He sighed. Such drama. She grinned and imagined the crinkles around his liquid brown eyes. "I mean, you're American, but—"

"Oh, thanks."

"See? Now I have to meet you to say sorry. So, where are you?"

She gave up. "Piazza di Trevi. But I still need the address. For the police."

"Okay, I'll text it. Just wait there." He paused. She heard the smile in his voice when he said, "Throw a coin in the fountain or something."

"Why?"

"It's supposed to guarantee a return trip to the city."

"Guarantee?"

"Yeah, well, probably doesn't include airfare."

She laughed despite her best intentions not to. "Just get here. Quick."

Romeo hung up. A moment later, her phone dinged with his text message. She forwarded the message to Morris, with a note to explain it might be the address for the courier who had picked up the Grantlys' luggage at the airport.

Morris texted back. "Thank you. WE WILL HANDLE THIS."

She sent a smiley, stuffed her phone in her pocket, and waited for the roar of Romeo's motorbike.

CHAPTER TWENTY

ENZO CLOSED THE DOOR to Bruno's apartment, pulled down his baseball cap, and descended the narrow staircase. His Beretta was still hot, but he tucked it deep inside his jacket pocket before opening the faded yellow door that led to the street.

Bruno had been a good man. In three years, he hadn't let Enzo down once. But this was different. The events at the airport could only be the work of the carabinieri. The raid on his office was definitely the ROS, and if the ROS were involved, Bruno was a liability. There was only one option to ensure his silence, and Enzo had taken it.

He turned left, and walked steadily down the residential street. He reached an intersection, and waited in the crowds for the lights to change before crossing the road. He felt good. Bruno had been the last link to his business in the U.S. except for Wilson Grantly. And Grantly would be done soon enough.

As he walked on, several cars raced past. Dark blue *gazzellas* with white roofs. Carabinieri. He stepped into a bus shelter, and watched them disappear on the route he had traveled from Bruno's apartment. His instincts told him to keep moving. But he needed to know.

He walked back to the intersection. The *gazzellas* were parked around the faded yellow door, and two carabinieri were standing guard. A couple was seated in the back of one of the *gazzellas*. The carabinieri must have entered the building.

Enzo's heart rate increased. How had the carabinieri responded so quickly? Had someone heard something? Seen something? He surveyed the street. Had one in the growing crowd of bystanders informed the police? He moved into a store entrance while keeping a clear view across the street.

The carabinieri at the door were waving people on. He took a deep breath. If an informant waited in the crowd, none came forward. But how else could carabinieri have arrived so soon?

The door opened, and a man in a dark suit walked out. He leaned into a *gazzella* and spoke to the people in the back. Enzo watched intently. Two people, long hair and short. A man and a woman. Bruno's neighbors, perhaps?

He shifted his weight. The man saw something and the woman pushed him to report it? Or the woman was the witness, and he had encouraged her to talk to the carabinieri? Enzo gripped his Beretta inside his pocket. Whatever the course of events, he might have to deal with them both.

The man in the suit went back into the building. The couple followed before he could get a good look at them.

He watched and waited. Minutes passed.

The faded yellow door opened, and the couple walked out. The female first. The man holding her elbow. She leaned on the building wall, her face blanched, and her hand on her chest as she struggled to breathe. She was slim, but he knew she had

stamina. And courage. She'd been the one at the airport. She'd
chased the courier through the car park, and made the ROS run
for their money. He clenched his jaw. Now she was here, with
the ROS, at Bruno's apartment.

Three motorbikes roared down the street, bounced onto the
sidewalk, riders dismounting in one swift movement.

Enzo clenched his teeth. Paparazzi. Just what he needed.
They must have been listening to the police channels as such
leeches normally did. They dispersed into the gradually thinning
crowd, cameras clicking.

The woman let go of the wall, and stretched. She was
recovering from the mess in Bruno's bedroom. Enzo grunted. He
didn't blame her. Even with the silencer, the close range shot had
almost taken Bruno's head off.

The woman walked back to the *gazzella*. The man was
talking to her, but she seemed to be ignoring him. She waved her
hand. From her wide-open mouth, he guessed she was angry.

Enzo breathed deep. First the airport, and now here? She was
no longer an oddity. She was part of the Grantly affair. Perhaps
even the reason the Grantlys and their money had not arrived.

He clenched his fist around the grip of his Beretta. She'd
arrived from New York City on Flight 12, the Grantlys' plane.
The plane on which his brother was also to have been a
passenger. Perhaps she knew something about Luigi's
disappearance. Perhaps she'd been involved there, too.

And if she was, if she'd done something to stop Luigi?

He frowned and narrowed his eyes to pinpoints.

He would deal with her.

He would teach her not to thwart his business, too.

She would learn.

Very, very slowly.

CHAPTER TWENTY-ONE

ENZO WATCHED AS MORE police cars arrived. A crime scene van parked close to the growing line of flashing blue lights. He found a *trattoria*, and took a tiny table with a view of the scene. He ordered ravioli and the house red without looking at the menu.

The man and the woman remained by one of the cars, frowning, scowling, and engaged in earnest discussion.

An ambulance backed up to the yellow door. Flashguns went wild. The paparazzi were as giddy as football fans at a tournament. The carabinieri pushed them back.

The paparazzi rounded on the woman. The man did his best to dissuade them. The last of the reporters to leave scribbled in a notebook before moving on.

The waiter returned with his glass of wine. Enzo took a mouthful, as he watched the reporter stuff his notebook in a backpack, and stand by a motorbike, his arms crossed, waiting for his photographer.

Enzo dropped twenty euros on the table, and left before his pasta arrived. He donned sunglasses and crossed the street. Smiling, he approached the reporter. "*Salve.*"

The reporter shrugged.

Enzo pointed to the waiting ambulance. "What's going on?"

"Someone died."

Enzo waved to the line of police vehicles. "Is all this usual?"

"Only if you get shot."

Enzo raised his eyebrows. "Ah."

The reporter called to his photographer, who waved and ignored him.

"You're not interested?" Enzo said.

The reporter looked at him. "He's not a Hollywood star."

"Wasn't a star before he died, you mean?"

"He was bankrupt. Once owned a winery in Tuscany, I guess." The reporter nodded to the woman. "Not like her."

Enzo glanced at her. "She's a Hollywood star?"

The reporter screwed up his face. "Would I be standing here if she was?"

"You just said—"

"She's an American."

"Oh."

Enzo turned his back to the woman. "What's an American doing here?"

The reporter shrugged.

"You must have some idea?"

He shrugged again.

"I thought you guys knew everything."

The reporter laughed. "The guy she's with is FBI."

Enzo pushed his eyebrows down. "FBI? In Roma?"

"Yeah, well. Yanks? They're everywhere these days."

Enzo nodded toward the ambulance. "You think this is one of theirs?"

The reporter shook his head.

"But FBI?"

"Maybe he was an informant."

"And he got shot?"

The reporter scowled. "Who said he got shot?"

Enzo gave him a flat smile. "You did."

His scowl evaporated. "Oh."

Enzo glanced at the American woman. "She's kind of nice."

The reporter groaned. "Is that what all this is about?"

"All what?"

"You. Asking questions. If you want her name, all you have to do is ask."

Enzo frowned. "You have it?"

"I'm a reporter, I know everything. Remember?" He waved at the woman. "Jess something or other."

"And him?"

The reporter sneered. "Who are you after, her or him?"

"No, I just—"

The man grunted. "Morris. The carabinieri call him Special Agent Morris." The man laughed. "Special Agent? Can you believe it?"

Enzo laughed with him. "Americans. They all think they're Hollywood stars."

CHAPTER TWENTY-TWO

ENZO WALKED AWAY FROM the reporter and the police, his pace measured, and his head down.

He had not expected the FBI, and it was an additional complexity. They were obviously working with the ROS. He frowned, how was the woman involved? She'd been at the airport chasing Bruno, only to be chased herself by the ROS. It didn't make sense.

He turned a street corner. Were the FBI arrogant enough to simply invade another country and act as if they still had all their powers? Perhaps they weren't FBI at all? Perhaps they were CIA faking a cover? The CIA certainly weren't above such operations.

Then again, the woman had been shaken by the appearance of Bruno's body. Surely not the response of a trained agent, FBI or CIA.

Had the Americans found Bruno? Passed the information to the ROS? Would that explain why they were left in the car when the Polizia entered Bruno's apartment? Or had the ROS brought the FBI in on the operation? He shook his head. It was an unpleasant thought. It would mean Bruno wasn't the last loose end he would have to tie up.

He took the steps down into a metro station. The ROS and the FBI? Things were getting uncomfortable. He'd been careful coming here. Checking for a tail, doubling back, using different routes, but now he'd have to reconsider his options.

He pulled a ticket from his pocket, and passed through the turnstiles and down to the platform. A sign said the train was due in seven minutes.

He'd hoped to be at the very same spot an hour earlier, and his plan in much better shape. He put his hands in his pockets. He'd been lucky, dealing with Bruno moments before the law arrived. And not just the Polizia but the ROS and the FBI. And the woman.

The FBI would be an additional challenge. He bit his lip. There again, they might be an opportunity. To close down his operation for a while, maybe even a year or two, he needed money.

He grinned. Yes, the presence of the FBI could be a very good thing because Wilson was still alive. The Americans insisted their government would pay no ransom for hostages, but that was a lie. He knew from experience.

And the Americans always had plenty of money.

CHAPTER TWENTY-THREE

Jess breathed deeply, and let go of the wall.

The terrible image of the man's head, cleaved open, swam in and out of her mind. The apartment was small, squalid, and liberally splashed with the late tenant's blood and gray matter and, well, other body fluids. She'd seen corpses before, but this one was viciously slaughtered.

Morris tapped her arm. "You okay?"

She nodded.

"You shouldn't even be here."

"You wouldn't be here if it wasn't for me."

"Maybe not today. But we were tracking him down." Morris sighed. "We'd have gotten here."

"I guess."

"We were too late anyway."

She scowled. "I passed the information to you as soon as I received it."

"I know." He shook his head. "It was a regret, not a complaint."

She breathed out through her nose. "We missed him by minutes." She looked up and down the crowded street. "He might even be nearby."

"He's gone." Morris shook his head. "He wouldn't stay here after the swarm of law enforcement showed up."

She looked back at the first floor apartment window. "You'll get something from this that will help with Wilson Grantly, right?"

"Maybe."

"Crime techs?"

"You saw them. They're working on it."

"What about cameras on this block?" She looked up and down the street. "There must be something?"

"Probably, but not inside the building. But even if we see him walking in the street, who's to say the body wasn't already like that when he arrived?"

"But why would he be here at all?"

"Maybe he's a friend?"

"Was a friend."

"We were too late, Jess. I know that. Vanelli knows that."

"Yeah."

"You're a civilian." Morris frowned and swiped his palm over his face. "Vanelli doesn't think a civilian should be involved here."

"Well I am involved. I was involved before he was."

"He's not wrong. This case has turned out to be much worse than expected."

She frowned. "You should have thought of that before you asked me to interview Wilson Grantly back at that coffee shop in Dallas."

"I didn't ask you to chase them down. You know I didn't."

"Them? You say it like you know Ficarra killed this guy."

"I'm not blind to other possibilities, Jess, but..."

"So, arrest him."

"We need evidence." Morris shook his head. "So far, the only evidence we have is that he's Luigi Ficarra's brother. We have nothing to connect Enzo to Luigi's crimes. Maybe we'll get something here with the courier. But I doubt it."

"Follow him, then. Surveillance. He'll screw something up. They always do. And when he does, you can grab him."

"The Italians have to follow their legal process. I can't change their law."

"Why not? Enzo Ficarra is not following the law."

"They have nothing to pin on him. If they did, he'd be in custody already. You saw how fast they move when they've got grounds."

"You call that nothing?" She gestured to Bruno's apartment. "You're just going to wait until he shoots someone in broad daylight with the cameras rolling?"

"Of course not." Morris shook his head again. "Vanelli is pushing for approval. He might get it as early as tomorrow. Believe me, Jess, he wants Enzo just as much as we do."

"What about Wilson Grantly?"

Morris sighed. "We want him, too, but we don't know where he is."

"Enzo's got him."

He nodded. "But where?"

"Exactly. That's a damn good reason to follow him."

"We want to, Jess. It's just—"

"The law. The process. People have to get paid. Too few resources, too many crimes. Blah, blah blah." She waved her hand to dismiss the excuses she'd heard way too many times before. "Yeah, so you said. I'll mention it to Wilson Grantly, should I ever see him alive."

"We should have Enzo under surveillance tomorrow." Morris took a deep breath. "There was another man at the airport, as well."

Jess leaned forward. "And?"

"And you don't know this."

"Who was it?"

"He wore a baseball cap. Kept his head down. Disabled the camera in the elevator."

She frowned.

"He was in the elevator at the airport for a couple of hours."

"What elevator?"

He nodded to the apartment. "The one the guy in there used."

"What was he doing in the elevator for two hours?"

Morris rolled his eyes. "He didn't want anyone to know he was at the airport."

"So, it was Enzo?"

"Maybe."

She screwed up her face. "He spent two hours in an elevator, and you can't find any clues it was Ficarra?"

"Hundreds of people go through the elevator every day."

She sighed.

"But he did leave us something," Morris said. "A hubcap. From his car."

Jess said nothing.

"Soil samples showed two possible areas." Morris sighed. "Big areas, unfortunately. And neither are anywhere close to where Ficarra lives."

"Which is?"

"Off limits to you. And I mean it. We need to be squeaky clean when we arrest him." He paused. "And I don't want him to notice you."

She raised an eyebrow. "Near here?"

"Might be."

"Might be, what?"

"I meant he might be around Rome, or he might not."

"Boy. You're really making progress."

Morris scowled. "Thank you."

She looked at the sidewalk. "We just need to get closer to Enzo."

"You definitely don't need to get an inch closer to him. In fact, I'd like it if you went back to Denver and put an entire ocean and half a country between you and him."

"I was speaking figuratively. Besides, I have my double-barreled friend." She patted her pocket where the Heizer rested comfortably against her side.

"For emergencies."

"What else would they be?"

"Yeah, well. Keep out of this, and you won't have an emergency."

She nodded. "Just tell me if you find something."

"Like Wilson Grantly?"

"Yeah, like him, or a grave for Enzo Ficarra."

CHAPTER TWENTY-FOUR

MORRIS SAT AT THE small desk he had been assigned outside Vanelli's office in the Raggruppamento Operativo Speciale building. He hung up the phone, swept the papers from his desk into the top drawer, and locked it. He found his way through the maze of desks to Vanelli's office. His door was open. Morris walked straight in.

Vanelli sat behind his desk. Two stone-faced carabinieri Morris recognized from the airport tapes stood on either side.

Vanelli cleared his throat. "We have a problem."

Morris settled into a chair directly in front of Vanelli's desk. "What problem?" He resisted the temptation to add, please don't let it be Jess.

Vanelli held up a sandwich bag by its edges. Morris leaned forward, his eyes drawn to a bloody finger in the center of the plastic. The nail had turned white and the flesh was pale. Patches of skin flapped at the cut end, marble white bone glowed in the center. The whole thing floated in a splash of blood.

His skin crawled. He clenched his jaw before he asked the question to which he suspected he already knew the answer. "Whose is it?"

"DNA will confirm, but," Vanelli passed over a photocopied piece of paper. "This tells us the owner is Wilson Grantly."

Morris let out a deep breath. Wilson Grantly's finger in a plastic bag wasn't good, but at least it wasn't Jess's. "I can get comparison samples from his parents."

"That isn't the only issue." Vanelli nodded to the paper.

Morris read. The note was addressed to him. It was short. "Wilson Grantly for a million euros. Be at your phone at six." He blew out a long breath. "How the hell does he know my name?" He glowered at Vanelli.

Vanelli raised his eyebrows. "Your reporter friend, perhaps?"

Morris tossed the paper on the desk. "That's ridiculous."

Vanelli picked up the paper. "It is addressed to Agent Morris of the FBI."

Morris clenched his teeth. "We're all agents."

"No one here refers to you that way." Vanelli smiled flatly. "In case that's what you're thinking."

"Some do."

Vanelli glowered.

Morris took a deep breath. "I don't know what to think, but Jess wouldn't spread that around. She's got a vested interest in keeping this quiet."

"She didn't seem very happy at the apartment yesterday."

"She was frustrated with our progress. She thinks we should have Ficarra under surveillance already."

"I share her frustration, but I'm sure you're aware how successful any prosecution would be if we didn't follow procedure." Vanelli leaned forward. "She's a reporter. And a celebrity one at that. She's only interested in her own fame."

Morris leaned back in his chair. "She risked her life in the U.S., and again here, in the hunt for justice. I won't even deign to answer that."

Vanelli frowned. "Whatever that means."

"It means, no matter what you think, she wouldn't have revealed my name to Ficarra."

"Perhaps there are other ways the information could have leaked out." Vanelli sniffed. "The real problem is the demand."

"A million euros? For Wilson Grantly?" Morris shook his head and clenched his jaw again. "We don't negotiate with terrorists. And we don't pay ransom."

"Neither do we." Vanelli picked up the plastic bag. "But..."

Morris crossed his arms. "The Grantlys don't have anything like that amount of money."

"And your government?"

"It's not up to me."

"The note says we have until six o'clock tonight."

"We should be focusing on finding Ficarra and bringing him in, not paying him off and leaving him out there to do this again."

"We are. But we have to cover all angles in parallel, as I'm sure you're aware."

Morris eyed the finger on Vanelli's desk. "You going to have that analyzed?"

"Naturally."

"And the surveillance?"

Vanelli nodded. "Approved an hour ago."

"Good."

"Um, hmm," Vanelli hummed. "There is just one small problem."

Morris cocked his head.

Vanelli's smile was rueful. "My men can't find him."

CHAPTER TWENTY-FIVE

JESS WALKED TOWARD HER hotel, using her phone for directions. She kept to broad streets, sacrificing speed for safety. She passed under an archway into the Piazza Navona. The square wasn't as large as she imagined, or perhaps it was the density of outdoor cafés that reduced the space. The café tables were filled, and lines of hungry diners waited patiently.

Tourists ringed street performers who variously juggled, unicycled, and painted their way into the crowd's hearts, and particularly, their pockets.

She worked her way past the fountains, pausing at the last one to consider if she had ever seen so many statues of naked men in one place before when her phone rang. Her publisher.

"Carter?"

"How're things, Jess?"

She frowned. "Two calls in two days? I wouldn't get this much attention from you if I were standing in your office."

"Now, now. I'm always interested in my star reporter."

"You mean, you're interested in when I'll have publication-ready copy."

"Oh Jess! Twist the knife, why don't you?"

"Yeah, yeah." She smiled. It was the first genuine smile she'd felt today. "You'll get it when it's ready."

"Actually," he drew out the word and his tone became serious, "I'm worried about you. The last time we talked, you left me concerned about your safety. And despite your callous characterization of my motives—all lies, by the way—I still am."

"Well, I'm still alive, if that's what you mean."

"I figured." He laughed. "The dead generally don't answer their phones."

She realized she was staring at a man in the barest of loincloths wrestling a fish, and turned away.

She cleared her throat. "Come on, Carter. What's on your mind?"

His voice dropped an octave. "You are okay, aren't you Jess? My offer to get our man in Paris down to you in a few hours stands. Or I can get you a bodyguard."

"I'm okay."

"All you have to do is ask."

"Really, Carter. I have the FBI and the carabinieri here to protect me, and everything is under control."

He grunted.

Jess waited as long as she could bear for him to speak again. She gave in first. "Is there anything else?"

He took a deep breath. "There is, actually. You remember Osborne?"

"Mr. Happy?"

"Yes. The man for whom the phrase, never have so few

complained about so much to so many, was invented."

Jess laughed. Carter Pierce was good for her spirits, if nothing else. "Please don't tell me something bad has happened to him."

"Nothing of the sort. He must have received a better offer. Handed his notice in this morning, packed up, and left. I did consider pointing out that his contract stipulated a month's notice, but given the circumstances…"

"You're mean, Carter."

"I like to think of myself as honest."

"Then you're honestly mean."

He laughed and she joined in. "But you should be here. People are smiling. Laughing. They have a spring in their step."

"Mean, mean, mean."

"Perhaps a tiny little bit. On the plus side, stories are being written, articles are being made. Productivity is up."

"As I said, mean, mean, mean."

"If I could just get something from my star reporter—"

"When it's ready, Carter. And not before."

"Well…I'll wait if I must." He sniffed as if he was crying. A joke. They both laughed. "Look after yourself, Jess. And come back in one piece. Soon."

She said her goodbyes, and terminated the call.

She liked the office. She worked there sometimes. She liked the people. Mostly. Now that Osborne was gone, she'd like it a lot more. But office life wasn't for her. She needed to be out, doing something. Keeping herself busy helped her to cope with Peter.

She returned her phone to her pocket and kept moving.

CHAPTER TWENTY-SIX

AT SIX O'CLOCK, MORRIS sat facing Vanelli at his desk, a phone between them. Coiled wires snaked out of the phone to two headsets, one beside each of them. Large foam pads covered the earpieces and microphones.

On the other end of the desk, Luca Russo, a fresh-faced college-aged guy, studied a computer screen, a stack of blinking lights and electronics next to him.

Two of Vanelli's men leaned against the back wall of the room, holsters bulging under their suits.

A woman who had introduced herself as a wellness and stress counselor relaxed in the only soft chair in the office. After Vanelli had told everyone that this was Morris's show, she had asked him one question.

"Have you done this before?"

Morris nodded. "Twice."

"And?"

"One saved."

"And one lost?"

There was a long silence before she looked at Vanelli. "You two do have something in common then."

Vanelli looked at Morris, and shrugged.

The wellness and stress counselor leaned back in her chair. "Fifty-fifty. Better than most in these situations."

Morris took a deep breath, and let it out slowly. The Italians had a weird way of dealing with stress.

The phone rang. He placed his watch on the desk in front of him. The men leaning on the rear wall turned to the computer screen. The college-aged guy started tapping keys.

Vanelli donned his headset. Morris did the same. He took a deep breath, and pressed the answer button. He listened for a moment. A high frequency buzz faded in and out in a regular rhythm. A deeper rumble persisted, stopping momentarily every few seconds.

Morris cleared his throat. "Morris."

A mechanical, synthesized voice crackled in his ear. "Is the money ready?"

"Who is this?"

"Answer the question."

"I need to know who I'm talking to."

"Is the money ready?"

Lines traced their way across a map on the computer screen, ending in a yellow star fifty miles north of Rome. Vanelli nodded, and the men leaning on the rear wall left the room, closing the door silently.

"We need more time," Morris said.

"No."

"It's a lot of money. It can't be arranged in an instant."

"You've had all day."

"It's not that easy."

"It's not that easy to send another finger, but I will."

Morris forced himself to breathe.

"Or maybe you want something bigger?" crackled the mechanical voice.

"Who am I dealing with?"

"Someone not that stupid."

"We have to know."

Morris waited. The high frequency buzz filled the line, the bass rumble keeping up its syncopated accompaniment.

The young guy adjusted a dial on the electronics.

Morris checked his watch. Twenty seconds. The maximum period of silence his training had recommended. He breathed out. Relaxing his muscles, calming his voice box. "How do you know my name?"

He heard clicks, and perhaps the slightest sounds of breathing through whatever electronics were distorting the man's voice.

"How do you know my name?" he repeated.

The silence on the phone continued. He opened his mouth to speak, but the metallic voice grated back at him.

"Left or right?"

Vanelli looked at him.

Morris licked his lips. "Don't do anything rash."

"So, you have the money?"

"We still need more time."

"Then choose, left or right."

"These things—"

"Left or right!" The voice buzzed and rattled like an angry snake.

Vanelli's finger hovered over the mute button. Morris

nodded.

"He's going to crack," Vanelli said.

"Even if we hand over money, there's no guarantee. And we know nothing about him."

"You've got one last chance."

Morris took a deep breath, and clicked the phone off mute.

"I need to talk to Wilson Grantly."

"No."

"I need to know what we are paying for."

Heavy breathing hissed and fizzed in his ear.

Morris licked his lips. "If you can give me that, I can take it to my superiors."

The hissing breaths continued.

Morris pushed his eyebrows together. "They might agree to your demands."

"Take them what I gave you."

"Just put Wilson on. I need to talk to him."

"Piss off."

"I need—"

"You need the money."

"I need proof of life."

A twisted grunt burst from the phone. The metallic voice swore. "Proof of life? Proof of life? Maybe I should send you proof of death."

"I need—"

The buzzing stopped, and the rumble was gone.

The young guy's hands raced between buttons and knobs, tweaking adjustments to the electronics.

Morris licked his lips, and spoke into his microphone. "I need proof of—"

The young guy shook his head, and leaned back in his chair. "We lost him."

The stress counselor let out a deep breath. "Let's hope that's a temporary condition."

CHAPTER TWENTY-SEVEN

MORRIS'S PHONE RANG, WAKING him five minutes before his alarm clock. He fumbled for the noise, and recognized Vanelli's number. "Morris here."

"We have another problem."

Morris closed his eyes. "You've found Wilson Grantly's body?"

"No."

Morris opened his eyes, and exhaled. "No news is good news."

Vanelli said, "My men were unable to locate Ficarra or the phone."

"Your men? You waited for them to drive out of Rome to—"

"Please, Agent Morris, credit us with some intelligence. My men informed the local Polizia. They were at the phone's last known location within minutes."

"You're right." Morris grimaced. "Sorry."

"We are all feeling the pressure, *signore*."

"Yes." Morris took a deep breath. "Any surveillance cameras near the location?"

"It's a small provincial village. Popular with tourists. But no cameras."

"So, Wilson could be anywhere."

"Assuming he's still alive."

Morris bit his lip.

"But, that's not the problem," Vanelli said. "American news networks are reporting a shooting."

Morris frowned. "What shooting?"

"Luigi Ficarra."

"Damn."

"As you say. It confounds our investigation, and raises the stakes."

Morris pressed the palm of his hand on his forehead. "I don't know how…I mean, it certainly didn't come from the FBI."

"Your Miss Kimball is press."

"I told you before, she wouldn't release anything."

"Perhaps, but I'm sure she knows plenty of people who are."

"What news networks? How many? We kept it under wraps this long, we might be able to quash the story."

Vanelli sighed. "It's out there, on the Internet. Even the BBC has it."

"So, Enzo knows."

"Possibly."

"Certainly." Morris swallowed. "We have to find Wilson Grantly."

"Trust me, I am trying. In the meantime, I'll leave Miss Kimball to you."

CHAPTER TWENTY-EIGHT

JESS WOKE FACING THE heavy drapes across the French doors to her balcony. Light crept around the folds in the fabric. She pulled the duvet tighter. The temptation to order room service was strong. It took five minutes for her to decide that abandoning her 600-thread-count cocoon for breakfast on fine white china and silver cutlery was a fair exchange.

Minutes later she stood in the shower, hot water playing over her shoulders and the heady scent of a giant cube of lavender Marseille soap tingling in her nose.

The towels were thick, the corners embroidered with the hotel's logo. She dried off, and sat at an antique dressing table. Morning light poured in through sheer curtains, making patterns that danced across the room. She fixed her hair, touched on light make up, and pulled on jeans and a silk top. All she needed now was breakfast.

She opened the door from her room. Her phone rang. It lay on the nightstand, forgotten as she basked in luxury. One day, it would be a call about Peter. Or Peter himself. Her skin tingled. It was a call she prayed for and longed for. What better day for news?

She reached the phone on its fourth ring. "Hello?"

"Morris. You seen the paper?"

Her shoulders sagged. "No. Just going to breakfast."

"Don't."

"Why? You caught Enzo?"

He snorted. "No. Vanelli can't even find him."

"You're kidding?"

"I wish. But that wasn't why I called. You're in the news."

"Me?"

"That's what I said."

She grimaced. "Sorry."

There was a moment's silence. "No problem. But someone blew it. Put your name out there."

"Someone? About what?"

"Luigi Ficarra."

She sucked air through her teeth. "*Foto Oggi?*"

"No. U.S. media."

She scowled. "It won't have come from my magazine."

"You're sure about that?" Morris's disbelief fairly oozed through the phone.

Her expression hardened. "Really."

"It came from someone."

Jess put her hand to her forehead. "Osborne."

"Who?"

"Mr. Happy. My publisher just told me Osborne quit. No proof, but he was always one to spoil the party."

Morris sighed. "Either way, you're in the news. Visible." He cleared his throat and rustled a newspaper. "Reporter shoots suspected blackmailer."

She sighed. "Which newspaper?"

"A bunch."

"Does it mention he took cyanide?"

"No."

She sighed. "So, everyone is going to think I killed him."

"It does say blackmailer."

"Suspected."

Morris blew out a long breath.

She swallowed. "What page?"

"Three."

"He committed suicide in the end."

"They don't mention that."

"It makes me look like a killer."

"No matter what it makes you look like, he was Enzo's brother."

"He might not read page three in the U.S. newspapers."

"Jess, it's out there. Online. Searchable."

She coughed.

"Besides, his brother didn't turn up. Enzo's going to be searching for him."

"Is that why you can't find Enzo?"

"I talked to him." Morris took a deep breath. "He's demanding money for Wilson."

"Do you know it's him? Do you have proof?"

"Don't get interested. You're leaving."

"Wilson's alive, right?"

Morris sucked air through his teeth. "Hard to say."

"How did he make contact?"

"None of your business. I only told you so you get the point.

Enzo might have disappeared, but he's demanding money for Wilson. He's going to be looking for his brother."

"And I've been named."

"Exactly. So get packing. Stay in your room, and I'll be there in thirty minutes."

"What?"

"Your time in Italy is over, Jess. You're leaving."

CHAPTER TWENTY-NINE

JESS STUFFED THE LAST of her clothes into a suitcase she'd bought from the hotel gift shop, and rearranged the contents twice before the case would lock. She looked over the cabinets, checked the bathroom counter, and gave the closet a once-over before wheeling her case to the door.

Sunlight speared through the windows, casting patterns on the carpet. The honeyed wood of the antique furniture glowed, and the balcony begged her to sit and stay a while.

She sighed. Damn Enzo Ficarra.

Her watch read eleven o'clock. Four hours before her hastily arranged flight took off. She opened the door, dragged her case into the hall, and cursed Enzo Ficarra one more time.

The elevator dinged. She grabbed her suitcase, and ran. A hand jutted out, holding open the doors. She slowed her pace. Fingers curled around the door, gripping it tight.

Her heart thumped against her ribs. Stay in your room, Morris had said. It seemed melodramatic, but now?

She pushed her hand in her pocket, and gripped the Heizer. The elevator door buzzed. She took a deep breath. She was being stupid. It could be anyone. A stranger trying to help. An ordinary, everyday pleasantry. She approached the elevator doors.

"Down?" said a man's voice.

She took a breath. "Yes."

A face appeared around the door. A face with lines and wrinkles. Salt and pepper hair. Spectacles. Tanned skin. Kind blue eyes. She breathed a sigh of relief. Not Enzo Ficarra.

She stepped into the elevator.

He held his hand over the buttons. "Lobby?"

She smiled. "Please."

The doors whirred closed, and the elevator descended.

The man grinned. "Enjoyed your stay?"

"Yeah."

"Rome," he said. "Never gets old."

She nodded.

He winked. "It's a joke."

She tried to laugh. "Right. Yes." She raised her eyebrows. "Very good."

The elevator bumped to a stop. The doors opened with a ding. The man gestured for her to go first. She headed straight for the concierge desk. The man strolled out through the main entrance.

She took a deep breath, and let it out slowly, relaxing her shoulders. She was worrying needlessly. There were a dozen guests in the lobby, half a dozen staff at reception, a cluster around a woman at the concierge desk, and two bellboys at the door.

She was perfectly safe. No one would do anything criminal in front of so many witnesses.

She rolled her head around, stretching the muscles in her neck. She was being ridiculous. Her imagination was working overtime. She was fine. Safety in numbers.

She took an armchair in front of an ornate fireplace. There were no flames, just an arrangement of dried flowers and herbs. She basked in the aroma, and people watched.

A young man at reception placated an unhappy customer with a strong Scottish accent. At the concierge desk, the woman did a brisk trade in pamphlets, drew circles on maps, and gestured directions to a steady stream of customers. The disgruntled Scotsman left the hotel. A couple walked in, arm-in-arm, and disappeared into the elevator.

Jess took a picture of the fireplace, and admired her handiwork on her phone.

"Miss Kimball?"

She spun around. The young man who had been on the receiving end of the Scotsman's wrath stood behind her chair.

"I'm Santo Mola." He smiled. "Agent Morris wants me to inform you that he is waiting."

She looked at the front of the hotel. There were no cars parked on the forecourt.

"He's at the rear. Quieter, he said."

She looked the man up and down. He had been behind reception only a few minutes before. He picked up her suitcase. "I can show you the way."

Jess stood up. "Lead on."

Mola carried the suitcase with ease even though he looked thin and frail. They worked their way along corridors, through a loading dock, to a door labeled "Car Park."

Mola opened the door. She glimpsed a black blur, and heard a crunch. Mola crumpled to the floor. Her suitcase tumbled sideways. She stepped back, reaching for her gun.

"Don't move."

Enzo Ficarra stood in the doorway, a large gun held in his outstretched hand. She saw the barrel and its rifling in painfully exquisite detail.

He jerked the gun in her direction. "Hands by your sides. Turn around."

It was the first time she'd heard his voice. She took her hand from her pocket, and turned her back to him. He spoke English with almost no accent. Like a television news anchor.

He ripped her messenger bag off her head, scraping the strap across her ear. She jerked away from the pain. He emptied the bag's contents on the floor, kicked her phone across the loading dock, and tossed the bag behind some boxes.

He pushed her hands behind her. She heard the buzz of a zip-tie, and felt its unforgiving nylon bind her wrists. He rammed a ball of cloth in her mouth, and wrapped tape across her face, fixing it in place. She gagged, and pushed at the cloth with her tongue.

He kept his gun on her as he pinned a note to the doorframe with a knife.

He checked the car park before jamming the gun in her back. "Out. Ford. On the right." He shoved her through the doorway with the barrel of the gun.

She stepped over Mola, and exited the rear of the building. The Ford was close. The engine was running. The trunk was open.

Enzo dug the gun in her back. "Get inside."

She climbed in. He pushed her head down, and slammed the trunk. She blinked. Slivers of light crept in around the corners of the lid.

She heard the driver's door open and close. Enzo raced out of the car park.

Acceleration rolled her backwards, jamming her face against a piece of metal. He braked hard, and she slid into the back of the rear seats. Her bound hands burning on the carpet.

She levered herself around using her forehead to lift her from the trunk's surface until she had her feet braced in one wheel arch and, her shoulder in the other. The force of the car's acceleration and braking strained at her abdomen, but it was worth it to stop the carpet scraping on her arms.

She twisted her hips and rotated her shoulders, easing her hands toward her pocket, and the two-shot Heizer. Her weight rested on her wrists. She clenched her teeth, and shuffled more weight onto her shoulders.

Her fingertips brushed the edge of her pocket. She fumbled the fabric between her fingers, pulling it closer. The car turned a corner, stealing it from her grasp. She took a deep breath and arched her back hard, reaching her pocket. She felt the geometry of the Heizer's patterned metal surface. She teased it closer to her palm, wrapping her fingertips around the grip. She stretched the fingers of her left hand, freeing the gun from the fabric, and pulled it into the palm of her right hand.

She breathed out, emptying her lungs and relaxing her muscles before breathing in again, and pulling the gun from her pocket.

She unwound the twist in her hips and shoulders, and stretched her back. Her joints clicked.

She squeezed the Heizer and checked that the safety was on.

She didn't have a plan, but she was armed, and would have the element of surprise. She hoped that would be enough to get free. After that, she'd run.

She rotated her feet toward the rear of the car, and rolled on her side. She couldn't see the gun behind her back, but she felt sure she could point it straight at anyone who released the trunk. She squeezed the gun.

If she missed, she would only have one more shot to adjust her aim. She shoved that thought to the back of her mind.

Her heart hammered in her chest. What if he had an accomplice? What if she needed more than one shot? She breathed in and out. Something was better than nothing. She had to use her advantage while she had it.

She rolled her head back, stretching her muscles. Whatever happened, she'd bring Enzo Ficarra to justice one way or another.

She settled down, listening to the rhythm of the car's engine and brakes, the creak of the suspension, the rumble of passing trucks. The traffic thinned out. Stop and start gave way to long periods of constant speed and sweeping turns. They were out of the city.

After what she guessed to be an hour, Enzo changed down through the gears. The car slowed before bumping onto what felt like the hard shoulder. Jess rolled her shoulders and redoubled her grip on the tiny gun. Her fingers rested on the safety.

The engine stopped. She took a deep breath. The silence was shocking. No cars, nothing to echo from walls, no hubbub of life. They must have been in the middle of nowhere.

Her heartbeat picked up speed.

The car door opened. She felt the car rock as he got out. She rolled on her side, angled the gun upwards, and flipped the safety.

This was it. Showtime.

He walked around the car, his shoes crunching on leaves and

branches. She held her mouth half open to silence the sound of her hard breathing. She rubbed her finger against the trigger, teasing it, feeling the weight of its pull. He walked alongside the car. She jolted as he rapped on the trunk.

She panted, and adjusted her grip. First shot, center mass. She had to be quick. The daylight would be blinding, but his silhouette would be clear. As soon as he opened the trunk. No delay. No thinking. No chance for him to see what was happening.

The sound of his steps on the undergrowth receded. She angled her head, triangulating his direction. He was walking toward the front of the car.

She swallowed. He wasn't opening the trunk? She sweated. He was going to leave her. She rubbed her brow on the carpet. Was he going to dispose of the vehicle with her in it? A bomb, a cliff, or, maybe a fire?

Her breathing raced beyond control. The darkness pressed in on her. The cooling engine ticked through the car's steel. Gusts of wind hissed through cracks and gaps. Birds called, long and pitiful.

Her heart banged against her ribs. Her pulse throbbed in her throat. She sniffed the air, dreading the scent of gas.

She had to find a way out. If he set fire to the car, he might stay and watch, but she would have to escape the trunk to have any hope of surviving. Even if all she could do was run, it was a chance.

She twisted her hands, wiping them, one at a time, on her sleeves as best the zip-tie would allow without letting go of the gun.

She hefted its diminutive weight. It took a 9mm round, but would it have enough power to break open the latch on the trunk? She adjusted her grip on the gun. If the first shot didn't open it, she would have no choice but to fire the second. Her element of surprise would be gone. Enzo would return and could easily put rounds through the car's thin skin. She breathed. Two shots? Would the latch survive two shots?

Would she?

She twisted her head. Was the latch in the center of the trunk, or to one side? It was too dark to see. She swallowed. She hadn't noticed as he pushed her in.

She licked around her mouth. Where the hell was he? What the hell was he doing? And worse, what was he going to do?

She forced her lungs to slow their sprint. Her arms ached from pointing the gun. Her spine felt locked in its arched position. She stretched her toes, and flexed her legs. She had to focus. She had to choose. Burst out, or wait for him to appear? If she could only free her hands, she would stand a fighting chance.

She stopped her breathing. She heard footsteps on the undergrowth. Getting louder. Heading toward the car. Enzo returning? Or someone else?

She checked her aim, ensuring her shot would be above the lip of the trunk, but low enough to hit something vital. She frowned. What if it was someone else? A passer-by?

She took a deep breath. She had to wait. She couldn't shoot a bystander. She had to identify Enzo before she pulled the trigger.

The footsteps grew louder. She rechecked the safety, and tightened her finger on the trigger. The footsteps stopped. One of the car's doors opened, and the vehicle rocked as someone sat in the driver's seat. Had Enzo returned? Or was it someone else? And what had he done while he was gone?

The starter motor churned, a mechanical squeal that sounded long overdue for oil. The squealing stopped, but the engine didn't catch. The keys rattled in the ignition, and the birds resumed their calls. Jess forced herself to breathe.

The keys rattled again, and the starter motor began its churn. The car shook, the engine laboring. The churning stopped and the quiet returned.

A man swore. Enzo's voice. The seat back separating them muffled the sound, but she was sure. His seat creaked. He muttered. Then nothing but silence. He didn't move, didn't speak, and didn't try to start the car.

Seconds felt like hours as she lay with her back arched to bring her gun up, ready to face him. She breathed deep. Light trickled in through gaps around the number plate and taillights. She moved her feet. One of the holes was big enough to push a pen through.

She eased her knees up to her chest, and rotated to bring her face close to the hole.

He laughed. "We'll be there soon. Though you might be happier where you are."

She bit her lip.

The keys rattled, and the starter motor churned.

She shoved her eye to the hole, blinking and squinting. The car was on an unmade path off a main road. Trees lined either side. They were heading into a forest.

Across the road were houses. Vacation rentals. Small and brightly painted. Thin iron gates guarding their short driveways. Jaunty black and gold lettering proudly announcing their names.

There were no lights visible in the windows, and no cars in the driveways. She blinked. Straining to the left, she saw an elderly lady in a garden, digging, a wheelbarrow at her side.

Jess breathed hard. If she broke out of the trunk, could she make it across the road? And if she did, what protection would an old lady be? Or would she just invite a monster into the old woman's life? Jess sighed. Better to stay where she was. For now.

The starter motor squealed. The engine caught, spluttering, idling rough until Enzo brought up the revs, smoothing it out.

Across the road, the houses waited patiently for their guests, oblivious to her plight. She longed to run for the protection of their walls, but she knew it was fruitless, he would find her, and kill her, and anyone who stood in his way.

Enzo engaged first with a crunch of gears. He drove forward twenty yards, and stopped. She saw a wide gate swaying in the wind. Enzo stepped out of the car. She saw his back as he closed the gate, securing it with a rusty chain and padlock.

She pulled back from the hole as he turned to walk toward the car. She was laying the wrong way around. The gun was pointing into the car. If he opened the trunk he would see her and the gun.

She swung her feet around to rotate to her prone position, her back arched and the gun pointed upwards, ready to fire on him. She panted. Sweat dripped from her forehead. She squeezed the grip of the Heizer.

He walked past. The gravel crunched under his feet. The car bounced as he sat in the driver's seat. His door clanged shut, and he drove on.

CHAPTER THIRTY

THE FORD BUMPED OVER the rough lane. Jess lost her purchase on the side of the trunk and thumped into the seat back that separated her from the rest of the car. The car jolted over a hump. She lurched into the air, her head banging against a metal spar along the top of the trunk. She crashed down, her back landing on her hands, twisting the gun from her grip.

Her fingers scrabbled for it, but came up empty. She rolled over, hoping to trap the gun under her body, but she felt nothing.

The Heizer had disappeared.

The car turned a bend, shoving her head first into the side of the trunk. She pushed back with her shoulders, turning herself over, and staring into the blackness between her and the seat back, praying for a glint of gun metal.

She saw it pressed into the gap between the trunk floor and the seat back. Different shades of black in the darkness. A glimmer. Far from her hands.

She pulled her feet up, twisting her leg over to bring the toe of her shoe down on the gun. The car bounced. Her weight shifted, and her shoe mashed into the gun's grip. She forced her forehead against the seat back, bracing herself. The car jolted again, snapping her head back. Her body bounced and lurched. Her legs stiffened to brace against the movement. Her feet pressed down. Down against the Heizer. Down and forward.

Forward through the gap.

She dragged herself along the seat back with her feet, burning her elbows on the trunk floor, angling her arms behind her, fumbling for the gap and the gun.

The car bounced and shuddered.

She felt the carpet and the back of the seat. Different textures on her fingertips. She probed the line where they joined, ramming her fingers into the space till they hurt. She twisted her hands, searching up and down the gap.

The gap.

Tiny and thin.

Like the Heizer.

Her eyelids sank down. The air eased from her lungs. Her stomach churned.

It was gone.

The gun was inside the car.

CHAPTER THIRTY-ONE

MORRIS STOOD AT THE hotel's rear door. He squeezed the phone, and took a deep breath. "There's no other way to say it, we were too late."

"She's gone?" said Vanelli.

"Out the back. He left a note."

Morris stared at the long knife pinning a piece of white card to the doorframe by a wickedly sharp looking point. He bit his lip.

"And?" Vanelli said.

"And, what?"

"What does it say?"

Morris read the note aloud. "4:00 p.m. Your office."

"That's it?"

"Apart from the fact it's pinned to the doorframe with a knife."

Vanelli whistled. "The hotel cameras catch anything?"

"She walked to the back of the hotel with a man from the

reception desk. Young guy. Santo Mola. Run him through your system, but my gut says he was duped. Someone, probably Ficarra, coshed Mola on the head, and pushed Jess into a white Ford."

"His face?"

"Baseball cap."

"License plate?"

"The cameras aren't good enough."

"I'll have traffic get us footage around the hotel. Where's Santo Mola now?"

"He's on his way to the hospital."

"Talking?"

Morris grunted. "Nothing much to say. Thought he was taking her to meet me."

"Can he identify Ficarra?"

"It was a heavy blow. He's fading in and out. So probably not."

Morris clenched his teeth, and took a deep breath. "Look, Ficarra only took her because she shot his brother. That could have happened whether she was here or in the U.S."

Vanelli took a deep breath, and exhaled slowly. "I have a forensics team on the way. We can search the traffic cameras from our office. Get what you can from the hotel."

Morris grunted.

"And Morris?"

"What?"

"This is Italy. You have no jurisdiction. You're our guest. No right to take this into your own hands."

Morris snorted. "Like that makes any difference. Ficarra's already taken this out of both our hands."

CHAPTER THIRTY-TWO

THE FORD CAME TO a halt. The engine died. Enzo got out of the car. Jess twisted, bringing her legs around, ready to kick at Enzo. The trunk popped open. Daylight glared. Enzo stood to one side. She kicked, swinging her legs in a wide arc.

He caught her feet with ease. "Now, now." He grabbed her other foot, dragging her legs over the lip of the trunk. "Play nice, and we'll both get what we want."

Again, she noticed that he spoke English with almost no accent of any kind. He might have been an American. Maybe he was.

She pulled herself up by her abs. He put his hand under her arm, and levered her out of the car. She breathed heavily. He looked a lot like his brother. Same black hair. Same dark eyes. Same sun worn features. The only thing lacking was a bullet hole. Unfortunately.

He smiled, and nodded to a ramshackle cabin.

She walked slowly, looking left and right. They were in a

small clearing in dense woods. Trails ran through the undergrowth. They had arrived on the only road in and out of the clearing. The ground was soft underfoot. The air smelled of vegetation.

Steps led up to the door. She climbed slowly. Birds cawed. Enzo removed a padlock, and the door creaked open. He pushed her inside.

The cabin had one room. A single substantial wooden pillar supported the roof. Mildewed furniture lay around the room, long ago rotted from damp. A lone plastic chair sat in a corner. She curled her nose up. The scent outside gave way to interior odors full of rot and decay.

Enzo closed the door. He unlocked a brass padlock on a large trapdoor. The door covered a shaft with a rusty iron ladder running down into the dark. He reached into the shaft and flipped a switch. A feeble light glowed some thirty feet down.

A tunnel. Another tunnel. Enzo Ficarra had a thing for tunnels. She'd never been claustrophobic, thank God. Jess sighed. She stepped back.

Enzo shook his head. "I will lower you down."

"No." She shook her head furiously.

"Yes." He took a leather harness from a collapsed chest of drawers, wrapped it under her arms, and buckled it under her chest. The leather stank.

She breathed hard.

He connected a rope to the harness, and looped it around the wooden pillar. "Sit on the edge."

She looked at the drop. "You can't be serious?" she grunted against her gag. "Just untie me."

He leaned back on the rope, taking the strain. "After your friends have paid."

She narrowed her eyes and stared at him. He wasn't insane. He knew precisely what he was doing. Cold, calculating. Not an ounce of madness evident in any of his actions or his manner. She shuddered. She was surely staring into the eyes of pure evil. Just like his brother. Maybe worse.

He nodded to the shaft. "Sit."

She knelt down, sliding her feet over the gap. Enzo pulled on the rope, and jerked her shoulders up.

"Over," he said.

She swallowed, and slid off the edge. The harness wrenched against her shoulders. Her weight shifted from her feet to her shoulders. The pull grew more intense, the harness forcing her arms further behind her. The nylon zip-tie cut into her wrists.

She dangled in the air, bumping against the rock, looking down the shaft. Enzo let the rope out in bursts. She grunted as each jolt wrenched at her shoulders and threatened to rip her arms from their sockets. She gritted her teeth until her feet touched solid ground.

Enzo pulled back on the rope, stretching her up onto her toes. He raced down the ladder, landing a couple of feet from her. He smiled. "It's easier going up."

She clenched her teeth.

He turned her around, and unclipped the harness, letting her down off her toes. Her shoulders relaxed and the burning pain subsided. She bit her lip, and fought back the desire to sigh.

He flipped a switch. Yellow pools of light sprang into life, revealing a roughhewn tunnel. Twenty yards away was an alcove, and beyond that a line of heavy wooden doors. He pushed her forward. The tunnel floor was uneven, no more than bare rock worn down by the passage of miners and whatever they had mined.

Enzo stopped her at the alcove. A coffee table was set into the space. There was a lamp on top. He switched it on. She looked away for a moment as her eyes adjusted to the lamp's glare, but not before she saw the table was covered with wide leather straps, much like the one Enzo had used to lower her into the tunnel.

Underneath the table were large black plastic bags. Industrial. Thick. Strong. Maybe even big enough for a body. She forced herself to look at them. Better to know what she was up against.

He pushed her forward. The ground grew rougher. She peered into the gloom. There was a line of doors on the right hand side. The first few were ruined, but those deeper in the tunnel seemed solid and held tightly sealed by large wooden beams.

"That one," he said, pointing.

She stopped at the door. A glimmer of light crept around its edges. He lifted the wooden beam and the door creaked open.

The room was carved from the rock. A small cave with only one way out. A dim light bulb glowing on the ceiling. A dirty mattress lay on a rusty metal bunk. Around the walls were a series of metal hoops cemented into the blocks.

Enzo pushed her inside. Mold assailed her nostrils. He tossed a plastic bag on the bed. "Lie on it. It'll ward off the damp."

He ripped the tape from around her head, pulling the gag out of her mouth. The tape tore at her skin and pulled her hair out by the roots, but she sighed with relief. She held her hands out behind her.

He shook his head.

She sank onto the plastic sheet.

He pointed to her feet. "Give me your shoes."

She didn't move.

He pulled a zip-tie from his pocket. "Or I can bind your feet together. Your choice."

She kicked off her shoes.

She looked at him, keeping her gaze low on his face, avoiding direct eye contact. "What's going to happen?"

He backed away to the door. "Simple. You will stay here until the FBI pays for your release."

He closed the door. There was a scraping of wood and metal as he dropped the heavy wooden beam into place. His shoes crunched on the rocks as he walked back up the tunnel.

The ceiling light went out. The image of the room and its pitiful light bulb faded from her retinas. She breathed out. Long and slow. The restraints cut into her skin, wild images raced through her mind, and the silence gnawed at her, but she was still alive.

She closed her eyes, and let the darkness swallow her and she wondered what Enzo would do to her when he found out she'd shot his brother.

CHAPTER THIRTY-THREE

ENZO CLOSED THE DRAPES, and switched on the light. The small rental home he had acquired was working out well. The owner had taken cash. Enzo had left the money in an envelope on the porch and the man had collected it. No forms to sign, no taxes to pay, no handshakes to make. Deal done. Anonymity for the price of two weeks' rent.

He pulled on a pair of rubber gloves, from a package that boasted they were flesh colored, though he'd never seen flesh that color, dead or alive. They muted his sense of touch, and would make his job more difficult, but fingerprints and DNA were more important than the ease with which he could work.

He opened a plastic carrier bag, and pulled out a bright red mechanical alarm clock and two small boxes. The first box contained a cheap mobile phone. He'd bought it at a village store, one he knew didn't have video camera surveillance. Inside the box he found the SIM card, but he didn't insert it into the phone. The last thing he wanted was a cell phone signal tracing his location.

He switched on the phone. The battery showed it was almost fully charged. A message in red text complained it was unable to find a network. He dismissed the message, and programmed a phone number into the ninth entry in the speed dial list. He pressed the nine key. The phone made a series of bleeps, and the programmed number appeared in its crude display followed by a message indicating the call didn't go through. He turned up the volume, and switched off the phone.

The second box contained two handheld radios, and a bundle of wires. He put the wires aside, and inserted the batteries in the first radio. Distorted classical music boomed. He turned the volume down, and tuned the radio to a frequency where he only heard static.

He turned the volume down on the second radio, and inserted its batteries. He tuned it to the same frequency as the first radio, and clicked a button marked Push to Talk. The first radio clicked. He tapped his finger on the plastic body of the radio, and heard the sound amplified through the first. Satisfied they were tuned to each other, he turned the radios off.

He pried the front cover from the phone, exposing the mechanism behind the buttons. He bent up the metal contacts for the nine key, so they could no longer touch. In the bundle of wires, he found two that had small clips on each end. He clipped one wire to each of the nine key's contacts.

He picked up the alarm clock. The plastic cover came away easily, and the mechanism slid out. He located the alarm bell and hammer, and detached a small coiled spring from the hammer. The alarm clock clicked as he wound it. He set the alarm for a minute in the future, and waited. When the alarm activated, the hammer flicked forward, and rang the bell once. Without the spring it stayed in place. No ringing alarm, just the simplest mechanical switch.

He attached the wires to the hammer and the bell, winding them around the metal multiple times to ensure a good contact. He wound the clock and set the alarm.

Gently, he placed one of the radios face to face with the phone, and wrapped tape around them both. He lifted the bundle into a plastic box, and switched on the radio, checking it one last time before placing the lid on the box and sealing it with tape.

He put the box in the carrier bag, and the trash in another. Even if the house was traced to him, he had no intention of leaving incriminating evidence.

He opened the drapes, picked up his car keys, and placed the bags in his car. He sat in the driver's seat, and studied a map. He would dispose of the trash in the village, but the box would require a much longer journey. He traced his finger along the country roads around Rome. He would travel to the east side of the city, to a small peak in the hills beyond Tivoli. A beautiful, rugged spot, with a clear line of sight to Rome. Ideal for radio reception and telephone calls. He would wind the clock, set the alarm, and at the appointed hour, the alarm would trigger an untraceable phone call to Colonnello Vanelli's office.

For what it was worth, he would give them their precious proof of life. Not of Grantly, but of the delicate Miss Kimball. He laughed. First Wilson Grantly, then Miss Kimball, then the FBI.

The Americans had blundered in where they weren't wanted, and now they would pay the price. A very high price.

Miss Kimball was far more valuable than Wilson Grantly.

She'd killed Luigi. He'd seen the news reports on the Internet. She'd shot his brother.

Simply thinking the truth reddened his face and raised his heartbeat pounding hard in his chest. He tamped his rage to a rigid level of manageable anger. There would be plenty of time for vengeance later.

His nostrils flared. His breathing slowed.

First, he'd collect the ransom.

After that, money wasn't the only price she would pay.

CHAPTER THIRTY-FOUR

JESS WATCHED. THERE WAS no light. Not real light. Just the flashes and blooms of her overstrained retinas, a wide-awake replay of the visions of deep sleep.

Her back ached. She shifted her weight as she half lay, half sat on the plastic bag on the old bed. She moved every few minutes, but numbness was setting into her arms and legs. She shivered. The cold penetrated her jeans, and she wished she'd worn a warmer shirt. How long had she been underground? An hour? Two?

Two hours. She bit her lip. The best chance of escape and rescue was always in the first few hours. She knew because of her work at *Taboo* with crime victims and their families. And she'd been told many times that her son, Peter, wasn't likely to be found because too much time had passed since he'd been kidnapped. Way too many years.

Immediately after any kidnapping, the captor was running on adrenaline that prevented him from thinking clearly, and the rescuers were doing the same. The rescuers became more acute, more determined, as they made progress toward the hostage. But the captor's high faded as fast as the drug drained from his bloodstream.

But two hours were two hours. Kidnappings had been solved after much longer times in captivity.

She breathed out. Enzo had left her. He had locked her up and, as far as she could tell, returned to the surface of the earth and driven away. Perhaps that made things different? Perhaps, with no immediate contact between them, her chances of escape and rescue would last longer?

She stretched her aching muscles as much as her restraints allowed.

Morris would know she had been taken because he'd been on his way to the hotel. He would have investigated when she didn't appear. He would have found Santo Mola, the man Enzo coshed. He would have reviewed the hotel's security camera footage, and the ones from the street. He would have seen Enzo, and tracked the car.

She grimaced. The houses she had seen from the rear of the car definitely weren't located in the city. They had lawns and gardens and views. Driveways with gates and rustic nameplates. They were on the outskirts of a town or a village, way beyond the city limits. There would be no surveillance cameras here.

So, they would know she had been kidnapped, and probably by whom, but after that she was on her own. If she escaped from Enzo's prison, she'd have to do it herself.

Escape? She pulled on the zip-tie. The possibility seemed remote. Even if she could break free, the door was thick, and the wooden bar sealing it shut was solid and heavy.

She shook her head and shrugged. An involuntary sigh

escaped her lips. If only she'd asked for some evidence that it actually was Morris waiting at the hotel. If she'd called him or talked to him, everything would have been different. One phone call. She bit her lip.

She hadn't taken Morris's warnings seriously enough. Or Vanelli's. He wasn't the world's greatest communicator, but if she had believed him, she'd be at the airport, sipping wine in the club lounge.

Enzo had been in control from the moment he kidnapped her. She sat in the blackness, and watched the speckles of light dance in her vision. Yes, Enzo was in control, and she was on her own. How would she change that balance?

Pins and needles ran through her right leg. She rolled sideways to relieve the pressure on her hips and stretch her leg. The tingling subsided.

Enzo had tied her up and locked her in, but he hadn't killed her. Did that mean he cared more for money than he cared about revenge?

Either way, he'd singled out the FBI to pay for her release, but would they? They had a well-known standing protocol never to pay ransom. She took a breath.

Damn. She sat as upright as her bonds would allow.

Ransom.

Enzo wanted to exchange her for money. Like Wilson Grantly. Enzo would threaten her life, maybe, she curled her fingers into fists, even harm her. There would be back and forth. Messages, demands. Morris would play for time. Trace phone calls. Fingerprint ransom notes. Analyze speech patterns. Anything for a lead. Until Morris would agree to the ransom in the hope of pulling off a sting.

Enzo would play them along. Morris would work night and

day. Everything would happen as she thought.

Everything except that Enzo wasn't planning to let her go.

He couldn't.

She'd shot his brother. She hadn't killed Luigi, but she could have. And if she hadn't shot him, he would have escaped. In Enzo's eyes, she'd killed Luigi either way.

CHAPTER THIRTY-FIVE

ENZO DELIVERED HIS PHONE call device to its appointed hilltop, and drove back to Rome. He pulled off the main road, unlocked the gate to his property, and drove on through.

Halfway to the cabin, he turned off the track and onto a wide walking path. Long grass and branches scraped down the sides of the Ford. The wheels fell into giant potholes, grinding the underside of the car against rocks and stones.

He didn't care. He would torch the Ford tomorrow.

The path opened into a clearing. He swung the car around, pointing it back down the route he had just taken, and stepped out.

The air was fresh with the scent of trees and a hint of salt from the coast a mile away. The tall trees and the sun's angle kept its rays from the floor of the clearing.

He rummaged in the trunk, and pulled out a pair of heavy gloves that reached his elbows. He tucked the cuffs of his jeans into his boots. Left leg then right. No need to invite trouble.

He pushed his way through the long grass to a clearing under a tree. Beside the tree was a green wooden box with a hole on one side and a handle on the top. He took hold of the handle.

The box squirmed in his hand. He peered through the hole. Tiny eyes stared back at him. Teeth and claws flashed. Rats. Good sized ones. He snapped a wooden cover over the hole.

Two. Not many, but he was out of time. He shook the box. He'd have to go with what he had. There again, two might be the best number. More might be overwhelming. He gave a flat smile. He didn't want things to come to an end too quickly.

The scratching and scuffling continued as he walked back to the Ford and dropped the green box in the trunk. He drove back through the grass and branches, over the rocks and potholes, down the wide footpath, to the lane and on to the cabin.

He took the box into the cabin, looped a cord through the handle, and lowered the rats into the mine. He climbed down, and flipped the switch that brought on the gloomy yellow lights strung down the tunnel.

The rats' scratching turned frantic. He shook the box to save them from themselves. The noise stopped.

He walked down the tunnel. The silence was oppressive, the jagged rocks and heavy earth swallowed every sound.

He found the door he wanted, and peered through the spy hole. Satisfied, he removed the locking bar, and opened the door.

"Hello, Jess."

She blinked up at him. Her knees were drawn toward her chest, her shoulders were rolled forward. Only the zip-tie holding her arms behind her prevented her from curling into a fetal position.

She said nothing.

He took another step into the room. "We need to talk. To

come to an agreement."

Her gaze flitted to the wooden box. She gave the barest of nods.

"The FBI will be paying for your release. They're obligated. They involved you. Or you involved yourself, and they didn't stop you. Either way, they are culpable."

She said nothing.

"So, why am I here?" He shrugged. "They will pay. They hate bad publicity, and I, or more correctly, you, could give them some very bad publicity. So, all they need is…encouragement…and that is where you come in."

He placed the box on the floor in front of her. The rats scrabbled, rocking the box. He pulled a cover from one side, revealing inner wire mesh. The rats flocked to the mesh and resumed scratching for freedom. They climbed over each other, squirming and wrestling for the best angle to gnaw through the wire.

Jess swallowed. Her eyes widened. White all but consumed her irises.

He nudged the box, sending the rats into a frenzy. "Two of them."

He waited for a gasp or some display of fear, but she kept her lips closed tight.

"Teeth and claws," he said. "And hunger."

She looked up at him but did not reply.

"In the wild, rats are always hungry. Never satisfied. It's their life. Their existence. They live from meal to meal." He kicked the box. "And if you leave them no choice, they will eat each other." He gave an upturned smile. "No qualms. No hesitation…no hunger."

"What do you want?" Her defiance was amusing.

He smiled. "If you leave them food, they will eat the food first." He raised his eyebrows. "Leave them a lot of food and they will eat for a long time."

She did not reply.

He sniffed. "I want you to understand."

"Understand what?"

He shook his head with mock sorrow, as if she was dimwitted. "I want you to understand what it is like."

She said nothing.

He smiled again. "When it is dark and they have food to eat."

In the hardened mask of her face, a tiny wrinkle appeared across her forehead, barely visible in the dim light. But he saw it. And he smiled again.

He scooped up the box by the handle, and stepped out of the room. He slammed the door and dropped the wooden bar into place.

Through the spy hole, he caught a last glimpse of her face. The defiant mask was gone. Deep furrows lined her forehead. She cringed and shut her eyes.

Mission accomplished.

He barely stopped himself from laughing.

Enzo adjusted his expression and stepped to the last door. He lifted the bar and swung the door open.

Grantly lay on the floor, his clothes covered in dried blood, his ruined hand cradled to his chest. He'd found swaddling and the blood had clotted. Precisely as Enzo had expected.

Grantly swung his head slowly toward Enzo. His eyes converged, pulling themselves back from whatever deep recesses they had found in the dark.

Enzo held the box behind his back, and smiled like a long

lost friend. "Hello, Wilson."

Wilson grunted, low, hoarse. He swayed his head side to side, trying to clear whatever fog filled his mind.

"Not long now," Enzo said.

Wilson made no noise.

"We are negotiating."

Wilson's lips quivered.

"I believe you may have a generous benefactor. Someone who will fulfill the promise your parents broke."

Wilson grunted.

"The FBI."

Wilson's gaze lurched in his direction.

"Ironic, isn't it?" Enzo tilted his head and ticked his tongue against the roof of his mouth. "The very FBI we did everything in our power to avoid will now pay your ransom."

Wilson moved his head. Enzo couldn't tell if he was attempting to communicate, or if he was about to pass out.

He kicked Wilson's leg. "That would be good, wouldn't it? I get the money, and you? You get freedom."

Enzo looked around the damp, bleak cell where Wilson had been confined for more than six days. "Freedom." He scuffed at the ground with his boot. "Probably seems like a lovely dream in here, but freedom for you is entirely possible."

He smiled again, showing a row of straight, white teeth. "You just have to do one small thing."

Grantly arched his eyebrows as if he understood. He nodded.

"Scream," said Enzo.

In one continuous movement, Enzo swung the box from behind him and lobbed it across the cave.

Grantly's head lurched to follow the box's path across his cell. It smashed on the wall. The lid broke off. The box and its contents scattered in all directions.

Grantly yelped.

Enzo leapt back, slamming the door shut behind him. He dropped the heavy wooden beam into place.

Enzo watched through the spy hole and waited a few minutes until the screaming started.

The rats were a psychological weapon. They would torment him. Deprive him of sleep. Needle at whatever was left of his soul. Constantly. Minute by minute. Hour by hour.

But the rats wouldn't kill Grantly. That was something Enzo would do himself. Eventually.

He took a deep breath. He didn't need Grantly or his pathetic quarter million dollars now. Kimball was a much more valuable prize. But Grantly would serve one last purpose.

Enzo returned along the tunnel, passed Kimball's door. The entire length of the walk from the end of the tunnel to the ladder, Enzo heard him.

Grantly was in fine voice. Yelling and screaming. Rasping, desperate, begging. The rats displacing his sanity. As planned.

Enzo laughed.

Five million Euro. Kimball would bring that much, at least.

The longer Grantly lasted, the more she'd be begging them to pay.

Her rescuers would be begging Enzo to accept it.

What a cheerful thought.

CHAPTER THIRTY-SIX

JESS CLOSED HER EYES, and listened as Enzo walked away from her cell. He opened another door. The tunnel's echoes confused his voice, and the heavy wooden door blurred his words, but his intonation was hard, questioning.

She frowned. Questioning who? She strained to hear, but there was no reply to Enzo's questions.

Wood splintered. Probably the box he'd carried.

The cell door scraped back into position.

Someone yelped.

There was a long silence before she heard footsteps. Enzo, heading closer. She shuffled backwards. He paused outside her cell. She took a deep breath.

The shout rang out. A terrified mixture of surprise and shock. Then another, and another.

Enzo remained outside her door.

The shouting grew into screams. Irregular staccato bursts that built until they rolled over each other. The notes rising and falling. Rasping over the gender. Hiding the owner behind their terror.

But she knew the owner, and the terror. She drew her knees toward her chest. Wilson Grantly. He was locked in the same tunnel. With the rats. Enzo had let them loose in a cell just like hers.

His talk. His vile superiority. His gloating. He'd carried out his threat. Just like he told her he would. She exhaled. Just like she knew he would.

A tremolo joined the screaming. Wilson moving abruptly, violently even. His screams doused in anger and venom. He thrashed, stamping, thumping, pounding, but the screams returned. The rats were terrorizing him, and he was trying to kill them.

Enzo walked away. He didn't speak, but his footsteps said all she needed to know. He was satisfied, contented, pleased with himself. She shivered. He was getting a kick out of his sick power.

She counted his steps from the door to the ladder. How many steps to cover the distance from her cell to the ladder? She counted the moments as she imagined him climbing up to ground level. How many rungs on that ladder? How quickly could she climb to freedom?

The light went out in the tunnel, and the coal black returned.

She shuffled her back against the cave wall.

Wilson screamed on.

She rolled her shoulders, curling her head to one side, willing the noise to stop. For her sake.

CHAPTER THIRTY-SEVEN

MORRIS RUBBED HIS EYES. Vanelli rolled the video back and forth. On a monitor between them, a man cartoon-walked in and out of Jess's hotel. She walked in front of the man, patiently reversing direction as Vanelli twisted a knob on the playback panel.

Two men to their right were hunched over another monitor, tracing the white Ford's journey out of Rome.

"It's him," Morris said.

Vanelli shrugged. "Hard to say."

"Has to be."

"His hat hides his face."

"Which proves it's him."

"We have too much experience with kidnapping here." Vanelli's sour frown revealed his feelings about the despicable crime. "No kidnapper wants to appear on camera. Believe me."

Morris rubbed his neck and stretched to relieve tight muscles.

Vanelli gave a pained smile. "I want Ficarra as much as you do, I want her back as much as you do. But we can't jump to conclusions. That would be foolish."

"Her name is Jessica Kimball."

Vanelli's face was expressionless. Sometimes it was impossible to read the man. Did he care about Jess Kimball? Or only about keeping his name out of a failed investigation in the press?

"And Enzo's disappeared. *Poof.*" Morris snapped his fingers and opened his hand to the air like a magician. "One minute he's the family man, the next he's gone on a business trip, according to his wife. Makes no sense."

"We still have to keep an open mind." Vanelli shook his head. "There are clues. We will find them."

Morris picked up a sheaf of papers and shook them. "I questioned everyone. No one at the hotel remembers seeing the man. Even the idiot who carried his message couldn't identify him in photographs."

"Exactly."

"Exactly, what?"

"Exactly why we need to keep an open mind. This isn't about catching Enzo, it's about saving her…*Signorina* Kimball."

Morris closed his eyes, and breathed out.

"Our forensic people are still at the hotel." Vanelli patted his shoulder. "There's still time for them to turn something up."

Morris opened his eyes. "But how much time does Jess have?"

CHAPTER THIRTY-EIGHT

JESS CLENCHED HER FISTS, driving her nails into her palms. Wilson's screaming had slowed, but still there were moments of madness. Thrashing and grunting, but never speaking.

She'd called his name. Quietly at first, but growing louder until she was yelling. Shouts and screams were all he returned. For a while she wondered if it might be someone else. Another poor soul trapped by Enzo. But the man was Wilson Grantly. She was sure.

She leaned back against the wall, her arms numb, and her hands throbbing from the zip-tie's relentless grip. She flexed her shoulders again, rolling them, stretching within the limits of her arms' position.

What did Enzo want? What was he going to force her to do that made threatening her with rats, and forcing her to listen to someone else's torture, rational in his mind?

She snorted. What made any of this rational? She'd involved herself in cases before, but this? She'd ignored the professionals who dealt with monsters like Enzo every day. She shouldn't have. She knew better. Monsters were always lurking. She'd learned that when her son was kidnapped.

She twisted her head left and right, peering into the blackness. Was this what Peter was suffering? Was he locked up like her? Cold. Lonely. Unbroken?

A pain formed in her chest.

Did he think she had abandoned him? That everyone had abandoned him? She squeezed her eyes shut. She *had* abandoned him. She had broken her ritual. She had left the country, and broken the close contact she kept with all her sources of information. The pain in her chest grew unbearably sharp. She took a deep breath. She had left him. Not in spirit. But in mind. Yes, she clenched her teeth, she had let him leave her thoughts.

His face flashed before her. The infant he'd been when she saw him last. The age-progressed image she carried with her constantly. She imagined his body, lying on a cold, hard floor. His arms and legs bound. His clothes in tatters.

She swallowed. Tears stung her face and lips. She bent her knee to wipe her nose.

What would happen to Peter if she didn't make it? What would become of him? Would a nameless lunatic decide his future the way Enzo was deciding hers?

Wilson screamed.

She lifted her head.

He thrashed, and cried out.

She took a deep breath. She squeezed her eyes closed. She would not become rat food for a madman. She would not abandon Peter. No matter what.

She breathed out, relaxing her muscles, letting the pain flow out of her body.

Enzo Ficarra.

She breathed in. She wasn't afraid of Enzo Ficarra.

She spoke his name. And again. Louder.

"Enzo Ficarra," she yelled.

She tipped her head upwards. "Enzo Ficarra!" she screamed.

Down the tunnel, the thrashing and groaning stopped.

Goosebumps ran over her skin. She straightened her back. She didn't have much sympathy for Wilson Grantly, but they had a common enemy. A moment's connection. A shared strength.

She breathed in.

Enzo Ficarra.

Whatever the bastard had planned for her, she'd have a better plan for him.

She massaged the back of her head against the rock.

A plan for Ficarra. She let the words roll around her mind.

Good words, but what plan? What were his weaknesses? Her strengths?

She shuffled back against the rock, bringing her knees up to hold herself upright. What strengths did she have? What advantage?

She chewed the inside of her lower lip gently and stared into the blackness.

Planning.

She furrowed her brow.

Planning. She was planning.

Whatever she thought she could do was more than Ficarra would imagine. The bonds, the threats, the rats, the cold and dark. He thought she would be broken and distraught. He thought he could ignore her now. That she'd given up.

He couldn't be more wrong.

She took a deep breath.

She'd been to the edge, perhaps, but she hadn't fallen in.

Not yet, at least.

So, what did he want? Why was he threatening her with the rats, when he already had her bound and locked up in a place where no one could possibly find her?

She moved her arms, shifting the pain of the plastic cutting into her skin.

The sharp, hard pain in her chest subsided.

Ficarra wanted the money, of course. He wanted to exchange her for money. Ransom. Good, old-fashioned ransom.

Yet she'd seen him. She'd seen her prison. She might find it again. The FBI and Vanelli's carabinieri would find plenty of evidence here to convict him and put him to death. With her help. She knew who he was.

Enzo Ficarra. Family man. He owned a business in Tuscany. Generations of Ficarras had lived there. He wouldn't simply fold his tent and disappear.

No. He intended to return to his life as if he'd never kidnapped her. Never tortured her. Never let her hear Wilson Grantly's screams.

Which meant he couldn't let her go.

So, why the threat?

She nodded.

He intended to persuade her to follow his orders before he killed her. Not something he could force her to do, but something she would need to do of her own will.

She rubbed her tongue over her teeth as she considered possibilities.

Proof of life. Morris would insist. Vanelli, too, probably. They'd dealt with hostages before. Kidnap for ransom was a common thing around the world now. Protocols had been developed.

Proof of life would be the first step.

Enzo needed her to prove she was still alive. How? A photograph holding a currently dated newspaper? A video? A telephone call?

Any of those would work. They'd need to be done in real time. Morris and Vanelli would be recording and monitoring and dissecting the recordings to find her.

She nodded. Three options, but just one chance. Once chance to tell Morris where to find them. For Wilson's sake. For his parents.

And...

She fought back a lump in her throat. For Peter. No matter what happened to her, one day he would be free. One day he would know about her. She tipped her head up, moistness coming to her eyes. If she never made it out of this tunnel, if she died here, then she was sure as hell going to leave him knowing he had a mother he wouldn't be ashamed of.

She rolled her head around, quelling her tears. She breathed deeply.

She needed more than words.

She needed something concrete.

Something she could tell Morris and Vanelli to help them find her.

Something she could say aloud in front of Ficarra.

But what? What did she know that Morris and Vanelli didn't know already?

Not the white Ford Ficarra used to abduct her. Surely they would have seen it on the hotel surveillance cameras.

The length of the drive from the hotel to this place? She was imprisoned maybe two hours from Rome. She shook her head. Two hours. She didn't even know which direction they had traveled, and two hours made an awfully big area for a fruitful search. Ficarra would have plenty of time to kill them both before Vanelli's carabinieri could find the abandoned mine.

How many old mines were there around Rome? She didn't know. Maybe hundreds. The place had the look of being abandoned for decades, too. It might not exist on maps of any kind.

She kept going. Kept her mind occupied. Kept hope alive.

The lane they had driven down was an unremarkable country lane with a gate, as far as she'd been able to see from inside the trunk.

What about the woods? The cabin? The houses across the road from the gate?

She narrowed her eyes, thinking, remembering.

They were country houses. Painted white and the bold colors of houses by the ocean. They had names. Names.

She frowned, forcing the memory of her time in the trunk of Enzo's Ford into her mind.

She had seen nameplates. One was clear in her memory. *Vista del Mare*. Sea View. An almost comically common name, perhaps, but the other one?

She closed her eyes, and cast her mind back across the road. The sign was on the gate. White with a black border. Gold lettering danced in her mind. Collins? Collinas?

She shook her head. No, she'd seen two words. Collinas Vista? Ventura? The letters ceased their dance. Her eyes widened.

Collina Ventosa. Windy Hilltop.

Vista del Mare and Collina Ventosa.

Two names. Two houses. Side-by-side. Vista del Mare could be too common, but along with Collina Ventosa?

She breathed out. She had a clue. Not perfect, but something she might be able to work with.

She rolled her fatigued and cramping shoulders. All she needed now was a way to tell Morris. Some way to write it down, or say it in a video. Some way that Ficarra wouldn't notice she was communicating her location to the FBI.

A thin line of yellow light appeared under the door.

Her skin prickled. She needed the answer fast.

Enzo was back.

CHAPTER THIRTY-NINE

JESS SHUFFLED DOWN TO the position she'd occupied before, letting her shoulders sag. Better to let Ficarra think things were going his way. The less threatened he felt, the more his vigilance would relax. She hoped.

The wooden beam lifted, and the door swung open. Enzo stood in the entrance.

He looked relaxed, dressed in normal looking jeans and a polo shirt. In his hands were two boxes, one green and wooden, the other translucent white plastic.

A weak scream filtered down the tunnel. A rasping, half-hearted effort, as if the once unimaginable had become commonplace.

"Wilson Grantly." Ficarra mimed sympathy, shook his head, shrugged. "But I expect you know that."

He stepped into her cell and placed the boxes on the ground.

"Only two rats in his box," Enzo said, preoccupied. "Not many really. But hunger makes all the difference."

Jess licked her lips and allowed the lower one to tremble. *Sick bastard.* She turned her gaze away lest he see the steel in her eyes.

He shook the wooden box. She heard scrabbling inside.

"Three." He shrugged. "Rat catching isn't an exact science."

He opened the white box, and lifted out a complicated looking radio. He pulled a wire in through the doorway, and plugged it into the rear of the radio, and sat on the box. "There is no way out of this cell. Whatever is in here when the door is closed, stays in here."

She stared at the green box and licked her lips again.

"You. The rats. The hunger. It all stays here."

She kept her lips pressed together as if to stop the trembling. Her nostrils flared anger, but he must have taken her expression as fear.

He leaned forward. "You understand what will happen to you if you don't follow instructions, yes?"

She nodded.

"Say it."

She swallowed. "Yes." Her voice was raspy.

He glowered at her, his lips pressed into a thin line.

"Then we will get along just fine." He waited for Wilson to finish a bout of screams, before clearing his throat.

"You will talk to the FBI. The people who brought you to this. Your friends, Morris and Vanelli." He kicked the green box for emphasis of his meaning. "You will tell them you are still alive. You will say you can stay alive for a mere five million euros."

He kicked the box again and the rats squealed. "You will not say anything else. Do you understand?"

She closed her eyes, and nodded. "Yes."

"They do not know where you are. You do not know where you are. Ms. Kimball." He waited for her to look at him. "One stupid action on your part, and you will die in this cell. Eventually." He nudged the rats into scrabbling with his boot again. "You understand?"

She nodded and cleared her throat. "Yes."

She swallowed. The thought of talking to Morris pulled at her gut. She'd made a hasty plan. Could she pull it off? Would Morris and Vanelli understand her hints? Her options were limited. This was the best plan she had to work with. Nothing more she could do. Yet.

Ficarra tapped his watch. "Five minutes."

She nodded. "I need water. My voice."

Ficarra reached behind him for a bottle of water and held it to her mouth. She sipped. Swallowed. She said, "Thanks." Her voice was stronger. Good.

Ficarra watched her carefully.

After she swallowed the water, she backed away from him, shuffling up against the cell wall. She couldn't mention their location. She couldn't casually drop in the fact she was being held in an old mine across the road from a couple of houses called…

She glanced in Ficarra's direction. His eyes were on her. She looked down.

House names. Could she hide them in her words? Vista del Mare and Collina Ventosa? Could she? She bit her lip. Would Ficarra notice?

She had to assume he would. She needed a code. She remembered Vanelli's skill with anagrams. Maybe she could tap into that. But how?

The letters danced in front of her again. Vista del Mare. She closed her eyes, and breathed out. She was a reporter. A wordsmith. She thought about the wordplay app she'd seen Vanelli using. The same one she played on her phone sometimes. How did *Warped Words* work, exactly? She shook her head to clear the brain fog and closed her eyes to recall.

The game supplied a row of letters. The player rearranged the letters as many times as possible in a short time frame. Each successful word added points. It was one of the games she was particularly good at. More importantly now, it was a game Vanelli played even better than she did.

Could she use the concept to devise a code on the spot? Using nothing but her wits?

She could. She had to. She had no choice.

Begin with Vista del Mare. One step at a time.

In her head, she saw the letters in a row.

She moved them around, looking for anagrams, different words from the same letters.

Mare? Rame? Meads? Travail, or Ravail?

She imagined that each guess returned the game's obnoxiously loud "wrong answer" buzzer.

She breathed to steady her nerves and tried again.

Travis.

Yes, Travis. Recognizable, at least.

Travis what?

Madel.

Travis Madel. That sounded like a real name, didn't it?

She counted the letters. One short. She had to use the extra e.

Make it Travis Madele. That could work.

Yes! She imagined the perky tone *Warped Words* sounded with each success.

Ficarra checked his watch. "Two minutes."

She breathed. One down, one to go.

But even if Vanelli decoded Travis Madele, one name would be useless. There could be thousands of Vista del Mares around Rome alone.

She needed to use the second name, Collina Ventosa. She moved the letters like tiles around in her mind's eye. She ran the virtual game faster this time.

Colin? That was a name. She counted the letters left over. Nine. What could she make of the remaining nine?

Ficarra switched on the radio. LEDs glowed, and blue numerals appeared. He flipped a couple of switches, and the speaker crackled into life. He plugged a microphone into an amateurish looking box with a large red switch.

Collina Ventosa swam through her mind. *Colin what? Colin who?*

"Bend your knees," Ficarra said.

She frowned.

"Bend them."

She complied.

He pointed a gun at the middle of her legs. "Say anything, and I blast off your kneecaps."

Her skin crawled. Cold sweat plastered her shirt to her back. She wriggled to free the fabric from her body.

"You will tell your friends you are still alive, and you want to stay that way." He waved the gun toward her knees again. "Understand?"

She swallowed.

He looked at her. Cold and long and hard. He moved the gun barrel slightly.

"Yes, yes." She nodded fast and breathed faster. "Tell them I'm alive, and they have to pay for my release. Five million."

"Euros."

She nodded. "Euros."

Her stomach churned. She wouldn't mind vomiting all over him. *Serve him right.* Still, she closed her mouth to slow her breathing.

He waved the gun back and forth at her knees. "The rats will love the blood if you make me shoot."

"I know. I understand. We need to keep calm—"

"*You* need to keep calm." His voice was cold.

She nodded. She clasped her hands together and squeezed. It was easy to show him she was terrified.

Vanesota, popped in her mind. She squeezed her hands into fists. She heard the cheery success tone.

Colin Vanesota?

But she needed to use the extra "l." How about Collin Vanesota? Did that sound even remotely like a real person? Did it use all the letters? Was it obvious enough? Hard to know. But it was her only chance. She had nothing else.

Enzo's radio buzzed into life. There was a metallic clang like an old-fashioned alarm clock, and then a rapid series of bleeps as a telephone auto-dialed.

She frowned. A telephone? He was calling them on a telephone? They would trace the call. They'd know where she was in moments. They could launch a rescue operation.

A distorted ringing tone came from the radio. Her stomach churned when she realized what he'd done. Cunning. Again.

He had linked the radio to a phone. Likely a phone a long distance away. She gritted her teeth. The police would get a fix on the phone, but not the radio signal. Not her location.

She bit her lip. Enzo wasn't a fool. She'd allowed herself to forget that momentarily.

The radio clicked and the ringing tone stopped. Someone had answered the phone. There were several moments of silence before Morris spoke. "Who is this?"

Ficarra flipped the large red switch. He spoke into the microphone. His voice came from the radio, distorted and harsh, filled with tremolo and echo. "You wanted proof of life."

Ficarra held the microphone for her. "Talk to him." He flipped the red switch back.

She took a deep breath. "Morris. It's me." Her voice was raspy, tremulous, tentative.

"Me, who?" Morris said.

She frowned. Cleared her throat. Spoke with as much strength as she could muster. "Jess. Jessica Kimball."

"I need you to prove it."

She looked from side to side. "We...we...I came to Rome three days ago."

He "uh, huh'd."

She breathed deep. What the hell could she say that wouldn't educate or anger Ficarra?

Morris spoke. "Where did we meet face to face for the first time?"

She swallowed. "Um...Dallas."

"Where in Dallas?"

She bit her lip. "A café...Café Bistro. We had coffee. And muffins. You arrived first."

Morris sighed. "How you doing, Jess?"

She breathed out. Her shoulders fell. She felt as if she was on the way home. She could be. If she handled this well enough.

"I'm good. I'm fine. I—"

Enzo poked her knee with his gun, and held his finger across his lips. He flipped the switch to the distorted position. "The stakes have gone up. So has the price. Five million euros. Used notes. Unmarked. I will detect any residue on them. Five million. I will call tomorrow. Ten a.m. Then you can have the precious Miss Kimball back."

"I can't get that much money overnight."

"Then try harder."

"There's a process. I have to—"

"Say another word, and she loses a kneecap."

Enzo had a cool, hard face. His gun was steady against her knee. She didn't doubt for a moment that he'd shoot her.

Seconds ticked by. Jess squeezed her lips together. Sweat ran down her forehead. The muscles in her leg knotted tight.

Morris grunted. "Where?"

Jess sighed.

"I will call you. Ten a.m.," Ficarra said.

"I need to know." Morris's voice was level and calm.

Enzo kept a stony face. Seconds ticked by. Jess's heart pounded. She forced herself forward, straining against the zip-tie around her wrists.

Ten seconds.

He adjusted his grip on his gun.

Fifteen.

She looked at Enzo.

Twenty seconds.

"Ten a.m. Tomorrow. I will be waiting," Morris said.

Jess gasped. Her shoulders sagged. A bead of sweat trickled down her forehead and dripped from the end of her nose.

"Put her back on," Morris said.

"Tomorrow," Enzo said, reaching for the off switch.

Jess leaned forward. "Please. Let me talk."

Enzo held his hand over the power switch.

She licked her lips. "I...I think I can help them. Get the money."

He breathed in and out. The air hissing through his nose. He withdrew his hand, and took hold of her leg, pushing the gun harder into the crook of her knee.

She swallowed.

He handed her the microphone.

Her heartbeat hammered in her throat. The gun pressed painfully into the back of her knee, but it was nothing compared to the pain a bullet would cause. What did it matter if he was planning to kill her anyway?

She took a deep breath. "Morris?"

Her voice buzzed from the speaker. Enzo flipped the switch, and her voice became normal.

"Morris?"

"We're going to get you out of this, Jess."

"Yeah. About the money. Talk to my magazine." She took a deep breath, and locked her jaw tight as she spoke. "Talk to Collin Vanesota. He's my boss. Or," she swallowed, suppressing her trembling voice, "or Travis Madele. Five million is small change to them. They got me into this. They knew the risks. They can afford it."

She paused. Her heart jumped hard in her chest. She took a shaky breath. "That's Travis Madele, Travis, like you'd expect, and Madele, M-A-D-E-L-E. And Collin Vanesota. C-O-L-L-I-N, V-A-N-E-S-O-T-A."

"Okay, Jess. Travis Madele and Collin Vanesota."

"Promise me you're going to talk to them."

Morris grunted. "Promise."

"They'll get the money. It's pocket change to them. They know what to do. They'll rearrange things."

"Okay."

"Wake them up if you have to. They owe me. Big time."

"I promise. I'll talk to them. Don't worry, Jess. It's going to be all right."

Enzo took the microphone, and flipped the switch. His distorted voice rasped from the speaker. "Five million euros. Tomorrow. No delays. No excuses."

He pressed a button on the radio. The LEDs went out and the numerals faded. He sat still.

She looked at him, straight on, unblinking.

He grunted, and put away his gun. "You did well."

He picked up the radio, and the rats, and left, barring the door with the wooden beam.

She closed her eyes, and rolled her head back. Beads of sweat ran down the side of her face. Her shirt clung to her back.

She had passed her message.

Enzo hadn't noticed.

She blew out a lungful of air, and prayed Morris and Vanelli could figure it out.

CHAPTER FORTY

MORRIS HUNG ONTO THE phone, straining to hear the last few whistles and pops as the call ended.

"Connection's gone," said Rosso, the fresh-faced guy, from behind his bank of equipment.

Morris sighed. He'd been quiet, firm, and reassuring on the call, but his blood was boiling. He took one more breath, and placed the handset back on the cradle. "We have to find her."

Vanelli looked at him from across his desk, and shrugged. "Of course." He leaned forward. "We will." He gestured to a giant map on the wall behind him. "I have twenty men searching for Ficarra, reviewing the tapes, conducting interviews, tracing the route the car took. If there's something to be found, we will find it."

Morris nodded.

Rosso hammered on a loud keyboard.

"Bad line," Morris said.

Rosso nodded without looking up. "They're somewhere quiet. No car noises. No city noises. No jets traveling overhead."

"Can the call be traced or not?"

Rosso nodded. "I have the phone number and location, but the radio…"

Morris frowned. "Radio?"

"Shortwave radio. Connected to a telephone. It'll be miles from their real location."

"You can tell all that?"

Rosso nodded. "From the sibilance. It's a cheap set. Probably just held a speaker to a microphone."

"Can the radio be traced?"

"Maybe. I just put feelers out to some people."

"Feelers?"

"On the Internet."

Morris's mouth hung open. "What?"

"Amateurs. People into shortwave. They might have picked up the signal. Might get a direction."

"Amateur radio? People still do that?"

Rosso glowered. "People still do."

Morris closed his mouth. "Well. Right. Good."

"Listen." A speaker on top of Rosso's pile of equipment squawked as he cued up a section of the phone call.

Morris's voice came from the speaker. "I need to know," his recorded voice said.

Rosso turned up the volume. Hissing and pops filled the room. Breathing. A rustling noise that could have been the poor line, or from wherever Jess was being held.

But there was another noise. Unmistakable.

Morris's skin crawled. He looked at Vanelli, who leveled his stare in return.

Rosso nodded. "Someone, somewhere, is screaming his head off."

CHAPTER FORTY-ONE

MORRIS WAITED IN THE lobby of the American Embassy until a heavyset man opened a plate glass door and beckoned him through, into the building's maze of gracefully aged corridors. They walked in silence until they reached a room with a very smooth, metal door. The man typed a number on a keypad, and the door opened an inch. He pulled it fully open, the air hissing around its edges, and gestured for Morris to enter.

Inside was a circular table and a dozen chairs, all dark wood. A large paper shredder sat in one corner.

In the middle of the table sat an enormous gray telephone. The number keys were pale, like the keys from an old cash register. There were two comically large lights on top, one yellow, one red. A single wire ran from the side of the phone to the wall.

The man waved at the device. "Usual thing. Fully encrypted. You know the number you want to dial?"

Morris nodded.

"A secure number?"

"FBI in DC. They're expecting me."

"Have at it then." The man backed out and closed the door. It sealed with a soft thump and a click.

Morris sat in front of the phone, lifted the receiver, and dialed his boss, the Assistant Director in charge of the FBI Dallas Field Office, Roy E. Ryans. The keys required a firm press and clicked loudly. The usual ringing tone followed by a series of beeps and buzzes took over, like an old dial-up Internet modem. The noises stopped, and his boss's voice came on the line.

"Morris?" Ryans' gruff drawl traveled clearly across the two countries and the Atlantic Ocean.

"Yes, Sir."

"Fill me in."

"We received the call from Kimball's kidnapper."

"Ficarra?"

"We believe."

"Evidence?"

"Nothing positive."

"Voice identification? Location tracking?"

"He used a scrambler. The Italians have recovered the phone he used, but it was connected to a shortwave radio."

"Prints? DNA?"

"It's clean."

Ryans waited.

"The Italians are trying to track the radio signal," Morris said.

"They had an airborne asset in place?"

"No. They...they're reaching out to amateurs...they're—"

"What?"

"Amateurs. On the…Internet."

"Say what?" Ryans was born in North Carolina and despite his training, his accent often revealed his early childhood origins.

"It was all anonymous."

"Anonymous? Nothing is anonymous if you're prepared to look hard enough." Ryans sighed. "And have they found anything?"

Morris said. "Not yet."

Ryans hissed through the slight space in his two front teeth. Morris could almost see the spittle pushing through the gap. "What does the kidnapper want?"

"Five million."

"Dollars?"

"Euros."

"How long have we got?" Morris could hear Ryans tapping a pen against the desk.

"Eighteen hours. Twenty, maybe."

"Maybe?"

Morris cleared his throat. "Someone was in severe pain in the background. On the call from Ficarra."

"Kimball?"

"No."

Ryans said, "I see."

"We think it could be Wilson Grantly."

"Connecting it to Enzo Ficarra." He sounded closer to approval than a moment earlier.

"Yes."

"That's something, I suppose."

"She also gave us some names."

"Kimball?"

Morris uh-huh'd. "Two people from her magazine. She

thinks they will pay the ransom. Said they owe her. I think she means for getting her into the situation."

Ryans took a deep breath. "A lot of people got her into this."

Morris rubbed his thumb against his forefinger absently. "Yes, sir."

"Whatever. Too late for regrets at this point, Morris."

Morris frowned.

"We don't negotiate," Ryans said. "Or pay off kidnappers."

"The Italians are doing all they can."

"If this goes south, the bureau isn't going to come out well."

"Sir—"

"Let me say that precisely." Ryans raised his voice slightly. "*We* are not going to come out of it well."

Morris clamped his jaw shut. "I'm not planning to let it go south."

There was a long silence.

Ryans grunted. "Give me the names."

"Travis Madele and Collin Vanesota. They work at her magazine. In Denver."

"Spell the names."

Morris read out the letters.

"Van-e-tossa?" Ryans said.

"Van-e-sota."

Ryans hissed through the gap in his teeth again. "They have to be New Yorkers."

Morris left the comment unanswered. That hissing sound drove him crazy. Besides, Roy E. Ryans thought any unusual names originated from New York.

Ryans huffed. "I'll have them contacted."

"We may have to go all the way."

"Pay him off?"

"At least a sting."

"Your track record for ops against this guy doesn't make that an appealing option, Morris."

"There are no appealing options."

Ryans fell silent.

"We will need the cash," Morris said.

Ryans grunted. "The embassy keeps a reserve for emergencies, but they may not have that much on hand."

"Five million."

"I know."

"Euros."

"Yes, Morris. I am aware you are in Italy."

"Sorry, sir."

"I'll have to bring it up with the director." Ryans paused. "Fifty-fifty chance he'll approve."

Morris sighed.

"I'll get back to you about the magazine people. But one last thing, Morris."

"Sir?"

"Don't screw this up."

CHAPTER FORTY-TWO

JESS BROUGHT HER KNEES up to her chest and shivered. The skin around her nails had turned milky white and her fingers were shriveled. Her lips were cracked and sore, and her legs were numb from the hard bed. She shifted her weight, sliding on the plastic bag. She shuffled back into its center to keep the worst of the underground dampness from seeping into her clothes.

Her stomach growled. She swallowed back bile that edged into her throat. It had been mid-morning when she was in the hotel, but time meant nothing in the dark. She'd slept and woken and slept again. Her eyes had night adjusted long ago, but there wasn't a glimmer of light to be seen. It was as black as she imagined a coal mine might be. A form of sensory deprivation, she supposed. Another of Enzo Ficarra's small tortures.

She leaned back on the wall. Now she was not only at Enzo's mercy, her life was in Morris and Vanelli's hands, too.

She rubbed her rough lips together. It had been hours since

she had conveyed the names. Morris would have checked at *Taboo Magazine.*

Her boss, Carter Pierce, would know the names were fake instantly.

But were the names enough? She hoped that Morris and Vanelli, working with Pierce, would find the anagrams, certainly. Would they find the houses before Ficarra killed Grantly? Before he killed her?

She bit her lip. There again, she wasn't in the houses. She was half a mile away, in the woods, in a mine under a cabin. She sighed. It might be too big a stretch.

She licked her sore lips, and regretted it the instant pain ran through the cracks. She hung her head down. She had to think of Peter. She would get out of here. She would get out, and find him. No matter what happened, she wouldn't let Enzo take away the one thing that mattered the most. Peter's life.

She took a deep breath and focused again on getting out.

There was only one way out of the cell. Through the door.

Then she would have to negotiate the tunnel, the ladder, and the forest that surrounded the cabin.

But first, she'd break free of the zip-tie binding her wrists.

She flexed her arms.

She rocked back and forth.

Zip-tie, door, tunnel, ladder, run.

It sounded so simple.

Temptingly simple.

Frustratingly simple.

She looked around her cell. She knew its rough outline. She stood, heels and back against the wall, and shuffled around the edge of the floor.

Her fingers searched the rock walls until she felt the wooden doorway at the roughest place on the walls.

An abrupt change in direction of the old stone. Inconsequential to the men who had hewn the space from the rock decades earlier, but not to her.

She shuffled her back against the sharp corner, testing it with her fingers. She arranged her wrists on either side, the zip-tie straddling the corner, and ground the heavy-duty plastic against the centuries-old rock.

The stone grazed the palms of her hands, and banged against her elbows. She angled her body forward, giving her arms slightly more room to move. She worked the plastic against the rock.

Fine grit fell through her fingers. Her skin grew raw as the plastic grew rough.

It was slow abrasion, but gave her hope and strength of purpose.

And she would need all the strength she could muster, if she was going to fight her way out before this cell became her tomb.

CHAPTER FORTY-THREE

MORRIS SORTED THROUGH HIS change to find the exact coins for a coffee from the vending machine outside Vanelli's office. The coins rattled as they fell through the slot.

"You realize no one here drinks that stuff," Vanelli said.

Morris shrugged. "I need the caffeine this morning."

The machine chugged. A bell rang. He slid open the drink dispenser door. There was no drink.

Vanelli laughed. "And that is exactly why no one here drinks that stuff."

"It took my money."

"It does. Every now and again. It's criminal, really." Vanelli grinned. "Perhaps you should arrest it?"

Morris fumbled for more change. Vanelli held out a handful of coins. Before Morris could take one, his phone rang. He looked at the display. "My boss." He pressed talk. "Sir?"

"Those names don't jive," Assistant Director Roy Ryans said.

"Sir?"

"We woke up the head of the magazine, and half his staff. There's no one who works there by those names. They've never heard those names before."

"Damn." Morris furrowed his brow. "Then it was a clue. Some kind of code."

"No kidding," Ryans deadpanned.

"Can the magazine fund the ransom?"

"Maybe."

"How maybe?"

"The publisher, a man named Carter Pierce, said they carry insurance for this sort of thing, but the insurers are wriggling."

"Swell." Morris bit his tongue and ran a hand over his head.

"Exactly," Ryans agreed. "Pierce is working on it. *Taboo's* a big outfit. Probably raise the money himself."

"Probably?"

"Pierce can afford it. But he has to transfer the money to Italy, and convert it into used banknotes."

"That can be done."

"It takes time, Morris. Don't make me tell you how long it took to build Rome."

Morris blew out a long breath. "So is the embassy our best bet?"

"They have the cash on hand," Ryans said.

"Then let's use that."

"First things first. To start with, the Director has to approve us to be involved in any kind of payoff."

Morris pressed his lips into a hard line. "And?"

"He hasn't returned my call."

"So, we're still at zero for the ransom."

"We're doing our best." Ryans paused. "You'd better do yours, too, in the meantime."

Morris grunted, "Yes, Sir," and ended the call.

CHAPTER FORTY-FOUR

VANELLI DUMPED HIS CHANGE back in his pocket. "The names aren't real?"

"Not even close." Morris shook his head. "She was clearly sending me a message. So she believed she was telling me something I should understand."

"But you don't? Understand, I mean?"

"Not yet. But I will." Morris dialed the FBI's Rome business office, and relayed the names to a female analyst with a strong Texas accent.

Vanelli called to the carabinieri officers working in the cube farm outside his spacious conference room.

He heard the keyboard clacking as the Texan started to search the databases. As he waited for her to check the names, a tide of officers swept into Vanelli's office.

Morris elbowed his way through the crowd to the rear, his phone pressed against his ear.

Vanelli wrote the names Jess had relayed on a wall-sized

whiteboard. People jostled for position to see clearly. The two carabinieri Vanelli used as daily muscle leaned against a wall near a filing cabinet.

Vanelli tapped the board. "The names the hostage identified as her bosses from her magazine in Denver are not real. Her magazine has never heard of them and doesn't know what the names mean."

Vanelli paced the small space in front of the board. "She was being clever."

"And damned brave, if you ask me," muttered the fresh-faced, nerdy Luca Rosso who stood beside Morris.

"What we need now," said Vanelli, "is to be as clever as Miss Kimball."

Clever. Jess was clever. Resourceful, too. Morris had been thinking about her message. What had she said? Right at the end after she'd offered the names? "Vanelli, can we hear the message playback? I only need the last few seconds. I want the exact words she said at the end."

Vanelli nodded toward Luca Rosso, who pushed a few buttons and replayed Jess's clues. *"They'll get the money. It's pocket change to them. They know what to do. They'll rearrange things."*

"That's it." A smirk lifted the corner of Morris's mouth. He slammed his hand on the wall. "Did you catch it, Vanelli?"

Vanelli cocked his head and lifted his palms.

"Remember that game you were playing at the stakeout? What was it called?" Morris stuffed both hands into his pockets. "Jess saw you. She watched you."

"*Warped Words.*" Vanelli nodded slowly. And then his lips parted in a genuine smile. "Anagrams. The names she gave us are anagrams."

Morris frowned. "So *rearrange* the letters. Let's figure this out."

"But what kind of words are we looking for?" a woman in the middle of the carabinieri crowd asked. "American names?"

"I don't think so. She gave us names because of the way she stated the message. But Miss Kimball is much more clever than that." Vanelli shook his head. He gestured to the entire front row of officers. "Get to the computers. Start looking. Names, sure. But not limited to American names. Include towns, villages, events, tourist locations, street names. Cover everything."

The front row filed out.

"First letters? CV? TM? Mean anything to the Ficarras?" said a blonde-haired guy.

"Maybe." Vanelli nodded for him to leave the room. "And look for anything in her past, too."

"No good matches against American names," said the Texan at the American Embassy through the speaker on Morris's phone, confirming Vanelli's hunch. "A few partials. Scattered across the country. None in Italy."

"Any connected with Miss Kimball, any of the Blazek extortion ring members, any name we've heard before during this investigation?" Morris ran splayed fingers through his hair. "Try Italy, Florida, Canada, Louisiana, and Texas. In that order."

"Checking now. Standby."

Morris covered the mouthpiece, and caught Vanelli's attention. "A few partial matches to American names. We're checking for any connected to Kimball, Ficarra, Grantly, or Blazek."

Vanelli gestured to the muscle men by the filing cabinet. "Prep the vans. Vests, guns, and radios for ten." He glanced in Morris's direction.

Morris nodded.

Vanelli's nostrils flared, and his mouth clamped shut. He breathed in and out. "Make it eleven."

They hustled from the room.

The Texan came back on the line and spoke in Morris's ear. "No one connected to Miss Kimball. A couple have lived in the same cities, and a few in New York where she works occasionally? Big place, doesn't mean much."

Morris sighed. "And the other locations?"

"I'm still checking, but nothing so far."

The room was empty. Vanelli turned back to his whiteboard.

The Texan continued clacking a keyboard in Morris's ear. "No towns, villages, or streets match. I have a giant list of anagrams. A couple of villages are close, but not identical."

"Close to Rome?"

"No. Close matches, anagram-wise."

Morris hissed through his teeth. "Where?"

"North of Turin. Three hundred miles, plus."

"Not likely he's taken her that far." Morris clicked his tongue and rubbed the back of his neck, thinking. "Send the close matches anyway. Anything you've got. And keep digging."

The Texan agreed and hung up. Moments later the email on his phone dinged. He flipped through long lists of computer generated anagram matches. Although none seemed likely, he forwarded the email to Vanelli.

Vanelli was scrawling on the whiteboard, writing names, crossing out letters, and wiping them clear to start again.

"Anything?" Morris called.

Vanelli shook his head without looking back.

Morris's email dinged again.

The red-haired woman returned, several pieces of paper in

her hands. Vanelli looked over her work, and they spoke in rapid Italian. Morris caught the words statues and parks.

His phone rang. He pressed talk without looking at the display. "Morris."

The Texan came back on. "Not great matches, but maybe."

He frowned. "Maybe what?"

"House names. Travis Madele is Vista del Mare."

Morris's skin tingled. "And Collin Vanesota?"

"Collina Ventosa."

"That's a house name?"

"Multiple times. They show up all over the place. Not only in Italy, but Spain and a few other places farther away. The words are pretty common." She stopped to inhale. "Vista del Mare means Sea View. Collina Ventosa means Windy Hill."

Vanelli had stopped writing on the white board. He was staring at Morris. Morris moved the phone from his mouth. "House names. Vista del Mare and Collina Ventosa."

Morris want back to his phone. "I want a list of everywhere those two names are in close proximity."

The Texan's voice hardened. "What do you think I've been doing? It's in your inbox."

"Got it. Thanks."

He brought up his email, and held out the list for Vanelli. Vanelli called an inspector into the room and set him to work marking the locations on the map behind his desk.

"Fourteen places where the two names are fairly close together," Morris said.

"Three are in cities," Vanelli said slowly, thinking things through. "We heard no city noises on the call. We can make them low priority, if not rule them out."

"Leaving eleven. And oddly, most are by the coast."

Vanelli's eyebrows shot up. "Vista del Mare?"

Morris rolled his eyes. "Sorry. Obvious."

Vanelli tapped the furthest pin. "Hundred miles. Winding roads. It'll take some time to reach."

He picked up his phone, and dispatched his men in three groups to survey the addresses. As soon as he placed the handset back on the hook, it rang again.

Morris watched Vanelli's face go through a series of contortions before he hung up.

"Let's go. When Ficarra calls again, it can be routed to my phone," Morris said.

Vanelli shook his head. "Your Ambassador Bell is in discussion with the Comandante Generale."

Morris shrugged and shook his head.

"The head of the carabinieri."

"I know who he is, I just don't know why our ambassador is here."

Vanelli smirked. "We're about to find out. They've requested our presence."

CHAPTER FORTY-FIVE

MORRIS FOLLOWED VANELLI INTO an elevator. "We haven't got time for this."

Vanelli stabbed the button for the top floor. "I can't ignore the Comandante."

"Can't you explain?"

"It's not him that's insisting."

Morris frowned. "Ambassador Bell?"

Vanelli pursed his lips.

Morris blew out a long breath. "What about your men?"

"They have the locations." He tapped his phone. "They will keep us informed."

They left the elevator, and stepped out into plush carpeting and a hushed atmosphere. Vanelli opened a large oak door with *Comandante Generale* engraved on a brass plaque.

They walked into a reception area. An imposing oak double door was opposite the entrance. The walls were covered with photographs of a man shaking hands with various dignitaries. The Comandante, Morris presumed.

A row of filing cabinets filled one wall and a young woman wearing a dark suit worked at a small desk. She stopped typing, and stood up, straightening her pencil skirt. "He's expecting you."

She stepped close to Vanelli, and whispered.

Vanelli grimaced. "None of us are happy."

The assistant opened one of the oak doors, and Morris followed Vanelli through.

The Comandante was a large man wearing a dark blue uniform. He sat at a broad, antique desk covered with papers, and an out-of-place flat screen monitor. On the wall behind him was a large painting of the carabinieri's seal.

The antique style of the desk flowed to several well-stocked bookshelves, a bureau, and the chairs in front of the desk. Morris recognized the diminutive U.S. Ambassador, Leonard E. Bell, seated in one of the chairs. He didn't rise or offer any greeting other than to glower over the top of his reading glasses at Morris.

Vanelli saluted. The Comandante said something unintelligible before gesturing to the empty chairs. "Sit."

Vanelli sat, his back perfectly straight. Morris took the chair opposite Ambassador Bell, who continued to stare.

The Comandante leaned back. "What progress?"

Vanelli took a breath. "The kidnapper is due to make contact in thirty minutes. We do not yet have the location of the exchange. The names Miss Kimball relayed were fake, we are therefore presuming they are a clue to her whereabouts."

"But you haven't located her?"

Vanelli shook his head. "We have a partial match of the names she gave to the names of some houses. We were just leaving to investigate."

"House names?"

"Locations where the two names are close together," Morris said.

The Comandante glanced at him, nodded, and turned back to Vanelli. "How many locations?"

"Fourteen. Eleven are higher priority."

"Too many," said Ambassador Bell.

"I have divided my men between the—"

Ambassador Bell cleared his throat. "I'm sure." He looked at the Comandante. "Miss Kimball is an American."

Vanelli turned to Ambassador Bell. "With respect, her nationality has no bearing on my actions in this case."

Ambassador Bell glanced at Vanelli. "An admirable sentiment." He turned back to the Comandante. "I would, however, like an embassy representative involved with your operation."

Vanelli frowned. "Representative?"

"Someone in country, who can assist."

Vanelli cleared his throat. "This is Italian soil. I have more than two dozen carabinieri and the Polizia for backup on the matter already. Your men will not be able to add—"

"I am charged to ensure our citizens are afforded every assistance."

Vanelli gestured to Morris. "You have your FBI agent already."

"I want a trained hostage negotiator. A man called Henderson. He speaks Italian." He glanced at Morris. "Fluently."

Morris leaned forward. "We've had no problem so far."

He took a deep breath. "Am I right in saying, you have never received any formal training in hostage negotiation?"

"I attended the course."

"Which, I understand, you did not complete."

"I had a case! A lead I couldn't ignore."

"And since then you have conducted two negotiations."

Morris closed his mouth.

The ambassador put his hands together. "Only one of which was successful."

There was a long silence.

Vanelli eased himself back in his chair.

The Comandante's chair creaked as he shifted his weight. He breathed in loudly through his nose. "In the circumstances, I believe we can accommodate an additional agent."

"Thank you," said Ambassador Bell.

The Comandante frowned. "This once."

The ambassador nodded. "There is one more thing. Since this case may well hinge entirely on the negotiations, Henderson will be in charge of our side of the operation." He looked at Morris. "That means you will take orders from him."

Morris ground his teeth.

Ambassador Bell looked away.

There was a long silence.

The Comandante grunted. "So, the other issue?"

Ambassador Bell raised his eyebrows. "You mean, the money?"

The Comandante nodded.

Ambassador Bell straightened his back. "We are working on it. We are not prepared to let anything happen to Miss Kimball."

"So, we can offer him the money," Vanelli said.

Ambassador Bell glanced at Vanelli. "As far as you are concerned."

Morris leaned forward. "As far as we are concerned?"

Ambassador Bell glowered. "There is an administrative matter to be dealt with."

"Then deal with it. When we talk to the kidnapper, we have to give a yes or no, not that we're dealing with an administrative matter."

Ambassador Bell leaned back. "I thought I made it clear, Agent Morris. Henderson is a trained hostage negotiator, and as of this moment, you report directly to him." The ambassador put his hands together, and intertwined his fingers. "So, it is his opinions that are important, not yours."

CHAPTER FORTY-SIX

MORRIS SHOVED HIS WAY into the elevator before the occupants had exited. They maneuvered around, staring.

Vanelli stepped in beside him, and pressed the button for his floor. "Walking out was not a good idea."

"The ambassador is an asshole. A sniveling, slimy, good-for-nothing son-of-a-bitch."

Vanelli grimaced.

"He thinks everything can be solved with the right paperwork."

"And you?"

"I know we need to follow process," Morris said. He jerked his thumb upwards. "I know it more than that bastard will ever know. And I know if we're going to find Ficarra, and pin this on him, we'll need to be absolutely squeaky clean. But Ficarra?" He shook a fist. "I know what we're up against."

Vanelli glanced at his watch. "What we're up against is time. He's due to call in fifteen minutes."

Morris exhaled. "I have to be there. I know what Bell said, but if Ficarra hears I've been taken off—"

"I know." Vanelli shook his head. "Despite your ambassador, this is Italian soil, and I am in charge. You're in on his call."

"And if he demands I'm the courier?"

Vanelli shrugged. "Then you're in on that, too."

Morris breathed out. "Thank you. I appreciate it."

The elevator bumped to a halt. Vanelli pressed the hold button, and kept it in. The doors stayed closed. He looked at Morris. "Has your ambassador closed your office?"

Morris frowned. "In the embassy?"

"In the alley."

Morris gave a blank stare.

Vanelli rolled his eyes. "Your so-called business office."

Morris sighed, and glanced down. "He's closing it. Yes."

"Everyone is being shipped back to the U.S.?"

"We will have a small staff. Liaison. Press releases, requests for information, stuff like that."

"A pity." Vanelli took his finger from the hold button. "We were hoping to set up joint operations."

The doors slid open.

"Joint operations?" Morris said.

"Your anonymous tip offs have been very useful." Vanelli stepped out of the elevator. "A little more information, a little earlier, and we might have stopped the Ficarras before all this started."

Morris nodded his agreement, and followed Vanelli down the corridor.

A man in a well-cut blue pinstripe suit stood outside the Colonnello's office. He held a briefcase in one hand, and thrust the other out to Vanelli. "Jeremy Henderson."

Vanelli shook his hand.

Henderson talked fast in Italian. Morris only caught the word "*ambasciatore*."

Vanelli grunted, and gestured toward his office.

Luca Russo, the fresh-faced telephone operator was ready at his stack of electronics. He glanced in their direction as they came in, and returned to his keyboard.

Vanelli sat at his desk. Morris took the chair directly opposite. Henderson remained standing.

"Special Agent Morris, it is my understanding that Ambassador Bell informed you that you are to take instructions from me, correct?" Henderson's tone brooked no argument.

Morris shrugged. "He might have mentioned it."

"I believe he did mention it. I am taking over this case."

Morris looked up at him. "The kidnapper referred to me in his notes. He requested to speak to me. Personally. So, I'm part of this case whether you like it or not."

"The ambassador—"

"The ambassador doesn't have a clue what is required to negotiate for someone's life. Nor does he have any idea what will be required if the negotiations do not succeed."

"I, however, am well aware of what is required for a successful negotiation."

"Well, you'll know that the last thing you want to do is change the kidnapper's point of contact."

"It has been done before."

"It's a blatantly unnecessary risk."

Henderson shrugged, as if Morris's view was worthless. "Your opinions are no longer relevant to this case. He gave me clear—"

"I refuse. I will not abandon Miss Kimball. Do you understand?"

Henderson huffed. "You are letting your personal feelings interfere with your work. Not a good method for a positive outcome to a difficult situation, in my experience."

Morris frowned. "And exactly what is your experience?"

"Many and varied, Agent Morris."

"You're not FBI?"

"This is Italy. The Italian authorities deal with the enforcement of the law in their own sovereign territory."

"So, what service are you with?"

Henderson scowled. "As I said, we do not need to concern ourselves with law enforcement—"

"You're not part of any investigative unit?"

The man glowered. "I am attached to the legal arm of the embassy staff."

"Attached?"

Henderson blinked.

"*Attached?*" Morris stood up and paced the room. "You're a paid contractor? That's it?"

"We provide—"

He scowled. "A beltway bandit?"

"I work hand-in-hand with the embassy, an extension of—"

"You mean, hand-in-pocket." Morris blew a long stream of hot air between his lips and ran both hands over his head.

"This is getting us nowhere. I have received the ambassador's instructions, and—"

"And I told you, we're close. But Miss Kimball's life still hangs in the balance. We don't dare screw with the kidnapper now." He stopped pacing. He stood inches from Henderson and stared straight into his face. "I'm not having a pompous jerk turn up now simply so the ambassador can claim some kind of victory at embassy cocktail parties."

Henderson folded his arms. "This isn't about claiming victory."

"Damn straight, it's not." Morris poked at Henderson with his finger. "Unlike you and your boss, I will accept nothing less than total victory. Miss Kimball back. Safe. Sound. Breathing. In one piece. And I want Ficarra facing life."

"Or the end of his life?"

He poked Henderson one more time, hard. "If that's what it takes."

"Agent Morris, you cannot—"

Vanelli held up his hand. "*Signori*. Agent Morris is assisting us with our negotiations."

Henderson put his hand on Vanelli's desk. "That—"

Vanelli leaned forward, his arms crossed, and met his eyes directly. "Negotiations that will begin in eight minutes. Sit down."

"We—"

"You have heard my last word on the subject, *signori*. Sit down, or leave. It's your choice."

Henderson scowled. He pressed his lips so thin they turned white. He glowered at Vanelli before sitting heavily in a chair.

"Are we ready?" Vanelli said to the telephone operator. Rosso nodded.

"Good." He looked at the ambassador's negotiator. "When the kidnapper calls, you will be absolutely silent."

Henderson gave the barest of nods. Morris didn't trust him an inch. But he had tougher things to deal with at the moment. As long as he stayed out of the way, the beltway bandit could wait.

Vanelli angled his computer screen so Morris could see a map showing the houses. Small blue dots marked the locations of the teams Vanelli had dispatched.

The room went silent.

Twenty-eight minutes later, Morris cross-checked the time on the computer.

Vanelli shrugged. "He'll call. He wants his money."

More minutes ticked by. One of the teams messaged Vanelli to report they had reached their destination. Ten minutes later, Vanelli received another message confirming that both the houses were clear. On the map, the blue dot headed toward its next destination. One down, ten to go.

The phone on Vanelli's desk rang.

The fresh-faced Rosso slipped on a giant set of headphones, pressed several buttons, and gave a thumbs up.

Morris picked up the receiver. "Morris."

A distorted metallic voice crackled. "You have the money?"

"Is Miss Kimball okay?"

"You heard her."

"Yesterday. I want to hear her today."

"Tough."

"I need to hear her."

"You'll be able to talk to her all you like, once I have the money."

"I need—"

"Do you have the money? Yes, or no?"

Morris licked his lips. "Yes."

"Used bills?"

"As you said."

"No tracers, no trackers, no powder?"

"Yes."

"I will scan the package before I let her go."

"We understand."

"You found my device? The telephone?"

"We did."

"Then you know that I am capable of detecting a tracker."

"Yes."

"If I find anything, I will retaliate."

"We understand."

"Against her."

"We understand."

"You'd better. This is a one-time offer. Screw with me, and I'll do more than screw with your precious reporter."

"We understand you. We have the money. We want this to go smoothly. Where do we meet?"

"You'll be told."

"I have to move five million. I need to know in advance."

"You'll be told when appropriate."

"I have to arrange transport."

"Then arrange it. I will call again in five hours. The handover will be an hour after that."

"That's not—"

The phone clicked off.

Henderson flashed a smarmy grin. "That went well."

It took every ounce of Morris's self-control not to punch him hard in the face.

CHAPTER FORTY-SEVEN

MORRIS GRITTED HIS TEETH. His breath hissed in and out through the gaps. Vanelli drummed his fingers on his desk. Rosso worked on his computers. The blue dots on the map inched along winding roads.

"What assets do you have?" Henderson said.

"Twenty-one men, all weapons trained. I can call on three helicopters. We have boats at several ports along the coast, and no shortage of Polizia." Vanelli straightened his back. "Believe me, I have no intention of failing to recover Miss Kimball."

"How many groups do you have investigating the hypothetical hostage locations?" Henderson asked.

Vanelli cocked his head. "Hypothetical hostage locations?"

"The houses." Henderson poked the map with his knuckle.

Vanelli grunted. "Three." He gestured to the map. "As you can see."

"How long will they take?" Henderson said.

"To do what?"

Henderson waved at the screen. "To look at all the houses. Interview people. Make sure she's not at any of these places."

"You understand this is very dangerous work?" Vanelli frowned. His eyes narrowed. "They could encounter the kidnapper at any moment."

"They're armed, aren't they?"

"Hostage situations can get very complex, very fast," Morris said.

Henderson grunted. "But can you search all the places in, say, four hours?"

Vanelli looked at the map. "Probably."

"Then Miss Kimball will be found before Ficarra calls back."

"That's not a certainty," Vanelli said.

Henderson stood up straight and buttoned his jacket. "A methodical search is all that is required."

"What do you mean, all that is required?"

"To rescue the hostage before the exchange is due." Henderson collected his briefcase.

Morris's fists clenched at his side. He knew what was coming. *Knew it.* "You're not getting the ransom money, are you?"

Henderson barely glanced at Morris. "I don't believe you are any longer in a position to ask that question. Or to require an answer."

Vanelli leaned forward. "But I am."

Henderson seemed unfazed.

Vanelli raised his eyebrows. "And?"

Henderson sniffed. "The U.S. government will do all that it can to enable the—"

Morris thumped the desk with his fist. "Bullshit!"

"The U.S. government is—"

"You heard him. He will retaliate against her." Morris waved at the phone. "Do you remember that?"

"I am not in a position to provide—"

"Get." Morris slammed his palm onto Vanelli's desk. "The." *Slam.* "Money." *Slam.*

Henderson did not flinch. "A properly conducted search will—"

Morris grabbed the lapels of Henderson's jacket, wrenching him forward. "Get. The. Money."

Henderson pushed against Morris's arm. Morris tightened his grip, crushing the jacket and raising it off his shoulders.

"Morris," Vanelli said.

"Understand." Morris shook Henderson's pinstripe suit away as if it were rotten. "If anything, I repeat, anything happens to her. I will be holding *you* personally responsible."

Rosso slapped a plastic ruler on Vanelli's desk. "I have some locations."

"Stay out of the way." Morris flung Henderson aside. Henderson tripped over his own feet and barely managed to avoid falling. Morris almost grinned. Too bad he didn't land on his ass.

Beside Rosso was a large sheet of graph paper covered with lines and tiny numbers. He gestured to the lines. "Tracks for shortwave radio activity in the last few minutes."

Morris studied the graph paper.

Rosso pointed to two lines that crossed. "Where there's an intersection, we have a position, otherwise we only have a direction."

Morris counted five intersections and twelve lonely lines. "How reliable is this?"

Russo shrugged. "It came from reports."

"The Internet?"

"Enthusiasts."

Morris's face crunched into a pained expression. "People still do amateur radio?"

Russo raised his eyebrows, nodded, and offered an I-told-you-so smile.

Vanelli copied the lines to the map on his wall. Morris's skin tingled as one of the lines ran close by one of the house locations, but by the time all the lines were on the map, all the suspect houses had lines nearby. He sighed. "It could be any of them."

Vanelli glanced at his computer. "My men are approaching the second location."

Twelve minutes later his phone rang. He listened for a moment before hanging up. "One house was empty. The other had one occupant, an old man."

Morris examined the lines on the map. "Jess wouldn't have taken such a risk for nothing. She was telling us something she thought we could figure out."

"Agreed." Vanelli nodded. "But what? The names don't match exactly."

"Gotta be the house names. The anagrams don't match anything else." Morris blew a stream of air. "So, she gave us two names. Anagrams. Most likely house names. What is she trying to tell us?"

"She could be in a house between the named ones?" said Rosso.

Vanelli shook his head. "My men checked the first location. No signs."

Morris walked to the map. The locations of the house name

pairs were marked with a blue pushpin. He worked from one to another, counting the properties between the suspect houses. "Three, one, none, two, four..."

Vanelli watched him. "The houses either side of where she's being held, maybe?"

"Maybe." The tingle came back to Morris's skin. "No! She gave us the names. That means she saw them, right? The house signs. Little plaques. On walls or gates."

"So?"

"She was in the trunk of the car. We know that from the hotel surveillance video."

Vanelli frowned.

"She had to see through a small gap, or a hole. Whatever it was, it wouldn't have been easy to see out of." He tapped the map. "And she saw two house names. So they must have been close together. Maybe even side-by-side. And it's difficult to see much from a small hole in a car trunk while it's bouncing around."

"They were stopped," Rosso said.

Morris nodded. "Uh-huh."

"They could have stopped anywhere," Vanelli said.

"She took a big risk telling us. So, they're important names. And she was in the trunk. So she could only see out of the rear." Morris shook his head and spoke slowly as he worked out the problem. "That means the rear of the car was pointing at the houses while they were heading away. We're not looking for the houses. We're looking for somewhere opposite the houses."

Rosso clicked his fingers. "The houses with no space in-between."

Morris tapped the one pushpin with no properties separating them. "Bingo."

CHAPTER FORTY-EIGHT

ENZO FICARRA CLOSED THE kitchen curtains in his rental cottage, and turned on the light. He pulled a new pair of latex gloves from a box, and snapped them on.

He secured a radio and a heavy-duty battery into a large plastic storage box. He hooked two thin wires from the radio and two thick wires from the battery to a white cube. From the white cube he ran two more thick wires that ended in thin, two-inch-long cylinders. Detonators.

From another box, he lifted five thick slabs of a soft waxy off-white material. He unwrapped two of the slabs, pressed them around one of the cylinders, and taped them to the inside of the plastic box. He repeated the process with two more slabs, and checked that the connections were tight.

He took the loose end of a hundred-foot coil of wire, attached it to the back of the radio, and left the coil outside the box. A hundred feet would be a long enough antenna for what he had in mind.

He taped the lid to the box, and placed the box in the back seat of the white Ford.

In the kitchen, he took out his last slab of the waxy material, and divided it in two with a kitchen knife. He pressed a detonator into each slab, attached a small radio, and wrapped the whole arrangement in a towel, sealing it with layers of tape. He placed the second bomb in the car next to the first.

He drove north for twenty minutes to an ancient market town and parked in the main square beside a glass and stainless steel phone box. As he made note of the number, he wondered how much more difficult the kidnapper's job would become as mobile phones eliminated the last public phone boxes.

He took the road east from the village. It ran alongside a sheer rock face that climbed twenty meters above him. After two miles, he reached a tunnel. It wasn't long. Two hundred meters. Mere seconds at sixty miles an hour. It was old, carved through soft rock in the early days of the motorcar. A direct path for farmers in the country to an ancient market town.

He grinned. Long ago, he had decided that tunnels were a seriously underused weapon in criminal endeavors.

Despite the tunnel's comparatively short length, the designers had the forethought to add a ventilation shaft. They had not been satisfied with a simple chimney, rising to the surface. They had installed an elaborate arrangement of steps and a storage building at the top of the shaft. The building adjoined a main road that led directly to the autostrada, Florence, and beyond.

Enzo slowed in the tunnel. The car behind him honked, then passed him. Enzo veered off into a small parking space beside the entrance to the ventilation shaft.

Enzo had chosen the location carefully. It was ideal for the handover, not that the ROS or FBI would be aware beforehand.

He visualized the final steps in his operation carefully, one final time.

Through some sense of duty or guilt, Agent Morris would carry the money. He would follow his instructions, and drive to the village to wait at the phone box for further directions.

From there, he would travel to the coast through the tunnel.

He would see Kimball at the ventilation shaft. He would stop.

Enzo would be there. She would have the towel with the explosives wrapped around her.

Morris's phone would be out of range. They would talk for a few seconds. He'd implore restraint. He'd make sure she was okay.

He'd hand over the money for the woman.

Enzo smiled. He would disable Morris's car. He would tell them not to follow him.

Agent Morris and Miss Kimball would never leave the tunnel. His second bomb would see to that.

The padlock on the entrance to the tunnel's ventilation shaft yielded to a short crowbar. He carried the plastic box up the first flight of stairs, placing it in a corner, and brushing dust and grime from the floor over it until it looked as if it had been abandoned years before.

He unwound the spool of wire that would form the antenna and laid it along the side of the steps, working his way higher and higher.

After a minute's climb he reached the storage room. He silently thanked his luck as the length of wire ended by the room's only window.

He taped the free end to the window, where it would receive a good signal.

He would leave Morris and Kimball stranded in the center of the tunnel. Even if they walked for the exit, they would never reach it.

The soft rock that had enabled the tunnel's construction would enable its destruction. The Semtex plastic explosive would collapse the whole structure.

From the window, he saw his old Fiat, still parked where he had left it days earlier.

The door from the storage room was locked, but as he rattled the handle, he knew it would give easily to outward pressure.

Satisfied his bomb was ready and his escape route good, he descended the steps. He returned to the Ford and rejoined the traffic.

After traveling a few miles, he turned for his grandfather's land.

He was ready for the exchange.

He was ready for his five million euro.

And, he gripped the steering wheel hard, he was ready to avenge his brother.

CHAPTER FORTY-NINE

MORRIS STOOD IN FRONT of the map on Vanelli's
wall, and traced a line from the pushpin that indicated the
side-by-side houses, across a small road and into a hatched
green area. There were no paths or buildings marked on the
land.

"A forest," Vanelli said.

Morris rubbed his finger over a tiny blur in the edge of the
main road. "An entrance?"

Vanelli stared. "Possibly."

"Vacant land."

Vanelli nodded.

Henderson stepped to the board. "So?"

Morris shook his head slowly. "People live in houses."

Henderson frowned.

Vanelli sighed. "If there's nowhere to live, maybe the
hostage isn't…still living."

"We need to go," Morris said.

"No," Henderson said. "The search teams will get there in time."

Morris shook his head. "It'll take too long. We need to go. Now."

"No," Henderson said. "All I hear is possibly, maybe, conjecture. In the balance of things, you are jumping to conclusions."

"It's all we've got," Morris said through clenched teeth.

"Vanelli is searching all the locations. Odds are he will find her."

"*Odds?*"

Henderson held his hand up in front of Morris. "And may I remind you, you are officially no longer in charge of this case."

"We have to cut down the *odds*. We have to go there first."

"No," said Vanelli.

Henderson smiled.

Morris looked slack-jawed at Vanelli.

Vanelli shook his head. "My teams have to work through the locations one at a time. If they jump around, they will waste time."

"And how do we know how much time Jess has got?"

Henderson squared up his shoulders. "Ficarra told us how long we've got."

Morris's eyes went wide. "And you believe him?"

"As the Colonnello said, he wants his money."

"Which you aren't even preparing."

"Because we are going to make efficient use of our resources, and find him." Henderson's tone was the same one he might offer to a recalcitrant child.

"But the houses?"

Vanelli shook his head. "It's possible."

Morris waved his finger at the pushpin. "It has to be there. It's the only thing that makes sense."

Henderson snorted. "The only thing that makes sense, Agent Morris, is that you are no longer needed on this investigation."

Morris clenched his fists, itching to punch Henderson this time for sure.

Vanelli stood up and looked at Morris. "I'm sorry, my friend. But I have to join the investigation." He gestured for Henderson to leave the office with him. "We can use my mobile command truck."

Morris clamped his jaw, hard, and did not respond.

Vanelli looked back from the doorway, and shrugged. "We have to play the *odds*. Investigate the locations methodically. These gentlemen can assist."

Morris didn't blink.

Vanelli pursed his lips. "And, I'm afraid, you are no longer in charge of the case."

Vanelli closed his office door. Morris watched through the glass wall. Vanelli walked to the elevator, herding the ambassador's man in front of him. He called two more officers from the cube farm.

Morris sweated. Blood pounded through his head. What was Vanelli up to? They had to go for the best chance. Play the *odds*. Damn it, Vanelli even said the same himself. And then he'd walked off with a pencil pushing overpaid contractor.

Morris turned, swinging his boot at a trashcan and kicked it across the room. It clanged off the far wall.

The office door burst open.

Morris turned to see Vanelli standing in the doorway. He darted into the office and reached for the bottom drawer of his desk, pulled out a bulletproof vest, and threw it at Morris.

Morris scowled. "What?"

Vanelli held out a jet-black submachine gun, the magazine longer than the barrel. "M12 Beretta. Can you use it?"

Morris nodded as he threaded his hand around the grip. "But…I don't—"

"The idiot is on the way to one of the locations. Ties up two of my Polizia, but it's probably a fair exchange." Vanelli pulled another Beretta from his bottom drawer. He raised an eyebrow. "You don't think I'm going to let him run the case, do you?"

"Not for a moment." Morris tossed the vest over his head. He headed for the door, buckling the vest around his waist. "But I owe you a new trashcan."

CHAPTER FIFTY

JESS TWIRLED THE REMAINS of the tie-wrap between her
fingers. Her wrists were raw with the constant rubbing against
the stone wall, but the plastic had finally snapped. She was under
no illusion about Enzo's reaction if he discovered her newfound
freedom. Whatever happened next, she had committed herself to
escape.

She scrabbled from the bed to the floor, bracing her back
against the metal frame, and aligning herself with the side wall.
She ran her bare feet over the rough stone, and the smooth of the
door, feeling for the boundary, getting her feet close to the edge,
and her legs coiled down for the most force and greatest
leverage.

Her hands trembled and her balance swam. She blinked hard,
and shoved the thought she hadn't eaten for at least twenty-four
hours to the back of her mind. She had to focus.

She took large breaths, deep and slow. Oxygenating her
body until her head buzzed. She clenched her fists, stretched her

legs, rotated her feet, stretching her toes toward her nose, working her muscles, settling her bones.

She rolled her shoulders, and shuffled back against the metal bars of the bed's frame. This was her chance. Her only chance.

The sound of boots on the wooden ladder were unmistakable. She counted the footsteps. Not because she knew how many it took to reach the door, but to prime her body and focus her mind.

Enzo's steps were crisp and measured. Inflexible boots pounded the concrete floor of the tunnel. Workman's boots. Cheap. Untraceable. Easily disposed of.

The footsteps stopped outside her door.

She took a deep breath, and held it. Her toes tingled. Goosebumps crawled down her back. She clenched her teeth.

Her cell was dark. She'd removed the bulb and shook it hard until she had heard the small wire inside break then placed the bulb back in its socket, the glass undamaged. A failed light bulb. An unlucky break, but an everyday occurrence.

She placed her hands together behind her back, as they had been when she was tied up, and peered in the direction of her feet. She saw only blackness.

Enzo's boots worked their way to the shaft. A click as he cycled the light switch. He walked back.

She forced herself to breathe out and back in. New oxygen. Recharging her muscles. Managing her fear. She shoved that thought to the back of her mind.

The wooden bar scraped from its rest. Followed by silence. Long. Hard. Testing and probing.

She breathed again. Quick. A short cycle of her lungs. Carbon dioxide out, oxygen in. Quelling the electricity in her before adrenaline overwhelmed her plan.

The door creaked. The movement of an inch. A faint glow broke through its rough edges. Thin light in the darkness, but not enough to see much.

He was suspicious because her light bulb didn't fire on. Waiting for a response. Keeping the advantage. Taunting her to escape if she dared.

She stole another breath, opening her mouth wide to hide the sound. She took her hands from her back, and gripped the bed. No point in deception now. When he opened the door, he'd see what he saw. She had to be faster than him. No other options would work.

The door sprang open, its metal hinges squealing. The tunnel's light wafted in. Feeble and dim, but to Jess's eyes, a torrent. She squinted, refusing her reflex to shut her eyes.

Enzo barreled in, elbow against the door, and his gun arcing around the room. He started at the head of the bed and scanned left, fearing the space behind the door.

Jess released her tension. Her electricity. Her fear. Anger fueled her now.

Her legs moved first. Muscles contracting. Electricity releasing.

The bends in her knees straightened. Her shoulders dug into the bed. Her back uncoiled.

Aligning her torso, shifting her weight, reinforcing her energy on a direct path to the supporting rock behind her.

Enzo stood no chance. He wasn't even looking in her direction.

Her ankles were braced. Her feet flew toward him first.

All of her strength, all of her fury concentrated to connect with such a small patch of bone.

Contact. Her heel, his knee. Bone against bone. Sideways.

Flexible cartilage and overwhelming force.

She felt his knee stretch and snap.

Her leg muscles jerked to a full stretch, pulling at her thighs, and wrenching her abdomen.

His knee bent unnaturally, horrifically sideways. Thank God.

His gun fired. A jet of light. The sound contained and concentrated inside the hard stone walls.

He pirouetted around on his good leg. His gun swept upward and his face turned toward her. He screamed. Rasping and guttural. Spitting and seething. Not words, but the anger generated from his pain produced a deafening, howling bellow worse than anything she'd heard emanating from Wilson Grantly's cell.

She coiled her legs, and jabbed again, aiming for his other leg. Punching her feet, and bracing her muscles.

The second time, her contact was weak. The angles were different. Her feet glanced off the side of his thigh.

His arms swung down, one hand grasping for his knee. He dropped his gun. It clattered against the far wall, lost in the darkness.

Jess pulled her knees in, rolling her momentum forward to rise up and run.

Enzo pitched down, his hands gripping his ruined leg. His forehead smashed into her face. Blunt and heavy. A blow and a push, shoving her backwards, rolling her over, his howls unabated.

She thrashed her arms, fighting to roll him off. He shoved back. Instinct. His muscles responded to the agony of forced movement.

She bunched up her knees, and rammed her elbow into his throat. He toppled sideways, gagging as he fought for breath.

Jess squeezed her abdomen, and pulled herself to her feet. She grabbed the edge of the door and propelled herself into the corridor. She slammed the door shut behind her.

Enzo's shocked groans turned from bellowing pain to roaring anger.

She lifted one end of the wooden beam and scooped her arm under the other. The weight of the timber wrenched at her back.

Behind the door, Enzo's groans turned to grunts produced along with scraping noises. What the hell was he doing?

She pushed the beam against the door, shoving it flat against the wall. The door shook. A jolt, hammering into her arms, shaking the beam.

Enzo refused to be locked in his own prison.

She heaved her shoulder forward, bracing with her legs, pushing the weight of the wood against the door, and ramming one end into the metal brace.

One side in place. One more to do.

Enzo screamed. Not pain, but primal anger. He shoved the door. It vibrated and the wood splintered.

Jess grunted, driving her body forward, clenching her teeth, and rammed the beam into the second brace, sealing the door. Sealing Enzo inside. In the total darkness.

She fell backwards, hands waving to catch her fall. She slammed into the rough rock, driving the air from her lungs. She gasped. Her left leg burned. She ran her hand over her jeans and felt a rip in the denim. Her hand came away wet and dark and bloody.

Enzo pounded the door. He cursed and swore and screamed. Hateful promises of pain and death.

She rolled onto her side, and pushed herself up. The rock floor cut into her bare feet.

The light that had seemed blinding when he opened the door, cast dim shapes and the blackest of shadows. She put her hands out, and stumbled forward. Her bleeding leg burned.

She struck the wall on the right. The bare rock scraped the palm of her hand. She pushed off toward the faint white light at the entrance shaft.

The floor became smoother. She kept moving, swinging her arms, keeping her momentum up and her weight off her gashed leg.

The shaft came into view. The ladder stretched up into the circular hole. All she had to do was make it to the daylight.

She was on her way. She'd get out of here alive. She almost laughed.

She felt relieved tears running down her cheeks and wiped them away.

A deafening noise erupted down the tunnel.

Her heart leapt into her mouth. She whipped around.

Flashes of light carved up the darkness. Wood splintered and cracked. Staccato noises echoed off the rough walls, loud and cackling.

She spluttered and choked.

Enzo had found his gun.

CHAPTER FIFTY-ONE

JESS THREW HERSELF AT the ladder. Daylight spilled down, too bright for her light-deprived eyes.

Her hands caught the ladder as the thundering gunfire stopped.

She looked back down the tunnel. Was he there? Had he escaped?

Her eyes darted left and right, probing the gloom.

She squeezed the ladder. What was she thinking? She couldn't control him now. She had only one option—run.

She put her good leg onto the first rung, and reached up, moving rung by rung, pulling with her arms to keep her weight off her gashed leg.

She heard another shot. More wood splintered and cracked. A growling roar.

Enzo was using his pain and anger to fuel brute force.

She escaped the cell, but she'd wounded an animal, and left it more dangerous.

She curled up, dragging her feet a rung higher. She worked upward, hand over hand, stretching for the light, her knees scraping on the rusty metal.

Her left leg screamed in pain. A bolt of fire seared into her thigh when she put any weight on her leg.

The circle of light above her grew closer. She stretched and grabbed and pulled, throwing her hands upward, straining at her abdomen to bring her feet up the rungs, before stretching and reaching again.

Down the tunnel, wood creaked. She heard grunting and straining. Enzo was still in the cell. She needed the door to hold for a few more minutes.

Above, she saw the cabin's ceiling. She pulled herself on up the rungs. Her hands reached the top of the ladder, a foot below the level of the cabin floor.

She gripped the last rung with all her might.

The pain in her leg was gone.

She was oblivious to the long drop and the narrow shaft.

She wrenched with her arms, drawing her whole body up six inches, stabbing her feet onto the next rung, pushing with her knees, and shoving herself from the shaft in one continuous movement.

Behind her, the cell door splintered and cracked. Old timbers crashed to the ground.

A long guttural scream, and then Enzo's voice shouting a solid stream of swearing and cursing.

She rolled onto the cabin floor, head spinning and lungs burning. She swept her gaze around the room. Empty.

Enzo hadn't brought any backup.

She dragged herself up, and hoisted the trap door closed. The clasp rattled. She ran her hands around the floor. The padlock was gone. She had no way to keep him in the tunnel.

"You. Will. Die," Enzo shouted. His voice was hoarse, his throat raw from his exertions. Worse, the sound of his shouting wasn't echoing down the tunnel.

Adrenaline prickled her skin.

He had reached the ladder.

She threw open the cabin door. Enzo's white Ford was parked outside. She lurched down the cabin's steps to the car. Her injured leg objected, but she pushed on.

The car was open. She ran her hands over the ignition switch, under the seat, and in the door pockets. No keys.

A duffel bag lay in the passenger side foot well. She ripped open the zipper, and froze.

Wires ran into a thick coiled towel. The other end of the wires ran to a small box. There was a large roll of duct tape. There was no doubt in her mind what Enzo had in store for her if the handover had occurred.

She let go of the bag, gingerly.

She needed a weapon and she knew where to find one. She stabbed the trunk release button, and levered herself out of the car.

"I'm going to kill you!" Enzo screamed.

Her heart pounded, and her skin prickled. A wave of heat washed over her. Her lungs worked overtime, straining to fill her blood with oxygen. She clamped her tongue against the roof of her mouth to stifle her voice.

Enzo was at the cabin door.

He leaned against the doorframe, his right leg raised off the ground, his right arm dark with blood. His open mouth was twisted to one side, drawing his nose off center. His eyebrows were pushed down hard.

"You're going to die." He spat the words, speaking from deep inside him, from force of will.

No time to search for her gun in the back seat. She dived for the car's trunk and threw the lid open.

Enzo limped toward the car, breathing hard and grunting back the pain of weight on his right knee.

The trunk was empty. She lifted the carpet, and wrenched the plastic cover off the spare tire.

Disposable gloves. Bright red reflective triangle. She threw them out.

The tire-iron. A two-foot metal bar bent into an L-shape. One end cast into a crude lump for a socket.

She whipped the tire iron from the car, and swung it in Enzo's direction.

He stopped five feet from her. Grunted. "You think you're going to stop me with that?"

She hefted the iron, holding it shoulder height, redoubling her grip.

He watched her hands.

She swallowed.

A twisted smile crept across his face. "All I have to do is get my gun."

He turned for the passenger door. Her heart went wild. Damn, Damn, Damn! Why hadn't she checked the glove compartment?

He limped a step, his back to her.

She had to strike first. She couldn't let him reach his gun. She took a deep breath, adjusted her grip, and swung for the back of his head.

He spun around, both hands out, the last vestiges of his sick smile still on his mouth. He grabbed the iron.

She strained, but he twisted, burning her hands, and levering the tire-iron from her.

She hopped back.

He laughed, and slapped the iron into the palm of his hand. "Well, well. Look what I have here."

She panted, and inched backward.

He limped a step closer.

The gash in her leg burned.

She looked around the clearing. She couldn't make a fast getaway, but she could move better than he did. And he couldn't chase her. Not rapidly, anyway.

"You're not going anywhere," he growled.

She inched away from him.

He smacked the tire-iron into his hand again and raised his eyebrows. "I'm going to enjoy killing you. For my brother."

She dived around the rear of the car, her legs pushing hard, the screaming from her thigh ignored.

He followed, scraping the tire-iron against the trunk lid. He was faster than she expected. Faster than her.

She whipped open the rear door, threw herself inside, and slammed the door.

He stood outside, watching her, his eyes wide, his nostrils flaring with each breath. Adrenaline was fueling him, too. He was naturally stronger than her, and he knew the car, the cabin, the area. He had the advantage.

Again.

She pulled back from the door. Through the window she saw the tire-iron. It swayed back and forth. She ran her hands over the front passenger seat. Could she use Enzo's bomb? Could she do anything with it?

Enzo lowered the iron, and reached for the door handle.

She threw herself at the door, hammering her fist down on the lock. There was a solid thump, the power locks sealing the doors.

He tried the handle. It clicked, useless. He let his arm drop to his side, and shuffled his weight on his one good leg.

She breathed.

His torso twisted, his arms flailed. She glimpsed the iron swinging. A long circular arc. Around his shoulder, over his head, and down toward the back of the car.

The rear window exploded. Glass flew. She whipped her hands to her face, and screamed. Slivers slashed her skin. Shards rained down on the rear seat, cutting into her thighs. She pushed back, sliding from the seat and thumping onto the floor.

Enzo swung the iron again and again, pounding the edges of what glass remained.

She whipped her head back and forth. She ran her hand over the carpet, and under the rear seat.

The rear seat, where she had lost her gun.

She shoved her arm under the seat, her fingers stretching, her palms brushing the carpet. The glass dug into her torso, and scraped at her hands.

She twisted her head to see under the seat, but the black carpet soaked up every glimmer of light.

There was a tearing of metal. She looked up. Enzo was stabbing the tire-iron into the door lock. He levered and strained, bowing the door. The side window exploded, raining more glass on her legs.

She thrashed her arm under the back seat, stretching her fingers, probing and searching. It had to be there. Unless he'd found her gun. Taken it.

Enzo twisted the tire-iron. The door locks thumped up. Metal squealed and the door bumped open. Forest air mixed with the decades-old dust of the Ford's carpet. Enzo slammed the tire-iron into the roof of the car, piercing through the headliner. He leaned in through the door. "You're mine."

She bent her knees, and punched her legs toward him. He moved sideways. Raising his bloodied arm and wrapping it around her ankles. He clamped down, locking her legs under his arm. She strained and kicked, but Enzo's grip was hard, and her angle not good.

He lurched back, pulling her feet out of the car.

She grabbed at a metal spar under the seat, tensing her muscles, and pulling herself inches back into the car.

He limped. Adjusting his position. Gaining better leverage.

She pulled on her legs. Harder this time. He moved backwards. Ripping her hands from the spar, stealing her only chance of resisting.

She flailed with her hands, searching for anything solid.

He pulled her legs from the car.

Her fingers caught something under the seat. A gentle touch. A glancing blow. Fast and brief. Once and gone.

She wrapped her fingers around an edge in the carpet, bracing herself. He pulled harder. She was half out of the car, her back on the doorsill, her abdomen exposed to him.

Her memory clicked. The touch. Brief and fast. Hard and flat. Angles and edges. A crosshatched pattern. Her skin tingled, and she lurched for the corner, her fingertips brushing metal.

He gave one more wrench, pulling her chest from the car, pinning her arms inside, against the sidewalls, under the seat.

She touched her gun. The Heizer.

He dropped her legs, and panted.

Her fingers slid over its metal. Skimming its grip, caressing the short barrel.

His eyes were narrow slits that bore into her. His breath hissed in sharp blasts through clenched teeth. He swung the tire-iron, low, left and right. He spat. "You should have stayed at home. You thought you were so damn clever, didn't you?" He grabbed her belt, yanking her up. "But you made a mistake."

He leaned down, his lips drawn back over clenched teeth. "You shot my brother."

She slipped a finger through the Heizer's trigger guard.

He raised the tire-iron behind his head.

Her fingers snapped closed around the handle. She twisted, levering her arm from under the seat, thrusting the gun through the door.

His eyes widened. The veins in his neck bulged. He tensed his shoulder, whipping the iron forward.

She fired. Arm straight. One shot. Center mass. Stomach, abdomen, chest. Three feet. She couldn't miss.

His shirt twitched around his stomach. His left side. The very edge of his silhouette.

His face froze.

His straight arm folded. The iron came down. Over his head. Socket end first. Loose and slow. Smacking into the roof. Skittering across its surface. Tumbling through where the rear window had once been.

Jess's belt slipped from his fingers. He doubled up, his hands clutching his side. A deep red stain growing on his shirt.

She pulled her legs up.

"It was his mistake." She punched her feet forward, ramming his shoulder back, twisting his head. His ruined knee collapsed.

She pointed the gun at his face. "And you've made the same error."

Enzo didn't move. His mouth hung open. His lips a wide twisted curl around his teeth. His arms hung loose around his abdomen.

Jess panted. She shifted her grip on the gun. Adjusted her aim. Focused on the point between his eyes.

His shoulders sank. His arms fell free. His back curled down.

She shuffled onto the doorsill, leaning forward, arms out, gun trained on his head.

He grunted. Panted. Groaned.

And lunged.

His arms lashed out. Grabbing her gun hand, turning it upwards, squeezing, crushing, prying.

Her fingers burned. She screamed. He twisted her arm, turning her sideways as her body fought to keep back the pain.

He twisted the gun in her hand. She flung a kick at his side. He grunted, and ripped the gun from her.

She lurched back into the car.

He pointed the gun. Eyes wide. Shaking and panting.

The gun wavered. He back-pedaled, putting the distance between her and the gun that she should have put between them earlier.

She blinked hard, sweat stinging her eyes.

He groaned. "I don't make mistakes."

He took a deep breath. Steadying the gun. Adjusting his grip. "And you've made your last."

His fingers curled tighter. The muscles in his arm bulged, bracing for the recoil.

Jess snapped her eyes closed. Jerked back. Brought her knees up. Curled fetal.

A single shot rang out.

Loud, close, heavy.

The last of the Heizer's barrels.

But she felt no pain.

Another shot boomed. Then a burst. Short. Hard. Crackling. Shaking the air. Scraping on her nerves.

She opened her eyes. Her head was on the floor between the front and rear seats. Her legs lay out of the car door. Across the clearing, the undergrowth swayed in the breeze and trees danced overhead. The sky blazed blue.

She breathed out. Ficarra was gone.

She levered herself off the floor. He lay on the ground. His legs twisted under him. Bloody holes peppered his chest. Glassy eyes stared from a frozen sneer. Blood drained from his mouth.

She swallowed hard, forcing back bile building in her throat.

Boots pounded in her direction. A lone figure. A large gun. A bulletproof vest. Head swiveling from car to cabin to woods. The gun following.

She rubbed her eyes. "Mm...Morris?"

He dropped to her side, his gun on Ficarra. His heavy boot kicked the body, to be sure.

Ficarra didn't move. His mouth hung open. His glassy eyes saw nothing.

Morris scanned the woods one last time then turned to her. "Both damn barrels, Kimball! Next time...use both damn barrels!"

She coughed and spluttered. Her lower lip trembled. She coughed. Tears streamed down her face, although she didn't feel them. Her chest heaved and bucked. She curled forward.

He put an arm around her shoulders.

She clung to him, trembling, eyes streaming. Her face rested against his shoulder. The bulletproof vest was rough on her cheek.

He patted her back.

She thumped his.

Seconds passed.

She choked and sniffed. She forced her mouth shut and held her breath. She pulled away from him.

Sweat ran down the side of his face. His bulletproof vest swelled and contracted as he gulped air. He scanned the clearing, training the weapon with his gaze.

She wiped her face with the back of her hand. "I didn't think you were going to make it."

He flashed a tight-lipped grin. "If you hadn't fired the first shot, I don't think we would have got here in time. We were way back. Going carefully. Slowly. We didn't know what was here."

She took a deep breath, and held it down lest the tears returned.

She wiped her nose again, and waved her dirty hand. "Sorry."

Morris grinned. "I've seen worse."

"Oh God!" She grabbed his arm. "Wilson Grantly." She twisted round to the cabin. "He's in there. There's a tunnel. And rats."

"Slow down, Jess. Vanelli is checking it out."

She frowned. "It might be dangerous."

He hoisted the gun. "We came prepared."

She looked around the clearing. "Just the two of you?"

"Yeah…well…long story. But he called the cavalry when we heard your shot. They're on their way."

She nodded. "I think there's a bomb in the duffel bag."

Morris peered into the front seats. "Right." He nodded and mocked. "Vital safety tip."

He helped her from the car to the other side of the cabin, away from the bomb, and Ficarra's bloody remains.

He led her to a fallen tree as a line of dark blue *gazzellas* raced into the clearing. Armed carabinieri poured out, taking up positions around the clearing, checking Ficarra's body, and descending on the cabin.

Morris briefed them quickly, pointing to the bag, and a man called for a bomb disposal squad.

She sat on the tree and panted, her arms wrapped tight around her.

The carabinieri emerged from the cabin carrying an overweight man. Jess had never seen Wilson Grantly, but she'd seen photos in his parents' home. He looked different now, but recognizable.

He groaned with every movement. His hair was matted, lacerations covered his face, and dark stains covered his torn clothes. They laid him on the ground as an ambulance arrived.

The medics went to work. Swabs and needles and bandages. They cut away his clothes, and fixed an oxygen mask to his face.

He grew quiet. Painkillers taking effect. They set up an intravenous drip, and loaded him into the ambulance.

One of the medics carried a bag over to her. He swabbed her cuts with anesthetic. He shone a light in her eyes and bandaged her thigh. He said something to Morris, and left.

Morris shrugged. "He thinks you should see a doctor."

She held up a trembling hand and swiped it through her hair. "No kidding."

Morris grinned and rubbed her shoulder.

The ambulance left, lights flashing and sirens blaring.

Vanelli emerged from the cabin, and walked over. He nodded in her direction. "You okay?"

She nodded.

A sheepish grin lifted his mouth. "Yeah. Stupid question."

She smiled. "But you figured it out. The anagrams."

Morris winked. "We're the FBI and the Carabinieri. We know everything."

She groaned. "Give me a break."

"You did good, Kimball." He grinned and patted her back again, as if he couldn't quite believe she'd survived. "You did good."

Her muscles protested her every move. The adrenaline was wearing off, but her hands still shook.

She looked at Morris. "You said, next time."

Wrinkles covered his brow.

She nodded in the direction of Ficarra's body. "Over there. You said, next time. Next time use both damn barrels."

He shrugged. "Friendly advice."

She looked at the cabin. "I don't ever want a next time."

"I have the feeling with you, there's always a next time."

She closed her eyes. They sat in silence.

Vanelli drew a car around. Morris opened the rear door, and helped her in. She sank into the seat, and laid her head back.

The winding coastal path back to Rome passed vineyards and olive groves and white crested waves breaking in rocky bays. Clouds nestled in an expanse of blue, small and puffed for the sole purpose of making the blue richer.

It was the dream of Italy. A beauty so strong it had given the Romans the confidence to strike out across the continent, and painters and poets inspiration across the centuries. But she saw none of it.

She was asleep before they reached the main road.

CHAPTER FIFTY-TWO

JESS SAT AT A breakfast table on the balcony terrace of her hotel, soaking up the warmth of the morning sun. Life bustled in the square below her. Waiters weaved between outdoor café tables, communicating in gestures and dispensing coffee. Mopeds threaded through traffic jams. Pedestrians dodged street sellers.

The fountain glistened in the sunlight. Tourists sat on the wall around the pool. Water splashed from an angel's trumpet. The occasional blast of a car horn echoed off the old stone walls.

Everything was chaos. Madness. And beautiful.

Someone cleared a throat.

She turned as Romeo placed a silver tray on the white tablecloth, and gestured to the plates.

"Cappuccino, cornetto, berries, and cream." He smiled. "Breakfast of champions, as you Americans say."

"What's that about Americans?" Morris stood in the doorway to the terrace, barely recognizable in jeans and a polo shirt. Vanelli stood behind him, immaculate in his dark suit, white shirt, and blue striped tie.

Romeo shifted his weight.

Vanelli said something in Italian, and Romeo left.

The two joined her at the table.

"How's the leg?" said Morris.

She patted her thigh gingerly. "Getting better."

"Good." He looked up at the hotel's façade. "Nice place. Pity you have to leave."

She grinned. "I have a day left."

He nodded. "More than me. My flight's in a couple of hours."

She scooped up a strawberry on her fork, and grinned. "Shame."

He smiled flatly. "I have to see the Grantlys."

She lowered her fork, and swallowed. "You've told them?"

"Not me. The office sent people." He waved his hand. "Not the kind of thing we do over the phone."

"No." She frowned. "I failed them."

He shook his head. "First of all, that would be a 'we,' not an 'I.' And secondly, he's alive. He'll make it. So, we didn't fail them. However, when he's well enough to travel back to the U.S., he'll be arrested and charged." He shrugged. "It's what would have happened anyway."

She sighed. "Doesn't make it any easier for the parents."

"Best that could be done," Morris said. "And they'll get their money back, so they won't live the end of their lives in poverty. That's no small thing."

They sat in silence for a few moments.

Romeo returned with a tray of espressos, handed them out, and left.

Vanelli savored the aroma. "You will return to Rome in the future under happier circumstances, yes?"

She shrugged. "I rarely take vacations, and it's expensive."

He shook his head. "Not vacation. You may have to return to testify."

"Testify about what? Enzo Ficarra is dead. He won't be brought to trial, will he?"

"My colleagues may desire an inquest. You did shoot him, after all. And the explosion in a tunnel near the old mine. We think Ficarra set the bomb planning to kill us after the ransom was paid. The timing works. You might help with testimony so we can close that case, too." Vanelli shrugged. "These matters are not in my domain."

She took a deep breath and nodded. "Oh."

"If it's necessary, can't she testify by video?" Morris said.

"Perhaps." Vanelli shrugged. "And there's the matter of a certain contractor favored by the ambassador."

Jess widened her eyes. "Who are you talking about?"

Morris grinned, lifted the coffee to his lips, blew on it, and placed it back in the saucer. "I will be coming back."

Jess looked at him. "Can't you testify by video?"

"Not for testimony." He shook his head. "Seems the State Department is having a rethink on its policy of closing down our business office."

Jess cocked her head. "Business office?"

A grin crossed Vanelli's face. "Miss Kimball, contrary to your government's assumption, we have known about the FBI business office for some time. We merely wish to put the cooperation on a," he raised his eyebrows, "more formal footing."

Morris nodded. "Seems the Comandante Generale was pretty

pleased. Toppling Ficarra could lead to more arrests."

"Which would be in jeopardy, if any of this was to be made public," Vanelli said.

"Er..."

He raised his eyebrows. "Prematurely. In a magazine, for example."

She sighed. "My publisher will hate me, but you have my word. Until you let me know it's safe."

"Excellent. We will do that." He finished his steaming espresso in one gulp. "And now, we should head to the airport." He stood and they shook hands. "A pleasure to meet you, *Signora* Kimball."

Morris scraped his chair back. "Don't know if I'll see you when you get back." He held out his hand. "But...you did good, Kimball. You did good."

She gripped his hand tightly. "You, too, and...thank you, for...you know."

"Shooting Enzo, saving your life, and generally pulling your butt out of the wringer?"

She laughed, and squeezed harder. "Yeah. All that stuff."

He squeezed back. "We wouldn't have made it here without you. It's been a pleasure." He glanced at the cloudless sky. "Make the most of your last day."

The men left her alone on the balcony. She finished her breakfast and her coffee, and closed her eyes, trying to forget the aches and pains that roamed her body. She listened to the sounds of cars and mopeds and the voices of a hundred languages. She listened until she was on the verge of losing consciousness.

"*Signora?*"

She opened her eyes, squinting in the sunlight.

Romeo held out a silver tray with a brilliant white demitasse of steaming hot espresso. "I thought you might need another."

She shook the fog from her mind, and cleared a space on the table. "You thought right."

He put the demitasse in front of her. "You're leaving?"

"One last day."

He grunted. "You know, it is said that the person who visits Rome for a week sees more than the person who visits for a whole year."

She grinned. "And what about the person who has just one day?"

He raised his eyebrows. "Naturally, they see a lot of Rome."

She cocked her head. "Really?"

"Really." He looked over the edge of the balcony. "There's the Pantheon, the Colosseum, the Vatican. They are all within fifteen minutes from here. And St. Peter's, the Galleria Borghese, the Piazza Navona, the—"

"Whoa." She held up a hand. "I'm not sure I'm up to it."

He nodded, sagely. "That is because you need a guide."

Her eyes widened. "A guide?"

"Someone who knows the city, the sights, the best places to eat."

She looked at his sparkling blue eyes and wavy blonde hair. "Oh? And let me guess, you just happen to know such a guide?"

He grinned. "None better."

She laughed, and downed her coffee, clinking the white espresso cup onto its saucer. "Then lead on, Romeo. Show me Rome."

THE END

ABOUT THE AUTHOR

DIANE CAPRI is the *New York Times*, *USA Today*, and worldwide bestselling author. She's a recovering lawyer and snowbird who divides her time between Florida and Michigan. An active member of Mystery Writers of America, Authors Guild, International Thriller Writers, Alliance of Independent Authors, and Sisters in Crime, she loves to hear from readers and is hard at work on her next novel.

Please connect with Diane online:
http://www.DianeCapri.com
Twitter: http://twitter.com/@DianeCapri
Facebook: http://www.facebook.com/Diane.Capri1
http://www.facebook.com/DianeCapriBooks

Printed in Great Britain
by Amazon